CAUGHT OFF GUARD

A SAMANTHA TRUE MYSTERY

KRISTI ROSE

KRISTI ROSE

CAUGHT
GUARD

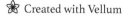 Created with Vellum

1

THE SECOND FRIDAY IN DECEMBER. MORNING

I SAT ACROSS THE VISITOR'S TABLE AND STARED AT AJ. THE inmates' orange Multnomah County jumpsuit complemented his light-brown skin. Slants of morning light broke through a narrow window near the ceiling, promising a beautiful, clear December day in the Pacific Northwest. Days like this during winter were such a rarity that locals would flood outdoors to soak up the vitamin D they'd missed over the past months. Yet AJ was stuck inside.

I picked at a chip in the linoleum tabletop, my nails scraping the plywood underneath. "I saw your mug shot. It's very flattering, so at least the media shows an excellent picture of you every ten minutes. The entire pro football league is likely jealous. You'll be known as the guy with the awesome mug shot."

I wanted to slap myself upside the head for saying something so stupid. He was in jail, charged with murder. He wouldn't care if his mug shot looked like a professional headshot. He was trying to salvage what was left of his freedom and would worry about his career next.

AJ dropped his head onto his arms, which were folded on the table. "Help me."

"I will," I said. "I'll check in on Troy every other day, and if you want, I can take Simon to my place. I don't know if they'll freeze your accounts, so last night, I paid all your bills two months in advance. I also moved money into Troy's account."

Troy was AJ's seventeen-year-old brother, and Simon was AJ's dog. And I was his girl Friday, a gig I did along with working part time at the online shopping department of my local grocery store. I'd become a professional private investigator nine months earlier and hadn't yet built my reputation enough to find steady work.

Without looking up, AJ said, "No, Sam, help me prove my innocence. I need to know I have someone on my side, trying to get to the bottom of this."

He lifted his head, projecting his fear and uncertainty with his watery gaze. The weight of it sat uncomfortably between my shoulders, pressing me into acceptance. I would not be a bystander in this travesty. At less than twenty-four hours in jail, he was already broken. Of course I was going to help.

"Don't forget you have Lockett," I said. "He's one of the best defense lawyers to date. I trust him with my life." In fact, I had trusted Tyson Lockett with my life in the past, and he'd come through. I was thankful he'd been willing to take on AJ's case.

"And I have you, right? You won't abandon me now, will you?" he pled.

I blew out a slow breath, trying to steady my nerves and hide my own fear. I was out of my element in Portland. Working as a private investigator in my hometown had been easy. I knew the cops. I knew the locals. Working outside of Wind River would be a new ball game, a playing field where the rules might be the same but the refs were unknown and could call the plays differently.

I put a hand on his arm and squeezed. "I'll do everything I can to help."

He looked over his shoulder at the guard standing ten feet away. In a hushed voice, he said, "Watch your back."

"You too." The one fact I knew about the case was that AJ was innocent. What I didn't know was if he'd been framed out of convenience or if he'd been a target too.

Six days earlier. Saturday.

Bang! The handgun jerked upward slightly as it ejected its payload.

"I'm hit!" Toby Wagonknecht, my IT guru, clutched his shoulder and dropped to his knees, bending forward in discomfort. The berries he'd picked moments before tumbled from his palm and onto the ground as he braced himself with both hands and groaned.

"It hurts." He moaned and rocked back. "I hate getting shot. I knew I should have stayed home."

I crossed the forest floor, my steps muffled by the fallen western hemlock needles.

"Be glad I shot you." I stood beside him and tapped the fallen berries with the toe of a hiking boot. "If you'd eaten these, the gastrointestinal grief they would've given you would've been far worse."

"You could have yelled a warning." He gripped his shoulder, red oozing between his fingers, a shocking contrast against his neon-yellow T-shirt. It made me think of ketchup and mustard.

I pointed my gun at his shoulder. "I think maybe red paintballs were a poor decision. From far away, that looks like actual blood."

"From up close, it hurts like hell."

"Worse than actually being shot?" I asked, hoping to give him some perspective.

He looked at me, wincing and clutching his shoulder. "I'm too emotionally scarred to answer that question objectively. Real gun, paintball gun—they both hurt." He moaned again. "I think I might need some chips or a burrito to distract me from the pain."

I rolled my eyes. "You and food. It's incredible you're so thin." *Waifish almost.*

He nodded toward something behind me. "Shoot her and ask her how it feels."

"Whoa." Precious came up beside me and swiped at the red oozing between Toby's fingers and played with it like a kid does with glue. "I knew I should've put money on you getting shot first." Precious, real name Erika Shurmann, was my best friend and sidekick.

I asked, "Who would you bet with? Because the odds would be wack if we all bet against each other."

"Leo." She gestured behind herself as if he were standing right there, which he wasn't.

The forest cloaked him—no telling where he was hiding. His Native American roots made him the favorite to come out of our work excursion unscathed. Leo had skills—aside from being one of Wind River's finest police officers, with a level head in sketchy situations, he could also track and live off the land for days with nothing but a piece of flint and a knife.

"Oh, look at those red berries." Precious stepped across Toby to reach for them.

He picked up his paintball gun and shot her in the butt.

"Yow! What did you do that for?" She spun toward him and smacked the gun out of his hand.

"Sam shot me when I was reaching for the berries. I thought that's what we were supposed to do."

I groaned and smacked a hand to my forehead. "Why did I think this was a good idea?" I said mostly to myself.

Then a tiny pine cone dropped in front of me. I looked up, and though the needles were thick and heavy and I couldn't see anything between the branches, I sensed more than saw Leo's presence.

I said to the tree, "You can come out. This was a bad idea. We can go back to camp and do... whatever."

We were staying at Sol Duc Hot Springs and Lodge and had the cabins for one more night. I'd planned to bring my friends—who also happened to be my investigative team when cases I worked on went sideways—out to the forest to teach them survival skills. But my plan was stupid. Precious and Toby had no desire to develop their survival skills.

The hemlock shook, and a few more pine cones dropped around us. A second later, Leo fell from the sky, landing on his feet in a squat.

He slowly stood and placed a hand on my shoulder. "Your heart was in the right place."

"That's not going to keep us safe."

Toby said, "I'm ready to go back to the cabin. They're having a fish fry today."

Precious oohed. "That sounds delicious. And I wouldn't mind a dip in the hot springs. It might take the ache out of this." She rubbed her backside while giving Toby a pointed look of anger.

He totally misread it. "Yeah, good idea. I can soak my shoulder."

Another groan escaped me, and Leo chuckled.

"Guys, you forgot why we came here. It wasn't for fish or hot springs," I said.

Precious adjusted her headband and smoothed her platinum hair. "But those are bonuses to being out here with all the bugs and critters."

How this woman spent one weekend a month sleeping in a tent while searching for Bigfoot was beyond me. When given a choice, she would pick room service and pampering over roughing it any day.

Leo cleared his throat. "The point is that all three of you have been victims of an assault. And Samantha feels responsible for you two when you help her on her cases. So maybe keep that in mind while we're out here."

Toby looked confused. "You didn't shoot me, Sam."

Precious said, "And you didn't push me down the stairs."

I looked at my two friends. "You both were injured because of my job. We're very lucky that none of us had more serious injuries. We have to get better at protecting ourselves. We have to get better at listening to our instincts. We need self-defense skills."

Precious shook her head. "But why here? I can take a self-defense course at the rec center."

Leo said, "You're part of the same Bigfoot research team that Tupi Whitehorse is on, yeah?"

She nodded.

"That takes you out into these Olympics once a month. Do you know how many people disappear in the woodlands every year? Around one thousand six hundred people since 2011. That's an average of seventeen people a year. That may not sound like a lot, but those are the ones we know of, and of those that disappear, only a small percent are found."

"Alive?" Toby asked.

"Or dead. But found." He crossed his arms and gave them both a steady, pointed look.

Toby grimaced. "And I thought the dark web was a scary place." He looked around the forest. "Now I have the creeps."

I watched Precious's face, seeing awareness dawn.

She said, "But I'm out there with a handful of others and Tupi."

Leo shook his head. "You can't always count on Tupi. He was saying at the last tribe meeting that he was stretched thin and might have to give up something."

I put up a hand, palm out. "Hang on. Let's just say this right now. You can't ever count on anyone." I pointed at Leo. "Pure luck that he saw me get kidnapped. As much as I'd love to know he or any of you will always have my back, that's just not realistic."

Leo sighed. "You've been hurt too many times already, and I haven't been there to stop it."

I looked at each of them in turn. "I never want to be in a position where we are counting on someone and our luck runs out. Do you get that?"

Toby and Precious nodded.

I said to Leo, "I absolutely hate having to call you when I'm in crisis. I aim to head crises off at the pass."

"That would be awesome. But you know you can always—"

"Yes, I know." I bumped my shoulder into his. "You're only a call away."

He winked as a smile played on his lips.

I blew out a sigh. So far, nothing about the trip was playing out like I'd planned, but I hoped this conversation would stick in their minds, and maybe we could try again another time.

I said, "So, a fish fry, huh?" and looked at my friends.

Toby rolled back his shoulders. "Actually, can we try one more time? I promise not to get distracted by the berries."

I said, "Little red round berries on a thorny bush called devil's club are...?"

Toby answered, "Not for human consumption." He gave Precious's backside a pointed look.

"Oh, that's right," she said. "Red berries bad. And since we're out here, we might as well try this weird-ass game of hide-and-seek again." She held up one finger. "But I'm gonna be honest. If fifteen minutes pass and I don't see or hear any of you, I'm gonna freak out. We came into this mountain forest together, and we're leaving together."

I looked between Toby and Precious. "Are you sure?"

They both nodded.

"Okay, I'll go back to the trailhead and wait seven minutes. Then I'll come in and start searching. Precious, start your clock then."

She smiled and nodded. "And let's make a bet. How about the first person to get shot treats us to the fish fry."

Toby pushed up off the ground. "Well, if we do that, then we might as well call it a day. We all know I'm gonna be the first hit."

Precious guffawed. "Try being positive. Visualize an outcome where I get hit or maybe you get Sam first."

"Or even me," Leo said.

"Never gonna happen," I said.

"As if," Toby said.

"Delusional much?" Precious asked.

Leo tossed up his hands in frustration. "Okay, then. If I'm so good and you all are so bad, then maybe I should be the one hunting you three?"

"Yeah," I said. "You should be."

Toby groaned. "I'm definitely going to need time with Lady M after this."

Lady M—Lady Marmalade—was a sugar glider and Toby's emotional-support animal, which he'd gotten after being shot earlier in the year.

Precious studied Toby. "I picture you sitting in the bathtub, holding Lady M and crying, with paint on your body while you rock back and forth. Don't do that. No matter what happens here today."

Toby rolled his eyes and headed down a trail. He stopped long enough to say, "I'm getting a head start."

"Oh," said Precious, "me too." With a dainty wave, she jogged down a different trail, her ponytail bouncing with each stride. She was dressed in camouflage yoga pants and a green T-shirt. I had to give her props for that.

Leo touched my arm to get my attention. "At least they're on board."

I nodded. "Yeah." I bit my lip.

"But?"

I faced him and locked our gazes. "But I have this dreadful feeling that something big and bad is coming and I'm not going to be able to protect anyone."

That feeling had been with me for more than two weeks, a foreboding I couldn't shake. It was the reason we were

there. I believed if a person could use their wits to survive in
the woods, they could use them in other places too.

"Maybe your feeling is more from the fact that you're
taking on more cases and you know, logically, that they're
bound to get tougher." Leo arched a brow in question.

"Maybe," I said. But I didn't actually believe that.

I'd grown up having to trust my instincts, and they were
sounding alarm bells. The best way to describe this feeling
was by using Shakespeare's words: "Something wicked this
way comes."

2

SATURDAY

AT SOL DUC RESORT, THE CABINS WERE SETS OF FOUR IN arched layouts. One firepit was placed centrally for easy access in each cabin cluster and was on a first-come-first-served basis.

We sat around the firepit, each stuffed to the gills from the fish fry—pun intended. Behind us, music floated from the resort as the occasional sound of laughter carried on the wind.

As I had been the first person shot, and by Toby to boot, I was much lighter in both funds and spirit. However, my thigh was aching where the paintball had made contact.

I pointed at Toby. "I have to say it again. What you did was clever."

He tapped his temple. "Thinking like a Jedi. A master of the dark web, such as I am; it's all about cloaking, right? When we're on the clear web and asking people to join us on the dark side, we use smoke and mirrors. And I thought, why not do that here?"

Leo chuckled. "So you tucked your neon T-shirt into a bush and hid across from it. Smart."

Toby stroked Lady M and beamed. "I was worried the pasty white of my natural skin would be as much a giveaway as the T-shirt. I thought about putting mud on my chest, but I didn't want to get my hands all grody." Toby was the cliché of a computer nerd. Tall, reed thin, with hunched shoulders, unkempt shaggy blond hair, an endless supply of ironic T-shirts, and a time dedicated to getting high. Everyone in town knew and often could be heard saying that Toby was unavailable because of "high time."

Precious tapped her beer to Toby's and raised it in the air. "To Toby, who embraced his inner native and won the challenge. And if that howl he did after shooting Sam is any indication of how he felt, he might have found his second calling."

Toby shook his head. "Smoking weed and eating pizza rolls is my second calling. Tricking hunters would be my third."

We laughed. The past year had been rough for Toby. He'd been shot, had to give up vaping because of the still unsolved vaping lung disease epidemic, and almost lost his emotional-support animal in a fight with an unstable bride. That last one was my fault, but still... Today his win was a good thing.

Leo leaned toward me and said under his breath, "You feel any better?"

I shrugged. "Maybe about Toby."

I glanced at my best friend. Six feet tall thanks to her German heritage, top heavy thanks to the Shurmann-women genes, and not intimidated by much thanks to a childhood stutter that only showed when she was overly stressed or scared, Precious never backed down from a rumble. But that was what scared me the most. One day, she would meet a foe that would outwit her.

I continued, "But I can't predict what's ahead, and I feel like there's too much unknown to prepare for."

"What are you two whispering about?" Precious asked.

I shrugged. "Just about ways to always be prepared."

She chuckled. "Would it make you feel better if I safety pinned a secret pocket with handcuff keys onto my pants every day like you did?"

Leo chuckled. "Did you really?"

I punched him on the shoulder. Being locked to a bike rack with no help was a situation I planned to never be in again. Being caught unprepared was a sore spot for me.

I ignored him and told Precious, "Yes, it would. And carry a stun gun or pepper spray at least."

Precious stood. "And aim for the throat"—she pretended to grab an imaginary man's throat—"and rip. Or aim for the twig and berries." She did a groin kick in the air, and both Leo and Toby groaned.

"On that note," Leo said as he stood, "I'm going to bed."

A quick glance at my watch told me bedtime was long past. The fire was low, other campers and cabin-stayers were straggling toward their beds, and somewhere off in the deep of the forest, a pack of coyotes barked and howled as they began their prowl. Though, to me, they sounded as if they were calling out a warning.

Leo squeezed my shoulder. "Native American lore says to see or hear wolves would be a bad omen. Be glad those are coyotes."

"Because wolves aren't in the Olympic National Forest," I pointed out.

"Yeah, can you imagine if you heard one? Even I'd be scared." He chuckled, gave my shoulder a final squeeze, then headed to the cabin he shared with Toby.

Toby stood as well. "I think I'm going to bed too. Too bad there's no internet out here, or I'd get online and brag to my friends, but I guess that'll have to wait."

I said, "Must be killing you to be device free."

He tossed his empty beer bottle into a recycling bin a dozen yards from the firepit. "Life without internet access is cruel and unnecessary."

Precious said, "Yet you survived and had a good day. I'll admit that I had a hard time with it at first too, but jeez, if we can't be off the grid for forty-eight hours without all hell breaking loose, then something is seriously wrong with the world. You know, I don't even know where my phone is right now. When's the last time that's happened?"

"Ten years ago?" I offered.

Toby gave a dismissive wave and shuffled toward his cabin.

I stretched and yawned.

Precious shook a finger at me. "You all are party poopers."

I rose from the log that served as my seat then kicked sand on the fire and made sure the embers had died.

"Come on, tomorrow's a long drive home," I said.

She grunted with disappointment then followed me to our cabin after tossing away her beer bottle.

· · ·

The next morning, we were up early and on the road. The drive south out of the Olympics to Wind River was slightly over five hours, not including stops. Both Precious and Leo had to be back at work on Monday, and I had babysitting duty. My six-year-old niece, Cora, was currently living with my parents while my sister was deployed. Rachel had left in late September and would be returning home in February. Having Cora around had been amazing, a wonderful chance to get to know my niece better and teach her bad habits, much to my sister's horror. And I was planning to take her with me the following day, to do a job—not a PI job; I'm not that careless. I also work part time for a second-string pro quarterback. I was the chief operating officer for his laundry, groceries, and dog.

The next day was dog-park day with Simon, and since Cora's school was closed for teacher inservice, I thought she would love to get some dog time in. Most animals are good for anyone's soul.

Besides, I had only one active PI case. I'd been hired by a woman to follow her fiancé to make sure he was telling the truth about how he spent his time. I followed him on Thursday and reported on his mundane day, to her relief. But she wanted two weeks of information, just to be safe.

The drive out of the national forest was quiet. I thought we'd all come to enjoy the experience of the peacefulness of being in nature. For me, being in the woods felt like being home. I loved camping and cooking food over an open fire. Having dyslexia meant school was hard for me. My dad recognized that and tried to find an outlet that built my self-esteem. Being outdoors became that thing. Leo's kid brother, Hue, is also dyslexic and one of my closest friends. When not out hiking or camping with my dad, I would hang out with Hue on the reservation and learn how to be still among the trees, how to fish with nothing but a branch, a line, and a hook, and how to make a gill net.

In nature, I found myself. I came into my own. And I disliked leaving it behind and heading back to a world where things automatically got harder.

"I know we just had breakfast," Toby said, "but we're planning on stopping for lunch, right? We're not driving straight through?"

We were in Leo's extended-cab truck, boys up front and girls in the back. The pause before anyone answered him allowed enough silence for us to hear his stomach rumble.

Precious lightly pushed his shoulder. "Sounds like you didn't have enough breakfast."

I handed him a protein bar over the seat. "It's gonna be a few hours at least."

He grumbled and took it. We drove out of the thick of the forest and east toward Port Angeles. I loved that the coastline of Victoria, Canada could be seen by looking north from the edge of town. I loved that pods of killer or gray whales could often be spotted right offshore.

We were closing in on Lake Crescent, one of the bluest lakes I'd ever seen, still easily thirty minutes away from the nearest town, when my phone chimed. Then Precious's phone chimed, also indicating missed calls and text messages. We looked at each other as we dug through our purses or backpacks for the phones we hadn't touched in two days. Leo's phone gave a shorter series of chimes, as did Toby's.

Precious said, "Looks like the world missed us." She looked at her screen, her brow furrowed.

I scrolled through a series of text messages from AJ and noticed he'd tried calling me seventeen times.

I told her, "These are all from AJ."

AJ was the second-string quarterback I worked for. Precious was his life coach as he strove to become a first-string NFL superstar. However, his current competition was a beloved All-Pro superstar.

"Mine too." She looked worried. "I hope he's okay." She tapped her phone three times then put it to her ear. "I'm calling him."

Leo met my gaze in the rearview mirror, a questioning arch in his brow. He was asking me if I thought that was the something I'd been worried about. I shrugged and gnawed on a thumbnail.

"Hi, AJ," Precious said. "I'm here with Sam, and we both noticed we missed a lot of calls and messages from you. Your messages were very cryptic. What's up?" She paused then said, "Okay, hold on." She looked at me. "He wants me to put him on speakerphone."

I asked the guys if that was okay, and they agreed.

"Okay, AJ. You're on speaker. And you should know there are two other people with us in the car." Precious identified Leo and Toby.

"Cool, cool," AJ said. "Hi, everyone. I have something exciting to share. Well, I mean it's bad but good. If that makes sense. I shouldn't be so excited, but I can't help it."

Precious cleared her throat. "Why don't you tell us what it is? We can take it from there."

"Our next game is this Thursday, and guess who the starting quarterback will be?" He couldn't hide the excitement in his voice.

"Seriously?" I said. "What's happened to McVay?"

Keith McVay had been the Portland Pioneers' quarterback and city superstar for the last five years. Something bad had to happen for McVay to not start.

"Yeah, seriously," AJ said. "Keith failed the mandatory drug-screening test he took Friday, and because he popped positive for illegal substances, he's been suspended for three games. I saw him yesterday, and he looks ravaged."

Both Leo and Toby shared looks of surprise.

Keith McVay popped positive? "Was it PEDs?" I asked.

When I was a kid, my dad, a reporter, had done an exposé on performance-enhancing drugs, turning a huge spotlight on the sport and the big business of winning. That was a time when the average citizen didn't know about PEDs.

AJ said, "That part I don't know. I don't care. I want to know if you all want to come to the game. Please say yes. Need my favorite girls there to support me."

Leo cut a side-eye toward me. He thought something was going on between me and AJ. The truth was that nothing was going on between me and anyone. When I found out I'd been married to a con man who played me for a fool, well, that kinda made dating unappealing. I hadn't gotten my taste for men back just yet.

Precious answered, "Of course we'll be there. We're excited for you. I'll be home later today, and let's talk then. Sound good?"

AJ said, "Yeah. Solid plan. Sam? You still coming for Simon tomorrow?"

"Yes, and I have your groceries to pick up as well."

"Put champagne on that list," AJ said.

Precious and I laughed.

I said, "I'm thinking Ralphs isn't going to carry the kind of champagne you want."

Precious said, "I'll take care of the champagne."

We ended the call moments later. I took a deep breath and tried to listen to my gut.

"Better?" Leo asked.

I shook my head. Whatever was making my spidey senses go off was still coming. And I was afraid the news with AJ might have been a distraction I couldn't afford.

3

MONDAY

I STOOD INSIDE AJ'S BACK DOOR, LOOKING OUT AT HIS PATIO, where Cora was playing with Simon, AJ's Airedale.

Precious and AJ were talking strategy on the couch.

AJ said, "After Thursday night's game, there will be three more before the new year. If I do well enough on the next two, I might catch the attention of a team who will be quarterback shopping in the spring."

I'd known Precious long enough to know what was coming next.

Precious said, "Okay. First, let's address your mindset."

I chimed in. "Never use the words 'if I'm lucky enough' or 'if I do.' That's negative self-talk. It's defeatist. You're already preparing for failure."

Precious snapped and pointed at me. "See, Samantha knows. Now I have to get it through your thick skull too."

AJ caught my eye, and I winked.

I said, "She's right, you know. The science behind the power of the brain is amazing. You work hard, AJ. You have talent. You've earned your position on the team. Now's your opportunity to prove you are more than ready. Success doesn't come because you got lucky in the games you start. Success comes with knowing you can handle any situation with confidence and skill."

He nodded, but the skepticism on his face belied his true inner feelings.

Precious slapped him upside the head. Ever since her concussion, she'd become noticeably more aggressive.

"Yow! What was that for?" AJ rubbed the back of his head.

Precious crossed her arms and sat back in the overstuffed armchair she'd claimed upon arrival, commanding AJ to sit on the ottoman so that he could face her.

"For two years, we've worked together, and I still can't get *you* to believe in yourself. Not fully, anyway. I'm down to trying more adverse responses."

"You plan on smacking me every time I say or think something negative?" He looked at me and smiled.

Precious said, "I can if you want. Or you can try harder. What do you think?"

"I think I'll try harder." He smiled.

Precious returned it. "A chance to prove yourself is what you've been waiting for, AJ. What you've been working hard on. Now is the time to show what an asset you are. No one will buy into you if you don't buy into yourself."

He nodded several times as if letting the words sink in. "I'm in the best shape I've ever been in. I've got my head on straight, mostly." He bumped Precious's knee with his fist in a teasing manner. "And I'm a damn good quarterback."

I said, "Now we're talking."

Precious said, "I'm going to talk to your agent so we all can be on the same page with the plan between now and when you land a starting position." She pretended to wipe away a tear. "I'll miss you when you're gone."

AJ laughed and rose from the ottoman. "You'll still be my life coach, Erika. Now, I'm gonna make a smoothie. Anyone else want one?"

I curled my lip. "Are you making that nasty-looking green drink?"

AJ furrowed his brow. "Hey, that green drink is part of why I'm in such great shape. You are what you put in your body."

"And I'm happy being coffee and carbs," I said without hesitation. "That drink looks toxic."

AJ made his way to the kitchen and pulled out his high-end blender. "Funny you should say that. The same day McVay popped positive on the test, I'd made him a green smoothie. Some of the guys teased me about spiking his drink so I could get some playtime." He chuckled and shook his head. "It wasn't funny then, but it's funny now."

After a quick glance at Cora to make sure she was okay, I joined AJ in the kitchen. "Wait, what did you just say? No one really believes you spiked McVay's drink, do they?"

AJ dumped an assortment of green veggies and an unpeeled kiwi into the blender. "No. Well, for a moment I wasn't sure because Coach asked me to prove it."

I gestured for him to continue.

"I said they should test all of us. Me and two other guys also drank the smoothie."

I glanced at Precious, my mind plotting out all the possible nefarious scenarios. I asked AJ, "And they tested everyone?"

AJ nodded. "Everyone who drank the smoothie. No one else popped positive."

I asked, "And the green smoothie you made... Did you make him one and then you a different one, or was your pour from the same blender as his?"

AJ's finger hovered over the blender's power button. "Same pour."

"And were there witnesses to all this?"

He nodded then jabbed the button, which filled the room with the loud whirring of blending fruits and vegetables. When the blender held nothing but a light-green sludge, AJ turned the machine off. "You're making me nervous with your questions."

Precious slid onto a barstool and leaned against the counter. "I think Sam is asking these questions out of precaution. We don't want that story to get repeated. Especially to the media. We don't want it to become a rumor or gossip. Even if they are joking. Stupid stuff has a way of sticking. And if McVay's been caught doing something illegal, it's not like he's going to just fess up."

I added, "She's right. He's likely going to try to deflect, and that could mean putting the spotlight on you and the drink you made him."

AJ poured his smoothie into a large cup and topped it with a lid and straw. "I made enough smoothie that day for four of us, in one blender."

I asked, "Were you the one who handed McVay his drink?"

AJ shook his head. "I poured it into four glasses on the counter and turned back to wash out the blender. The guys were all there waiting, and each took his own glass."

"You saw that?"

AJ squinted as if trying to remember. "They were in the room when I finished making the drink, but I didn't see each of them take a glass. When I turned back, only one glass remained, mine, and the others were drinking the smoothie." He shrugged as if it wasn't any big deal.

I hoped he was right. My stupid feeling of unease was strengthening, creating a knot of tension between my shoulders. Maybe I was trying to make the situation with AJ the cause because, all things considered, that situation was doable. Manageable. Fixable.

Gathering all the facts would put me at ease. "So others in the room will be able to say McVay took his own smoothie."

AJ thought for a moment. "Actually, Keith wasn't in the room when I poured the drink. I'm not sure where he was, but one of the trainers said he'd take it to Keith."

"Which trainer?"

"Brad. Brad Jenson."

I made a mental note then asked, "What's going to happen to McVay?"

AJ shrugged again. "Nothing. He'll serve a three-game suspension, probably pay a fine, and return to the field like nothing happened. He gets a little mini break. Keith McVay is untouchable. He's connected to the right people. In a few years, this won't be remembered."

In the current climate of persecution on social media, I found that hard to believe. But then, some people lived under a lucky star, and dirt didn't seem to stick to them. Maybe McVay was one of those. I made a mental note to ask my dad about him. Dad's years as a reporter, beat and investigative, would provide far more information than doing some online search.

"So," AJ said, after tossing his empty cup into the sink,

"you gonna continue to harsh my vibe, or can we just enjoy this opportunity?"

I laughed. "Yeah, sorry."

Precious said, "She can't help herself. This PI gig of hers has made her dark."

I laughed again but with false humor. Precious was right. In less than a year, I'd gone from being more optimistic to pragmatically fatalistic, no matter how hard I tried not to. Leo had warned me many years ago when I'd tried my hand at being a crime-scene photographer. And he'd been right. But the truth was that I would rather be a PI instead of what I used to do. Studio photography might be less risky, but taking pictures of devilish children dressed up as angels with their insanely neurotic moms had eaten away at my soul.

I clasped my hands in false glee. "Okay, all that aside. Who's super excited about seeing AJ play live? I know I am."

AJ broke out into a wide grin. "None of those hard metal seats for my friends. Nope. Clubhouse seats for you all."

I glanced at Precious. "I've never been in the clubhouse before."

She wagged her brows. "I hear the food is good."

We high-fived.

AJ slid three tickets across the counter toward us. "Who are you bringing?"

I said, "My dad, of course. He's a serious football fan."

AJ gave me a thumbs-up. "And you're cool keeping an eye on T-Roy while there? I know he's old enough to take care of himself, but it'll make me feel better." T-Roy was his nickname for his teenage brother, Troy.

I looked over my shoulder toward the bedrooms. "Where is Troy, by the way?"

Their mom lived in Arizona, undergoing treatment for cancer, and AJ was Troy's guardian.

"He's working at a video game store. Can you believe it?" AJ winked.

His brother had been arrested for shoplifting a few months back and had done his community service time in what was supposed to be a scared-straight program for wealthy kids. But when his instructor was murdered and one of the kids in the program accused, Troy had straightened up his act really quickly. That probably wasn't what the judge who'd sentenced Troy had in mind. But hey, whatever works.

Cora ran into the house with Simon on her heels. "We need some treats. I'm trying to teach Simon to shake."

AJ, who'd just picked up the blender to carry it to the sink, pointed at a canister on the counter. "They're in there."

Cora pointed at the blender. "What was that?"

AJ said, "A green smoothie. Very healthy and good for you."

In typical kindergarten fashion, Cora responded with absolute brutal honesty. "It looks like vomit. Alien vomit."

AJ looked at me and laughed. "She's totally related to you. That could've come from your mouth."

I grinned. "I take that as a compliment." I told Cora, "We have to be heading out. I'll bring you back to play with Simon another day."

She wrapped her arms around the dog's neck. "Can't I take him home?"

I knelt before my niece and said, "That would make AJ sad. Simon is his best friend. And besides, I happen to know that in the evening, Simon gets gassy and can stink up a room for hours. Like the smell of rotten eggs."

"Hey," AJ said with indignation, "he has feelings, and he can't help that he has a sensitive GI system."

Cora grimaced, her grip on Simon relaxing. "Maybe he should stay here."

Precious said, "Maybe you should give him some of that green vomit drink."

For a second, the tension I'd been carrying around eased as I joked with my friends and family. I wished whatever was coming would just come already. Let's get this show on the road so I can put it behind me. Though if this is how life is going to be from now on, maybe I should revisit studio or crime-scene photography.

Not for the first time did I wonder if I was cut out for the high-stakes lifestyle of a private investigator.

4

THURSDAY

GAME DAY

I WAS DECKED OUT IN MY PORTLAND PIONEER TEAM COLORS: dirty brown and puke green. Dad took it a step further and painted green and brown smudges under his eyes. I couldn't say the colors were flattering, but no one cared.

I'd grown up going to games because my dad and I were big Seahawks fans. But I'd never found my seats by taking an elevator to them. My pocketbook supported only tickets that required extreme stair climbing. I'd also never found my seat by going through a heated lobby with carpet, lounge seating, and a bar with a scattering of bar-height tables for mingling.

A host showed us to the box, but not before double-checking our tickets. Inside the box were cushioned seats set theater style for optimal game viewing. The temperature was a comfy seventy degrees. Outside, the weather was misting as Mother Nature alternated between sleet and rain.

"This is the life," Dad said and elbowed me.

"All your connections and never a clubhouse invite?" I tsked and shook my head in mock disappointment.

Dad chuckled. "Yeah, well, I was persona non grata for decades."

He'd even spent some time in the slammer for not disclosing his source on his PED exposé. After that jading experience, Russell and Elizabeth True moved their young daughters out of Los Angeles and to the small town of Wind River, where Dad became the owner and sole staff reporter for *The Wind River Journal*.

I tossed my plastic backpack onto a plush armchair in the front row and took the seat next to it. "Good thing that was a long time ago, because I had to give our names for the tickets." I waggled my eyebrows. "Or you'd be taking in the game like Keith McVay, from your couch by the flat screen. With Mom and Cora there distracting you."

Dad winked. "That's why you're my favorite daughter."

"This week," I said under my breath because Dad always told Rachel and me that each of us was his favorite daughter... as if he had others.

Precious moved my bag one chair away and took the seat next to me. Dad sat on my other side and Troy next to him.

Leaning forward, I told Troy, "I bet we seem silly to you. We're all excited to be here, and this is your standard now." I smiled.

He shrugged. "I don't come to the games often. Or if I do, I sometimes wait in the underground. Mom came once before she left for Arizona, but I haven't been up here since."

"Too bad your mom can't be here now," I said.

He nodded. "Yeah, because the time she did come, he warmed the bench the entire game. But she's watching today." He waved his phone. "And she's texting."

Precious looked around and sighed. "This is the life." She

pointed at a credenza at the end of the room. "Already stocked with food."

Troy looked over his shoulder at the hot plates and serving dishes. "AJ had to select the menu in advance."

I grimaced. "I hope he didn't put that green sludge drink on the menu. And I hope there's more than veggies."

Troy laughed. "Yeah, I told him I wouldn't go unless there were wings."

I high-fived Troy.

Precious asked, "So each box can have something different? Foodwise, I mean."

Troy nodded. "It's all about how much you want to spend."

Precious stood and smoothed her palms down the front of her jeans. "I think I'll go check things out. Get a feel for the place."

I pointed at the scoreboard outside the window. We were practically eye level with it, and I had an amazing view of the entire field. Luxury is awesome. "Game starts in fifteen. You don't want to miss kickoff."

She rolled her eyes. I stood and followed her out of the row.

She looked over her shoulder. "Are you coming with?"

I shook my head and pointed at the buffet. "I get a nervous stomach and can't eat during the game. I'm going to fill up now."

She was out the door moments later, her chuckle floating on the wind.

Dad, Troy, and I ate our body weight in wings while discussing the obstacles AJ might have in the game. The emcee of the game came over the loudspeaker to amp up the crowd. I glanced around for Precious. She'd been gone longer than I expected.

I said, "I'll be back. I'm gonna go look for Precious."

Dad arched his brows. "Don't miss kickoff."

I nodded then stopped outside the box, shutting the solid wooden door behind me. Then I noticed how quiet the lounge was, how the doors to the boxes offered a barrier to sound. I scanned the space to my right and left—no sign of Precious.

I was about to ask the attendant when I heard her laugh. Barely. It came from the box next to ours. The door wasn't fully closed, or I wouldn't have heard her at all.

I stepped up to the door and knocked. The act itself felt silly because I wasn't at a residence.

Nothing happened. I knocked again. Still nothing. Because the door was ajar, I pulled it open and looked inside. That box was far more active and crowded than ours. Twenty people milled around with glasses of champagne and plates of crab legs and oysters. I saw what Troy had meant when he said the menu could be customized.

Precious was standing in a circle of three men. She'd dressed in jeans, a white T-shirt tucked in, knee-high boots that were waterproof, surprising because they didn't look weather friendly, and a corduroy jacket. The jacket was tied around her waist, which only accentuated her endowed chest and small waist. Her act of football patriotism was a brown-and-green scarf around her neck. She blended in perfectly with the crowd in the room.

She put a hand on the arm of one of the men and said, "It's not about daydreaming the future but visualizing how your plan works, the steps you take to get to the goal. There's no such thing as a ceiling."

He looked besotted... and loaded, sporting a leather watch with a diamond-and-rose-gold face I recognized as a Breitling. His dirty-blond hair was receding slightly though he looked to be maybe mid-thirties. He had friendly blue eyes and one dimple on his right cheek. He and his two friends were taller than Precious, something I'm sure she appreciated as she stood at six feet.

I tapped her on a shoulder. When she looked over, I pointed at the scoreboard. "Two minutes."

"Yeah," she said. "I still have two minutes. Sam, meet my new friends. I met Austin when I was out exploring." She squeezed his arm then did the weirdest thing ever. She giggled coquettishly.

I'd seen the various stages of Precious flirting or in a relationship. And I thought I'd seen it all. But that giggle was like nothing I'd ever experienced, as if Precious was flustered. And a flustered Precious was as rare a sighting as Bigfoot. I was used to angry Precious and scared Precious.

Austin stuck out a hand. "Austin Strong."

As we shook hands, recognition dawned. *Holy crap.* Austin Strong was a tech mogul who'd gotten his start by capturing the market on internet privacy. About a decade before, spyware popped up that turned computer cameras into motion detectors and spied on people everywhere. Suddenly, women around the world, mostly college students, were finding videos of themselves on the internet —videos of them changing clothes, sleeping, studying, having sex, or doing many other random acts were being streamed for any pervert's pleasure. Strong invented software called StrongBlock to block the spyware. He became a billionaire almost overnight because of it. And he wasn't a one-hit wonder. Security was his thing, and he was one of the strongest voices advocating for ownership of data and online privacy.

And for all his good deeds, he then wooed the people of Oregon by purchasing a pro-football team and moving it to Portland.

"Samantha True," I said. "It's nice to meet you."

He gestured to his friends. "This is DeShawn Cook—you might know him as Lil' Megalodon—and Seth Painter."

Lil' Megalodon was a superstar rapper. A skinny, rail-thin white guy with a scruffy goatee and short dreadlocks, he'd managed to capture the hearts of the youth with his stand-up-and-fight raps cleverly done with classical music as the melodies. In truth, I had him in my Spotify playlist. His raps were great for inspiring perseverance while I went running. Hanging from his neck was a large gold rope chain and a megalodon tooth the size of my hand with fingers splayed. Down his right arm was a six-inch bandage.

"Yikes." I gestured at the bandage.

He glanced at his arm. "Got cut by those that wish to repress. Dirty blade. Had to get one of those stupid shots."

Tetanus. Thinking about it made my arm ache. "Scary," I said.

The rapper said, "Not for me. I will not be silenced."

Seth Painter stuck out his hand, and the conversation shifted.

I also knew Seth Painter—by name only, though. His family owned one of the largest insurance companies on the West Coast.

We exchanged pleasantries then were interrupted by the emcee announcing the coin toss.

I pointed toward the door. "If you'll excuse me, I'm going to go back to our box. I want to see kickoff." I could've watched it there but wanted to see it with my dad. And being around such influential and wealthy people made me nervous.

Precious said, "I'll go with you. Thanks again, Austin. It was such a pleasure to meet you."

He squeezed both her shoulders warmly. "Let's connect." After letting go of her shoulders, he tapped his shirt pocket. "I have your card. I'll be in touch."

"Enjoy the game," she said to the others and let me pull her from the room.

We said nothing in the hallway and stayed quiet until we took our seats back in our box.

"Where were you?" Dad asked.

I waved a hand dismissively. "Oh, just chatting with Austin Strong, Seth Painter, and Lil' Megalodon."

"What?" Troy said, nearly coming out of his seat. "Lil' Megalodon is here?"

"Yeah." I hitched a finger over my shoulder, indicating the box to our right. "In that box right there. If you hang out in the lounge area, you might actually run into him."

Troy stood.

I did as well and met his gaze. "I was kidding. Your brother will kill you if you miss his game."

Troy grimaced. "But Lil' Megalodon... I love him."

Precious said, "He's not going anywhere. When I was there, I noticed he stepped out to use the restroom instead of the one in the box. If the way he's chugging those Diet Cokes is any indication, you'll likely find him making a trip between quarters. Try then."

Troy gave it a thought then sat. "Okay. I'll do that."

Dad looked at me. "Austin Strong, huh?"

I nodded and waited. Dad knew everyone or something about them.

He said, "I did a piece on him right as he was coming out of college. Interesting interview. Self-made. He's successful because he doesn't take no for an answer."

"It's weird to meet billionaires my age," I said.

Dad chuckled. "Made you feel like a slacker, huh?"

"Yeah. A bit. Or more that they're so sure of their path." I'd long accepted that comparing myself to others was stupid. Maybe being dyslexic helped with that. I always knew I was different. I knew my journey wouldn't be like most people's. We all have our own paths and potential, and I was comfortable with mine. Mostly. But sometimes self-doubt crept in.

The crowd cheered, and I looked out the window toward the field. *Great, I missed kickoff.* At least I hadn't missed AJ's first play.

"Hold on to your titties, kitties. The fun is just beginning," Precious said as the teams ran out to line up for the first snap.

Unable to contain my excitement, I squealed and let myself get lost in the sport on the field.

I ended up standing for most of the game, yelling at the players on the field. The teams took turns alternating the lead, staying within three points of each other. AJ threw one interception but rallied hard, and in the end, the Portland Pioneers won by a field goal.

Troy pumped the air when the final whistle blew. "Today was epic. I got Lil' Megalodon's autograph, and AJ won."

I said, "And when you talk to him, make sure you reverse that order."

The plan was to head down to the tunnel that led to the

locker rooms. We weren't allowed into the locker rooms, but we could wait for AJ in a specified area. Getting to the family waiting area took us through a secret maze of back hallways and elevator rides. In the waiting area, other families and friends mingled. Security and local Portland PD stood between us and the locker rooms.

Troy nodded toward the cops. "What's that about?"

I'd only given the security a cursory glance but turned my attention to them fully. I'd been on a winning high and hadn't processed that the Portland PD wouldn't normally be present. Local PD were talking with the Pioneers' head coach in a tense exchange of words.

The locker room doors swung open, and the cops led out a man in handcuffs with a towel over his head, likely done as some attempt at privacy. He was dressed in jeans and a T-shirt, and if the moisture clinging to his shirt was any indication, he'd just come from a shower—a player.

"What the hell?" Troy said then rushed toward the towel-hidden man, only to be stopped five feet away by security. "That's my brother!" he yelled while fighting against the two men holding him back by his shoulders.

I pushed through the gathering crowd, the whirring sound of cameras and people whispering around me. How I managed I don't know, but I slipped through the hands of a security guard and rushed to AJ.

I walked backward, facing him as the cops continued to usher him down the tunnel toward the exit.

AJ had his head down but looked up at me through the folds of the towel. "McVay is dead," he whispered. "And they think I did it."

5

FRIDAY AFTER THE ARREST

I LEFT THE MULTNOMAH COUNTY JAIL, FEELING GUILTY FOR being able to walk away. The jail, housed at the Multnomah County Sheriff's Office, was located in downtown Portland and, if given only a quick glance, looked like any other office building—until one realized many of the windows in the middle section of the building were small slats wedged between concrete squares. The outside space was surrounded by a large chain-link fence with massive rolls of barbed wire at the top. Above the slatted windows were five floors of office windows housing the sheriff's department. I'd tried to go up there after meeting with AJ to talk to the arresting officers but couldn't get past the reception area.

The scale of the department was not lost on me. It echoed the severity of AJ's current state and how far removed from my element I was. That was no Wind River Police Department where the receptionist was someone I'd gone to school with. Heck, Wind River's police chief, D. B. Louney, had even cheated off me in chemistry.

I was stuck. I drove home chewing a thumbnail, scared

and unsure how I was going to help AJ. I'd thought to start
with the arresting cops, but they refused to see me.

At home, I parked LC, my ancient but hardworking
Wagoneer, behind my dad's newspaper and promised LC a
quart of oil first thing. LC, named after the explorers Lewis
and Clark because we had numerous adventures under our
belt, drank oil like there was no tomorrow. His monthly oil
budget was greater than my takeout coffee budget. And I had
a serious love for coffee not brewed by me.

Inside, I dictated a list of my thoughts to get organized,
and I stored it on my phone.

What I'd done: taken care of AJ's financial needs and
touched base with Troy, who was going to stay with his mom
in Arizona.

The media was all over the place, and the police had
trashed AJ's house, looking for evidence.

What I needed to do: pick up Simon, clean AJ's house,
find out who killed Keith McVay—*but how?*

I stretched out on the couch and pressed my palms to my
temples, trying to force myself to come up with the next
move. Maybe my uncertainty was immobilizing me. Maybe
my inertia was inexperience. But I was determined to not let
either of those be a reason I would let AJ down. But I was
seriously scared. I switched to my other thumbnail, having
gnawed the other one to the quick. From my backpack I took
out my iPad mini and searched YouTube for more how-to-
be-a-private-investigator videos, specifically on solving
murders. The pickings were slim, and some looked to be
presented by people greener than me. I was swiping with
frustration when someone rapped on my front door.

"Unless you have a crystal ball and can provide all the answers, go away," I said, having left YouTube and using a search engine to try to find higher quality information.

The door swung open, and Precious and Leo stood at the threshold.

Precious asked, "Is this a pity party?"

I glanced at her over my iPad and looked away. Tears threatened to break free, and I desperately didn't want to cry... at least not in front of Leo.

They stepped inside, Precious first.

She snatched the iPad from my hand. "What are you doing?"

"Looking for answers." I sat up and reached for the device.

She held it behind her back. "I had a feeling you'd be feeling rough after seeing AJ. That's why I called Leo and asked him if he might have any suggestions." She pushed my legs off the couch and sat down next to me. "Austin Strong called me. Offered to help AJ any way he could. Thanked me for getting Tyson Lockett as AJ's defense attorney and wondered how I managed that."

After the game, as the police escorted AJ off the premises, Precious had called Lockett as if she'd read my mind.

I said, "I'm surprised Strong is offering support. All the negative attention on his team can't be good."

Precious nodded. "They're getting hammered in social media."

Leo, in his cop uniform of navy pants and top with a gray undershirt, sat down on my other side. His shirtsleeves were rolled up, his eagle tattoo side-eyeing me.

He said, "It's all over the news too. They're making a big

deal out of anything and everything. Like the fact that Strong and McVay went to college together."

I snapped my head in his direction. "They did? Really?" I hadn't gotten the impression they'd known each other outside of the Pioneers. But I was no expert on McVay or Strong.

He leaned back into the couch. "Apparently."

I slapped myself on the forehead. "Man, I'm stupid. I should have Toby digging into everyone he can. I've been so focused on what I *can't* do that I forgot to look at what I *can* do."

Precious bumped me with her shoulder. "And now you know why we came over. I had a feeling you were feeling... overwhelmed. I mean, you made us go into the woods for scary hide-and-seek because, and this is all just my opinion, you're scared of failure. Which I get—"

I nudged her back with my shoulder—hard. "Get to the point."

Precious rolled her eyes.

Leo chuckled. "Precious asked if maybe I knew someone who might be able to guide you somewhat."

I looked between them.

Precious nodded. "Yeah, a mentor. We've all had them. Only you haven't. You gotta admit it's a brilliant idea."

She was right. The idea had merit.

I looked at Leo. "And you know such a person. An Obi-Wan to my Skywalker?"

Leo grimaced slightly. "Maybe not exactly Obi-Wan, but I've worked with this private investigator before. He's originally from Portland but moved out here a few years back when he retired." He made air quotes around "retired." To my questioning look, he said, "He only takes cases that move him."

To which I asked, "And before, he took any case?"

Leo gave a brisk nod. "Pretty much. He's a little rough around the edges, but he could teach you a lot. He's good at what he does."

Precious handed me my iPad. "You can't be dependent on YouTube to answer all your questions."

She's right. "What's his name?" I asked, wondering if I might have heard of him.

"Paul Bea," said Leo.

I asked, "What's the *B* stand for?"

"His last name."

I gave him a look to convey that I thought he was jerking my chain. "Yeah, I know it's his last name. And it starts with a *B*. What's the rest of it?"

Leo laughed. "Sorry, my bad. I get what you're asking. His last name isn't just the letter *B*. It's *B* and then an *e* and an *a*. Bea."

I snort laughed. "I got it now."

Leo knocked a fist against my leg. "Come on. Let's go meet him. He's at the dog park."

Precious was up and at the door in seconds, swinging it open and gesturing with a flourish for me to precede her.

The dog park was a two-acre parcel of land with chicken-wire fencing. The land sloped down a hill that led to a wildlife preserve. I would run by it on my jogging path. The previous year, the city had put in a fake fire hydrant fountain that spewed water with the press of a button and provided dogs with fresh water and a place to splash. I made a mental note to bring Simon there every day to burn energy.

Three cars were at the dog park. We'd followed Leo in

his police cruiser because he had to return to work afterward. Trailing behind Leo, we entered the dog park and were greeted by two ankle biters and three large dogs. Two of the larger dogs were Labs, and the other was a giant schnauzer. Across the field, two women were standing together, and standing as far away from them as humanly possible without leaving the park was an older man. He whistled, and the schnauzer took off in his direction.

One of the Labs jumped on Precious, and she knocked him down. Both smaller dogs were nipping at Leo's legs.

"Hey," Leo called out to the ladies, "you want to call your dogs?"

The ladies scowled, and one called the names of the four dogs... which in turned ignored her.

Precious leaned over. "See what he did there? He deduced that all these dogs belonged to them." She elbowed me in a hardy-har way.

Leo picked up a punctured and weatherworn tennis ball and tossed it across the field. The Labs followed it. The ankle biters circled us until Leo pushed them away.

I glared at her. "Duh. One, he knows this dude and, I'm guessing, knows what kind of dog he has. Two, the only guy here whistled, and his dog came running. That leaves the ladies with these dogs."

Precious gave me a puzzled look. "I was kidding." She grabbed my hands and inspected my fingers, with their nails chewed and mangled. "You're worse than I thought. Now I'm positive meeting Paul Bea is the right thing. You need to find some confidence. You need to visualize yourself being successful with this case, or your fear is going to consume you."

I nodded. The simple fact that I hadn't even called Toby

to get background info told me I was frozen with fear. I hadn't felt like that since I'd been a kid right before a reading test, which I knew I couldn't pass even if I had the cheat sheet... because I couldn't read a cheat sheet either. I'd felt like an imposter then, and I felt like one now, like I'd been playing at being a PI and had only gotten lucky. And maybe I had. But I thought I'd learned something along the way. Not drawing on that was making me nuts.

I turned to Leo. "We can take it from here if you need to get back to work."

He glanced at his watch. "I do. Are you sure?"

I nodded. "I got this."

Precious beamed and clapped in excitement. "We got this."

I continued nodding. "Yeah, we got this. Thanks for setting this up, Leo."

He left while Precious and I made our way across the field toward the older gentleman waiting by a bench. He was bent over, petting his dog, but stood as we approached.

Paul Bea was probably two inches shorter than me and sported a Bob Ross Afro. His skin was a slightly yellowish hue, like he'd been tinted by years of cigarette smoke... or had a liver issue. He had a large belly that pushed the waistline of his black jogging pants low. A black T-shirt and bright-white tennis shoes finished out the outfit.

I waved. "Hi Paul, I'm Samantha True. This is my friend, Erika Shurmann."

"Paulie. People call me Paulie." Paulie scanned me up and down. "I hope you're the PI because chesty here"—he jerked a thumb toward Precious—"would be perfect for trapping the wayward spouse."

Precious looked at me and said softly, "I'm gonna take that as a compliment. I guess."

I cleared my throat. "Yeah, I'm the PI."

Paulie scratched a dirty nail across his nose. "And you caught yourself the McVay murder." He gave a low whistle. "Nice."

I tucked my hands into my jeans pocket to keep from chewing them. "Only it's my friend sitting in jail, so it doesn't feel nice."

Paul held up a finger. "Lesson number one. Never make friends with clients, and never make clients out of friends."

"Thanks, Mr. Bea. Too late this time. But I'll keep it in mind for next time."

"Paulie." His squinty eyes darted between Precious and me. "So tell me about the case."

Where to start? I took a breath, ready to launch into AJ's story, but one of the Labs ran up to hump Precious's leg. She shooed it away like a person does a fly, but the brown dog kept coming back for more.

"Hey," Paulie yelled, "call your dog!" The irritation in his voice was coming through loud and clear.

"Here, Brownie! Come on, boy," one of the ladies said in a sickly-sweet voice.

Brownie continued to ignore her, his focus on molesting Precious. Paulie walked over to the dog and grabbed it by the collar. Then he stepped away from Precious and told the dog to scram, pushing him on the butt.

"Stupid woman," Paulie mumbled when he returned to us. "You know, she comes here with a laser pointer and tells people when their dogs have crapped. The laser points out where the pile is waiting to be picked up."

Brownie was between his owner and us, still eyeing

Precious but contemplating Paulie's alpha status. Paulie postured by doing a fake lunge, and the dog ran off.

I said, "You're kidding."

Paulie shook his head. "Okay, tell me about your client."

I explained AJ's situation and what I knew.

"Where do you plan to start?" Paulie asked.

"I have my IT guy doing background on McVay, and..." I wondered if it was a lie if I planned on having Toby do it. And who else should I look into? I had nothing.

"That's it?" he asked.

I shrugged. "Isn't that why I'm here?"

Paulie laughed bitterly. "Girl, if you don't know where to start, you might as well tell your friend to enjoy death row. Because Leo's right. You are in over your head." He shook his head then called to his dog. "Come on, Rocket, let's blow this popsicle stand."

Okay, maybe I don't have this.

6

FRIDAY

I TRIED NOT TO FREAK OUT IN FRONT OF PRECIOUS, BUT SHE knew me too well.

After we watched Paulie leave the dog park, she grabbed me by the shoulders and stared me hard in the eyes. "Do not freak out. Call Toby and start with that background check."

I gulped in air. "And then what?"

She punched me hard in the shoulder. "Come on, Sam. What is it you're really afraid of?"

Precious and I had been friends since early elementary school and had been through a lot. She overcame her stuttering, I my dyslexia. Being the kids that were different and pulled out of the classroom gave us something in common and forged a friendship that was deep and true.

I said, "I've only solved one case."

She shook her head. "That's not true. You've helped lots of people, and I think you should count the one back in college, remember? When you were the crime-scene intern and Junkies was robbed." Junkies was a local bar attached to a junkyard.

"I meant big cases. So, okay. Two," I said. "The situation with what happened to Carson was a matter of survival."

Carson was my husband, though not legally, as I'd found out when he died in a mysterious fiery car accident. And figuring out all the lies of my life was what had led me to become a private investigator.

Precious's grip on my shoulders eased. "And now?"

"Now, this is big time. It's AJ. This is life or death. And I'm scared I'm going to fail."

Precious smiled and wrapped an arm around my shoulder. We walked toward the gate.

"Sam, by doing nothing, you've already failed. And I know you as well as I know myself. You aren't good with failure. The reason you're chewing your nails is because you're doing nothing. So do something. Anything. Call Toby. Call the coach of the team. Call McVay's mother. But do something. Start somewhere. What's Lockett said?"

I stopped walking, turned my face up to the misty-gray sky, and sighed deeply. "Lockett. Duh." AJ's lawyer and my friend was going to be my first point of contact. AJ had asked me to help him, but I couldn't do that if Lockett thought I might damage AJ's defense. I looked back at Precious. "I know what to do now."

She shook her head. "You've always known what to do. It's only now that you're listening to yourself."

I smiled. "You're a good life coach."

"Duh," she said. "Also, Leo mentioned that if this meeting went sideways, you could find Paulie Bea at the gun range on Mondays and Wednesdays. Maybe you go tell him then what your plan is and see if he can help."

Paulie Bea might turn me away and laugh at me again, but having another PI for checks and balances wasn't something I could walk away from without trying again. I pulled out my phone and called Tyson Lockett, lawyer extraordinaire. We'd met because he was my not-so-legal husband's best friend. Tyson had helped me get to the bottom of Carson's death and lies.

Two hours later, I was dressed in my best black skirt, white button-down shirt, and a pink cardigan sweater and was waiting for Lockett outside the Multnomah County Sheriff's Office. My long hair was pulled back into a French braid, and with Precious's help, I'd even done my makeup. I planned to meet first with Lockett and AJ and listen to his recounting of events, then I was going to find the arresting cops and try again for a chat.

Upon my arrival, Lockett gave me a tight hug and a kiss on the cheek. He was tall, blond, and built like the surfer he was, with broad shoulders and a narrow waist. His skin was far too sun-kissed for our Pacific Northwest rainy season.

"Where did you come from? You have a nice glow about you." I hadn't seen him in several weeks.

He grinned. "Maldives. Nothing but pure tube riding." He mimed skimming a wave. "It was glorious."

"Sorry to drag you back to the world of glum." Surfing across the globe had to be far better than being a defense attorney.

"I was back for another case anyway, and my next trip isn't until February."

"I hope this is all over by then," I mumbled.

Tyson cut me a puzzled look. "Are you kidding? AJ has the dream team. Me and you. Two weeks." He held up two fingers. "We'll have it wrapped up."

"I hope you're right." I was sick of bemoaning my fears and didn't want to let Lockett down with them, but I also wanted AJ to get the best. "But if at any time you think another PI would be better for AJ, you let me know."

Lockett flung an arm over my shoulder. "What you may lack in experience you make up in grit. Let's get started."

Twenty minutes later, after a very uncomfortable pat down, we were seated in the same visitation room where I'd met with AJ earlier that day. That morning had felt like weeks before.

AJ sank into the seat opposite us, shoulders slumped. "I'm glad to see you both."

I made the introductions since they hadn't met in person —only a quick phone call during which Lockett gave AJ the rundown on what not to do while he was being held.

Lockett jumped right into it. "You won't be arraigned for a few days. The arraignment is where you'll enter your plea—"

"Not guilty," AJ said, sitting up suddenly. "I didn't kill Keith."

Lockett held up a hand. "I know. We'll get there. But first, you'll enter a plea of not guilty. Then we're going to try to get you out on bail. You might not like the conditions. We'll need to talk about your limitations. You're being charged with murder, so I'm guessing at a minimum they'll want a high bail and maybe even a tracker on your ankle."

AJ nodded. "I can live with that. Not that I have a lot of money."

Lockett pulled up his briefcase. "You play pro football. You're perceived as having money. And sometimes, perception gets confused for reality." Lockett pulled out a legal pad and a pen and scratched a few things at the top.

Up until then, he'd been nothing but professional, but I did a double take when I saw the pen. It was designed to resemble an ordinary pen found anywhere, but when it was held up to write, a film slid down the shaft of the pen to reveal the phrase "You've already lost."

I pointed at the pen. "What's that?"

Lockett held it up. "A message to the prosecution. Freaks them out every time. I had them made in bulk. Some say 'Bad call' or 'You're screwed.' They're my favorite." He turned back to AJ. "Now, why don't you start at the beginning? Why were you at Keith McVay's house Wednesday night?"

I took out a notepad as well. I knew my fear was keeping from firing on all cylinders. I also knew I couldn't count on Lockett's notes. Reading them would be a struggle because of his chicken-scratch handwriting and his shorthand, which didn't mesh with my own dyslexia-created code.

AJ wiped his hands down his face then looked at me with tired hazel eyes. His normally dark Mediterranean complexion was sallow.

I smiled softly. "I know this is hard. What was supposed to be a great day for you has turned into a nightmare. But we're going to get this worked out."

He nodded mechanically. "Throughout the day, Keith and I had been texting about the game. He was giving me tips about the opposing team and certain films to watch to help with prep. Around dinner, I asked him how he was holding up. He was pissed about the drug test and kept saying the lab got it wrong."

Lockett interrupted. "Yet he failed two more subsequent tests." He pulled out some papers he'd tucked under his notepad and flipped through them. "He demanded they try a different lab, which they did, yet he got the same results: a failed drug test."

AJ said, "Keith was adamant that the tests were errors.

He said he'd taken some painkillers after a car accident he had and was trying to find out if maybe that was messing up his test. We had a game the night after his accident, and he was pretty sore. He still played. He was sacked three times. Maybe he took more than he was supposed to take of the pain meds?"

My brain flashed on a news image I'd seen. McVay had been in an accident Thanksgiving weekend.

Lockett read from his secret papers. "Sunday evening, McVay was T-boned by a delivery truck a few miles from the Pioneers' training facility. He was taken to the hospital and given Cataflam, an anti-inflammatory, nonsteroidal drug. He was released that night. The drug in his system when he bombed his pee test was an anabolic-androgenic steroid. Not related."

AJ looked dejected. "You know, Keith told me that had he been driving his Porsche that day, he likely would have been killed in that accident, but he was in his Mercedes SUV. Pure luck, he'd said." AJ shook his head sadly. "Doesn't sound very lucky to me."

Me neither, to be honest. I made a few notes. "Is it normal for McVay to be at the training facility on a Sunday night?"

AJ nodded. "Yeah, there's no rest when there's games to prep for. He had specific days when he watched game videos. I had gone to the facility to watch videos too. We even went over some footage together."

Needing to understand the habits of players better, I asked, "You go even when you have a game the next night?"

AJ shrugged, confusion on his face. "Yeah. So?"

Okay, point taken. All that nighttime studying was normal regardless of the game schedule.

Lockett gestured for AJ to continue. "You were saying

that Keith was pissed about the failed test. Did he say anything else? Did he accuse you of anything?"

AJ cut his eyes to me then back to Lockett. "No." He leaned forward to rest his elbows on the table then his head in his hands.

Lockett said, "Tell me why there's speculation that you might have spiked his smoothie."

AJ sighed.

AJ and I filled Lockett in about the smoothie-making event, and I explained that the one blender and one pour meant they'd all had the smoothie from the same batch.

AJ said, "A few guys ribbed me about spiking the smoothie, but no one meant it. To prove the smoothies were spiked, we all volunteered to be tested that Friday too."

Lockett asked, "We?"

"Me and the two other guys who drank the smoothie. Four total if we count Keith." AJ gave Lockett their names. "And we all showed clean."

"What time was this?" I liked to see things linearly, and setting the time helped me.

AJ mumbled, "Around eight."

Lockett wrote on his notepad. "And you said the trainer delivered the drink. His name is Brad Jenson. We'll want to talk to him." He said that last part to me.

I wrote Brad's name on my pad.

Lockett continued. "How was Keith the week after the suspension? Leading up to your start?"

"He was acting a little weird."

"Weird?" Lockett asked. "Weird toward you, weird?"

AJ shook his head. "No, at least I didn't take it like that. I assumed his behavior was because he was going to miss a game. He's the ultimate competitor and hadn't missed a game in his career yet. Until now. But he was angry and jumpy."

"Jumpy?" I asked.

AJ nodded. "That's the best I can describe it."

"Tell me about the day before the game," Lockett said. "You went to McVay's house?"

"Coach was making him stay home. He'd work out at home, attended meetings remotely. I felt bad for him. Like I said, we'd been texting, and that evening, I offered to bring him some food and company. I figured he could coach me a little more. Maybe that would make him feel better. And I would reassure him that I wasn't out for his job."

"But you want a starting position."

AJ nodded in his hands. "Yeah, but that doesn't make me a killer. Every second string wants a starting position."

Lockett said, "So you go to his house..."

"I picked up takeout from an Indian cuisine place he likes in Portland."

"Any alcohol?"

AJ looked up at Lockett with an angry expression and shook his head. "No, I had a big game the next day. That would have been stupid of me."

Lockett looked at his papers again. "His urine analysis says he was drinking a lot the night he died."

"Anything else of interest on the toxicology report?" I asked.

Lockett shook his head, his attention returning to AJ. "Okay, you go to his house with curry and naan bread. Then what?"

"Yeah, how did you know that's what I took?"

Lockett tapped the papers. "Coroner's report."

"I get there, and it's weird at first."

Lockett probes. "What's *weird*? You've said that before. Explain *weird*."

"Keith. He's antsy, restless. When he opens the door, he looks past me like he thinks someone else is out there. Then gestures for me to hurry and come in."

That time, I interrupted. "Any guesses why?"

AJ shrugged. "The media had been hanging out there a lot. I figured that was why. Keith's in negotiations"—AJ closed his eyes and groaned—"he *was* in negotiations for his contract, and some reporters were dogging him about it. They picked up the hounding when he popped positive."

Currently, top quarterbacks were making fat money on their new contract deals. But if a player had a history of trouble or drugs, that deal could go sideways really quickly.

I asked, "Keith never popped before, right? He's squeaky clean."

AJ nodded, confirming what I'd thought. That was unlike McVay. If I'd had something happen to damage my reputation, I would be acting weird too.

"You go to Keith's. He invites you inside. You take curry and share a meal. Then what?" Lockett was gently grilling AJ, his questions on point and moving the information along.

AJ shrugged. "We watched some film, and he coached me a bit about the other team's defense. Prepped me."

"And?" Lockett probed.

"And then I left."

"What time was that?"

"About nine thirty. I remember thinking I could get home in time to watch *Ridiculousness*. That starts at ten."

"And you're sure no alcohol was consumed?" Lockett asked. "Think. Try to picture his place when you were there."

AJ pressed the heels of his palms to his eyes, and long seconds passed. "There was an open beer on the coffee table when I got there. He maybe took a few drinks from it, but he didn't even finish it while I was there." He dropped his hands. "He wasn't on a bender or anything."

"Did you get in a fight? Exchange heated words?"

AJ shook his head.

"You sure?" Lockett pushed.

"Yeah. I think I'd remember getting in a fight."

Lockett tossed his pen onto the pad. "It's amazing what people forget. McVay had a cut across his nose. Like he'd been punched."

AJ nodded. "I saw that. I asked him what happened, and he said he got it while having a trainer do reps with him. Said Brad came out to the house. Keith said one ball caught him off guard and got him in the face."

Lockett said, "Okay. We'll get you arraigned and try to get bail. I have a meeting with the prosecutor to see what evidence they have. They're dragging their heels with disclosure. This is a high-profile case already. You're gonna be persona non grata for a long time. If you don't have thick skin, you'd better get it fast. You don't talk to anyone but me and Sam. Understand?"

AJ paled and nodded.

"No phone-call confessions. No secrets that I have to hear from the other side. You go back to your cell and wrack your brain for what it is that the cops have on you, whatever it is that put you here."

AJ said, "I just thought wrong place at the wrong time."

"Maybe that's some of it. But that's not enough to charge you. But let's hope it is, because I can get that tossed out in a heartbeat." Lockett stuffed paper and pens into his briefcase.

"I didn't do this, AJ said. "I'm innocent, and there has to be a way to prove it."

Lockett gave a quick bark. "You ever heard of the Innocence Project? It's an entire team of lawyers helping to get wrongly convicted people out of prison. Besides, everyone says they're innocent. In this current day, you're guilty until proven otherwise, and social media will find a good conspiracy theorist to keep people believing there's always a chance you're guilty. Buckle up. It's going to be a tough ride."

AJ gulped.

So did I.

7

FRIDAY

AFTER ANOTHER REBUFF BY THE COPS HANDLING AJ'S CASE, I made my next stop the training facility for the Portland Pioneers, a massive three-story building in Troutdale, the length of three football fields. Behind it, those fields ran end to end, overlooking the Columbia River with stunning views of the Columbia River Gorge.

My goal was to talk to the trainer and anyone else I could get in to see then to head across the bridge back into Washington to follow my other client's fiancé. I knew where he'd gone the previous week, and I wanted to make sure he was doing the same, within reason, that week.

I parked LC in a visitor spot and checked under his carriage to make sure he wasn't going to leave a trace of oil. In the back of my Wagoneer was spare cardboard to slip underneath in case he had post trip drip. But for the moment, he was clean.

The grand entrance, two glass doors flanked by a wall of river rock, stood twenty feet tall. Stepping inside was like entering a high-end lodge with solid wooden beams running the length of the room and dark barn-board floors contrasting with light-green furniture. Hanging on the walls were banners of playoff championships—no Super Bowl wins yet. But if sports radio chatter was any indication, the team was getting close—well, had been getting close with McVay at the helm.

The receptionist was a cool number with a silver buzz cut and earrings the size of my palm. She met my gaze with a steely one of her own.

"How may I help you?" Her nameplate read Amber North.

I showed her my private-investigator badge. "Hi, I'm Samantha True. I was hoping I could speak with the trainer Brad Jenson."

She showed no reaction whatsoever. "About?"

Um, none of your business. I impersonated a fish for a few seconds as I searched for words. "I just need him to verify a few facts for me."

Her gaze flicked to my backpack, where I'd tucked my badge. "But you're not a cop."

I wasn't sure if she was asking or talking out loud. "Is Mr. Jenson here?"

She crossed her arms. "Leave your card. I'll tell him you came by, and he can call you if he wants."

"I only need five minutes of his time." That was kind of a lie. But I really didn't want to have to stalk Brad Jenson to find an opportunity to run into him conveniently.

Amber North stared back at me without blinking. I was pretty good at that game, having spent my childhood in stare-down battles with Rachel, but I didn't want to burn my bridge here, so I thanked her and headed out, not leaving a business card because I knew she'd probably trash it before I even made it out the door.

I leaned against LC and was staring at the building, thinking about another way in, when a Ralphs click-and-shop delivery truck came rumbling into the lot and drove to the end before turning the corner toward the back. I jumped into LC and followed, parking at the very end of the complex. I worked about ten hours a week at the Ralphs grocery store in the click-and-shop department. None of my coworkers would be making this delivery because the store I worked at was in Vancouver, and this delivery was likely from the Ralphs distribution center because the order was larger than what a store could accommodate. But none of that mattered. What did matter was that I knew how those deliveries went and thought I might have an opportunity I could work to my advantage.

I jogged along the side of the building—which had no windows, luckily—and around the back. The truck was backed up to an open doorway, and the driver was ringing a bell. Moments later, the back door of the building swung open, and a large dude in a white chef's coat came out. He and the delivery guy carried large boxes of food from the truck into the building. I waited until they were both deep inside the truck and slipped through the back door.

I entered a large room with some benches, lockers, and hooks to hang coats and whatnot. Another door at the other end opened into a hallway. Once in the hallway, I paused to gather my bearings, seeing four doors to pick from. Two were on my left, one marked Restroom, the other Storage. On my right, one door was propped open and showed the kitchen. Another door at the far end was marked Exit.

Taking the exit was likely what I wanted to do, but I

wouldn't know where to go from there. I couldn't just
wander the building.

Instead, I hurried into the prep area, hoping to not get
seen by the delivery guy or the chef. Two women my mom's
age were dicing vegetables. On the stove, four large pots
steamed. One quick whiff told me soup was on. And it
smelled yummy. The scent of chicken and herbs hit me first.
The next was the hearty smell of beef stew.

My stomach grumbled—loudly. One of the ladies dicing
looked at me and raised an eyebrow.

"Smells really good. I'm sorry to interrupt, but could you
point me in the direction of Brad Jenson? I'm supposed to
meet him, and I think I came in the wrong door. He's one of
the team trainers."

Now I had the attention of both, and my stomach
rumbled again. I tried to make my expression apologetic and
slightly pleading. The taller lady pushed her hairnet off her
forehead with the back of one hand and looked out into the
dining room. I followed her gaze and saw several of the
players huddled at a table, talking quietly with plates of food
between them.

One guy stood alone, leaning against a vending machine,
his attention on his phone. He was dressed in khakis and a
polo shirt, a team lanyard around his neck. His hair, regular
boring brown, was cut short and preppy. But he didn't look
preppy. He looked nerdy trying to be preppy.

The tall lady turned back to me. "That's him by the snack
vendor."

I smiled. "Thanks." Then I made my way out the exit.

I wasted no time making my way to Jenson but walked
with confidence and purpose, like I had every reason to be in
the dining room of the Pioneers' training facility. Being

proactive was giving me a head rush. Maybe I was finding my groove.

I sidled up to Jenson and asked, "How's it going?"

He jumped and nearly dropped his phone. "F-f-fine."

"Sorry. Didn't mean to scare you." I stuck out my hand. "I'm Sam."

He shook mine limply. "Brad."

"Yeah, I've been trying to meet you." I took a business card from my back pocket and handed it to him. "I work for AJ Gunn. And I need your help in verifying a few things."

"I don't know anything." He stepped away from the vending machine, and I moved with him, attempting to herd him back against the wall.

"I'm not saying you know anything. I just need you to tell me what AJ was doing on Friday the day Keith McVay took that drug test and failed it."

Brad looked over my shoulder, his face pale and his eyes darting. I didn't want to read too much into his reactions.

"I wasn't with AJ all day," he said.

I fake laughed in an attempt to ease his anxiety. "Of course you weren't. How could you be? But you were there when AJ made that nasty green smoothie of his, right?"

Brad nodded, looking as uncomfortable as before and clearly not responding to my pathetic attempts to relax him.

"And you saw AJ give McVay the smoothie?"

AJ had said he didn't give McVay the drink, but I wanted Brad's version.

"Yeah. McVay drank the smoothie."

"That AJ handed to him?"

Brad locked eyes with me for a millisecond then glanced away and shifted his weight. "I can't remember if AJ gave Keith the drink or not."

I nodded. "Okay. Understandable. You said two other guys drank that sludge that day. Maybe one of them will remember." I looked around for the two men AJ had said drank the smoothie.

Brad sighed. "I carried the drink to Keith. He was getting into the whirlpool. He was still a little sore from the accident. The day before, he pulled his quad and wanted to warm the muscles before stretching out."

"Oh, so you handed the drink to Keith?"

Brad shook his head, making me almost groan in frustration. "I put the drink on the table by the whirlpool. I think Keith was in the locker room, changing or something. I don't know where he went."

"Did you stay in the room with the drink until Keith came back?"

Brad looked at me like I was stupid. "No, I don't get paid to babysit a smoothie made of vegetables. There are other guys who need work done before they get on the field."

"And all this happened before the drug test Keith took?"

Jenson eyed me with skepticism. "Yeah, team meeting is where players find out if they have to do the mando drug test."

"And team meeting is at nine o'clock?" I was guessing.

"Ten."

So McVay had drunk the smoothie before the meeting, found out he had to test, peed in a cup, and failed the test.

I moved on. "How about Thursday? When you went to Keith's house to do reps with him. When the ball hit him in the face? Tell me about that."

"What are you talking about? I never went to Keith's." Brad's lip curled up slightly, only to drop seconds later. He stared at something over my shoulder.

I turned around to see a security guard watching us.

Brad said, "I have to go. I shouldn't be talking to you anyway."

I turned back to Brad, knowing things were likely to go downhill fast. "Me, specifically? How can that be?"

Brad rolled his eyes. "We've been forbidden to talk to anyone about the case except the cops, and even then, we need the team lawyer with us."

Lockett wouldn't hesitate to subpoena anyone in that facility. "Well, I have a few more questions. Are you telling me you didn't go to Keith's Thursday to work him out?"

Brad's attention was on the security guard. "You're about to get thrown out. You should run. And we never talked, if anyone asks."

With sarcasm, I said, "I appreciate your time, Brad. And if anyone asks, I'll tell them your lips were sealed. That it may have looked like we were talking, but you said nothing whatsoever." I stepped aside to give Brad room to pass because I knew I'd lost him, but I was annoyed with him. In a murder case, people should spill everything they know in the name of justice. I mean, never mind a person's life was on the line.

He took a step then paused. We were facing opposite directions, our sides aligned, when he said, "Tell AJ good luck. I'm sorry he got roped into this."

Brad scurried off like a nervous rat. Mouth agape, I watched him leave. The security guy moved toward me, and I skirted around the tables, keeping a large gap between us. Then I exited the dining hall the way I'd come, walking quickly through the hallway and back toward the kitchen like I was in a race. In a way, it was—a race to not get caught.

"Hey," someone behind me called. "Stop!"

I rushed outside through the door, bumping the chef as he was coming in.

"Sorry," I mumbled and jogged off toward LC, afraid I'd draw more attention if I broke into a full run.

I rounded the corner and jumped into LC through the back passenger door. I flipped over the bench seat into the cargo space, where I crawled under the handful of blankets I kept for when I was out in the woods. Afraid they'd grab my license number, I didn't want to drive off. But I didn't want to get caught sitting there either. My gut told me to hide and stay low, so that's what I did. Moments later, I heard the security guard talking, probably on his shoulder mic.

"No sign of anyone. Lot's quiet."

From the clarity of his voice, I figured he was standing nearby, close enough to look inside and spot me had I not covered myself. I waited for what felt like years but was likely minutes. Though the day was gray, misty, and cold, typical of Pacific Northwest winters, sweat trickled down the back of my neck, feeling like a spider scampering inside my shirt. I resisted the urge to brush the sweat away. I counted to one hundred, slowly, while listening. No sound. I moved one corner of a blanket to peek and check if the coast was clear. From my hiding spot, I could see one window. No guard. I pushed more fabric away to look out the back. No guard there either.

Slowly, I sat up. The coast was clear.

That's when I swiped at my neck and did a mini heebie-jeebies dance. Even though I knew logically what I'd felt, shaking the image of an arachnid was difficult.

Movement at the building's front caught my eye. Brad Jenson jogged across the parking lot to his car, a late-model, standard, boring, white pickup. He glanced at his phone and back at the building before jumping into his truck and peeling out of the lot.

I pulled my phone from my back pocket and dialed Toby.

"Dudette," he said after the first ring.

"Dude, ready to do some online sleuthing?"

"Hit me."

"I'd like you to find out what you can about Brad Jenson. He's a trainer with the Pioneers. And Keith McVay as well." I wracked my brain for anyone else he might look into.

"Worked on McVay the day your pal Gunn was arrested. I'll send that to you now. I also did Gunn. I'll get started on this Jenson person." Cooing filtered over the line.

"Ah, tell Lady M I said hi." I'd gotten attached to Toby's emotional-support animal. "And thanks for being one step ahead of me on this one."

Teamwork makes the dream work, unless someone on your team slips you a mickey that gets you to pop positive on a routine drug test.

8

FRIDAY

As I was crossing the bridge into Washington from the Pioneers' training complex, the ramifications of working with AJ began. I was headed to downtown Vancouver to follow my other client's fiancé when my cell rang. Because LC doesn't have a working stereo, I had my earbuds in and was listening to Spotify when the call came through.

The screen showed my client's name.

"Hello, Samantha True speaking," I said with a smile. That was one case I was happy to have because I knew I could do it with my eyes closed.

"Hello, Samantha. It's Renee Foote."

"Hello, Renee. How are you? I'm on my way now to spend the afternoon watching Jon. If he's as predictable as I think and as loyal as he seems, I should find him right where he said he'd be."

She cleared her throat. "That's why I'm calling. I'm sorry, Samantha, but I need to cancel my service. I mean to say that I want you to stop following him, that I'm good. We can be done." She groaned.

"You'd like to end the job?" I exited the highway, but instead of heading in the direction of Renee's fiancé, I pulled onto the shoulder. "Is everything okay?" I had only one day of data on Jon, and she'd been adamant about getting two weeks of observation.

"Yes."

"So you no longer feel worried about Jon?"

She groaned again. "Ugh, it's that... I like you, Samantha. From the moment we met, I didn't feel embarrassed sharing my fear with you. But it's that..."

I waited patiently.

She sighed. "On the news earlier, there was a shot of you and a lawyer coming out of the Multnomah County jail. I guess you're also working the case of that murdered quarterback."

"Is there a problem with that?"

I had no idea we'd been caught by news cameras. I'd seen them, but none had rushed us like I'd seen in the movies. Tyson and I strolled to our cars and drove away unharmed.

"Yes," Renee said. "I think this guy they arrested did it, and I don't want to be associated with your company. It makes me feel dirty. And they're saying awful things about you on social media. Is it true your husband was a bigamist?"

I groaned, keeping it in so that she couldn't hear. I rested my forehead on my steering wheel and said, "I'm sorry that you feel that way, Renee. Used to be in this country people were innocent until proven guilty, not the other way around. If you'd like, I can refer you to another private investigator." I didn't know anyone but Paulie Bea, but I thought that was the professional thing to do.

"I found one. His name is Paulie Bea. He said he knew

you. Said I was doing the right thing if I wanted to keep my situation under the radar."

Of course he did. "Well, sounds like you're all set. Thanks for being honest with me, Renee. I'll send all my notes and my final invoice tonight. Good luck."

"Thank you, Samantha," she said, then disconnected.

I banged my head softly against the steering wheel. Paulie Bea. I had an incredible urge to kick him in the shins.

I pointed LC toward Wind River and headed home. I had dictated my notes about Renee's fiancé's whereabouts and sent them to Toby to edit. Proofing is not my super skill. After a quick call to him, he sent Renee a final invoice and all the documentation I'd accumulated.

Back roads were my path home—houses on large plots of land, some with horses, goats, and a few cows. Mount Saint Helens sat on my right side, watching from afar. Seeing the volcano with its snowy peak was a boon. Typically, the skies were too cloudy for such scenery.

I contemplated swinging by my parents' to see Cora, but my frustration was too fresh, and I didn't want my niece to think she had anything to do with that. As I drove past the dog park, I caught a glimpse of a person who looked like Paulie Bea and his dog walking the width of the park.

With a sharp jerk of the wheel, I pulled into the dog park, my sudden declaration spraying gravel and mud. I threw LC into park and jumped out. Paulie's dog, Rocket, met me at the gate, tail wagging. I scratched him behind the ears.

"Sorry you have a butthead for a master, Rocket," I mumbled, stomping over to Paulie.

He held up his hands in protest. "Hey, can I help it if your clients don't like you?"

"How did she even find you? I thought you were retired."

Paulie shrugged. "I do good advertising. And I can target people on Facebook. I've been in this business long enough to know you weren't going to keep all your clients."

"Why did you even take the case?"

Paulie pulled a treat from his pocket and tossed it to Rocket. "Easy money. She said the fiancé had done nothing wrong the week you watched him. I can spend one week in my car watching a numbskull."

He was dressed in the same tracksuit as that morning even though I felt like three days had already passed.

"Well, surprise, I only surveyed him for one day. So it's more like you have thirteen left."

Paulie shrugged as if to say that was no biggie. "You got any more clients you want to hand over before they jump ship?"

I threw up my hands in disgust. "I thought you were supposed to be helping me, not stealing work from me."

"I am helping you. Freeing up all your extra time so you can try to get your murderer friend off the hook."

"He's innocent."

Paulie rolled his eyes. "They all say that. Lesson number one, Samantha. If it walks like a duck, quacks like a duck, then it's a duck."

"There's nothing but circumstantial evidence that points to AJ."

Again with the eye roll. I wanted to smack him upside the head.

"Yeah, because fingerprints on the dumbbell aren't proof."

My mind did a quick calculation even though I wasn't sure what Paulie was talking about. "AJ had been to McVay's house before. They're professional athletes. It makes sense they might have worked out together that night." My response made me feel like a genius.

"Yeah, true. Except this particular dumbbell was the murder weapon."

I narrowed my eyes. "How do you know that?"

Paulie tossed Rocket another treat. "I have friends and keep my ear to the ground."

I rolled my eyes with great exaggeration because Paulie was talking in riddles. "Which was it? You asked someone or overheard something?"

He smiled. "Caught that, did you? Good. You might be able to do this job after all. I had lunch at a favorite cop stop in downtown Portland. I chummed it up with one of the cops who works in the evidence room at the county jail. He let it spill."

Note to self. Learn where cops hang out. Leo was easy. He hung out with me or on the reservation, doing work for the tribe.

Paulie said, "You have to see both sides every time, the entire time. Or you're going to miss what's right in front of you. You can't afford to be shortsighted."

"Lesson number one?" I raised an eyebrow in question.

"Two. The duck comment was the first lesson."

"Hey," someone called from across the park.

Both Paulie and I turned to see one of the women that had been at the park earlier.

I pointed in her direction. "Is it weird that she's here again at the same time you are?"

Paulie grunted. "No, it's just bad luck."

The woman held up a flashlight whose beam was like an

oversized laser pointer. She directed our attention twenty feet to our side.

"Your dog crapped right there. Pick it up." The flashlight made a circle around the area where I was guessing a pile of dog poo was waiting.

Paulie said, "You know, when I retired, I thought I was leaving the a-holes behind. Guess not."

"How legit is this thing about the dumbbell and fingerprints?" Part of me hoped he was pulling my chain.

"Came straight from the evidence clerk's mouth. Who, I might add, is a Pioneers fan, so that should be kept in mind."

"But evidence is evidence. How would being a fan affect that?"

Paulie pulled a poop bag from his pocket and looked me in the eye. "Ever hear of evidence gone missing? Logged in wrong?"

I nodded and followed him as he went toward the waiting beam of light.

"In this case, your pal has the people against him. They're fans of McVay. He's the guy who was going to take them to the Super Bowl. If he re-signed, that is."

"Now we'll never know."

But I got what Paulie meant. Lots of hopes and dreams were pinned on McVay. And in my line of business, I'd seen people do terrible things over hopes, dreams, greed, pride, and anger. These reactions were disheartening, really. My mind raced as I tried to pull out tidbits that would need to be fleshed out. I needed to talk to Lockett and wanted to talk to my dad.

I took a step to leave before turning back toward Paulie. "Thanks."

"Anytime."

I nodded. "Renee Foote case. I think he's an up-and-up guy. At least, if he's out fooling around, then it's with someone in his office or not every week."

Paulie nodded.

I seemed to have gained a mentor, which was good because if what he said was true about AJ and the finger-prints on the dumbbell, I was going to need all the help I could get.

9

FRIDAY

I PULLED INTO THE ALLEY NEXT TO MY APARTMENT AND LET LC rest. He would need some oil before I went out again, but his engine needed to cool first.

My apartment was the second floor over the offices of my dad's newspaper, *The Wind River Journal*, and had two entrances—one from the side stairs up to a balcony and my front door, the other a staircase in the back of my dad's offices, which opened near the back door of my apartment. I chose the latter because I needed a good, hearty father-daughter talk to ground me. A lot had happened that day, and I was feeling... a lot of conflicting emotions.

I entered the paper from the front and waved to my dad's right-hand woman, Stella MacInerney. With essential oils on hand to fix any ailment and a sharp tongue to keep people in place in case the ailment was their behavior, Stella knew everyone and saw everything. She was just as valuable a source as the paper itself, if not more so. She was on the phone when I came in and waved me over. I noticed as I passed that she'd dropped her voice, sounding smooth and sexy. Stella had buried three husbands, and I wondered if she was currently working on number four.

The offices of *The Wind River Journal* opened into a lobby blocked by Stella's desk. Behind her were two offices to the left and two storage rooms to the right. The center was the bullpen, but Dad didn't staff in-house journalists. Anyone he hired was freelance. Behind the bullpen were the kitchen, the restroom, and to the far right, the stairs to my apartment.

Dad's office was the last room on the left. He was at his desk, squinting at some papers, his glasses atop his head.

I took after Russell True. Taller than most women my age —except Precious, who had me by two inches as she was six feet—I had my father's blue-green eyes, smattering of freckles, love of the outdoors, and insatiable curiosity for information. Only my curly reddish-blonde hair came from my mother.

"Hey, Daddy-o. If you wore the glasses, it might make seeing the papers easier." I plopped onto the couch across from his desk.

The couch used to be in my parents' TV room, but once Rachel and I moved out, my folks got new furniture.

"Sammy," he said with a smile and folded the papers, slipping them under his desk calendar. "It's a great day for a dad when their best kid comes by."

I chuckled. "You're just saying that because Rachel isn't near to hear it."

She was, in fact, on a naval carrier somewhere in foreign waters.

"Maybe," Dad said. "Maybe not." He narrowed his eyes. "What's wrong?"

I sat back, surprised he noticed. *Am I so transparent?* "What makes you think something is wrong?"

"You're here. Usually, you're on a run or upstairs on the balcony, relaxing."

True. "That doesn't mean anything is wrong." I tried to relax into the couch but couldn't get comfortable.

"And you've got a crease between your brows. You get that crease when you've got something on your mind. Something you can't work out." He did a backward wave, gesturing for me to spill. "Tell your old man what's wrong. Is it the AJ Gunn case?"

I sighed, nodded, then let my head drop back against the couch. "He's innocent. I know he is."

"But...?" Dad's coaxing was soft.

"But what if he's not and I'm on the wrong side of this?" I couldn't even look at him as I said it. Feeling like a traitor to AJ, Lockett, and even Precious, I stared at the ceiling tiles.

"Is it the fingerprints on the dumbbell that give you pause?"

I lifted my head to look at my dad, incredulous. "How did you know?"

He shrugged and sat back in his office chair, reclining enough to put his feet up on his desk. "I have connections."

I tossed my hands up in frustration. "Why does everyone have connections but me?"

Dad chuckled. "You have connections. You just don't have these connections. But you will. Keep at it, and they'll come with time." He met my gaze. "You think the prints on the dumbbell are the smoking gun?"

I shook my head hesitantly. "I've seen people convicted for less. I can reason out why AJ's prints might be on the dumbbell. I'm worried that I'm letting my emotions tell me what's in front of me, which is what I want to see and not what might actually be there. Does that make sense?"

Dad nodded. "Yep, and because you're hesitant, that means your checks and balances are working. Have a little faith in yourself and know that nothing is instant but"—he ticked off items on his fingers—"instant coffee, instant mashed potatoes, or rice—"

"Okay, I get it." I laughed.

"But you don't feel any better, do you?" He studied me.

"No." I shook my head. "This case is hard. At first, I was stuck and taking no action. Now, I'm taking action and feel like everyone else is ten steps ahead."

"You know what I always say. Maybe you should get some distance so you can see the full picture. Go work on another case. Take your mind off this, and—"

"The problem will solve itself," I said, finishing what he'd been saying since I could remember. "I don't have any other cases, Dad. My one case dropped today. She didn't like that I was on AJ's defense team."

Dad's face got serious, and he swung his feet off his desk then stood. The papers he'd slipped under his calendar earlier, he pulled out and carried over. He sat next to me on the couch and handed them to me.

"Your mother will be ticked that I showed this to you, but I think you need to know what you're up against. This is going to get worse before it gets better."

I unfolded the pages and recognized them to be a printout of an article from Dad's online version of the paper. The timestamp told me the article had been posted that morning, Dad being the writer. In summary, the article was about AJ's arrest and McVay's death and career as the Pioneers' quarterback.

"I heard he was up for a new contract or something." I needed Dad to help me understand football contracts.

He nodded. "McVay was at the end of his rookie contract. Currently, the top quarterbacks are getting contracts for eight to ten years and hundreds of millions of dollars."

"And McVay was in that caliber of QBs that could get a big payout?"

McVay and the Pioneers did have a winning record, with several playoff visits.

"Yep," Dad said. "This year looked good for them to make the Super Bowl too. Both the offense and defense were playing tight. Believe it or not, that's got lots of people upset. Not that McVay is dead but that the Pioneers won't make it now." He shook his head in disgust.

I did believe it. I scratched my head. "Could another team have had McVay killed to stop their playoff and Super Bowl run?" Though that was a stretch, I'd seen weirder reasons.

"Sure, but that's unlikely. It's more likely someone had a beef with McVay, and now he's dead."

"AJ didn't have a beef with McVay."

"He wanted a starting position, though."

"Yeah, but he doesn't get that in jail. He's not stupid. He's not going to kill a guy and think the coast is clear for him to become the savior of the Pioneers."

Dad squeezed my shoulder. "Sounds like you know how you feel about AJ's guilt or innocence."

I nodded slowly, thinking about how I'd instantly defended AJ because it had felt right to do so. "What do you know about anabolic-androgenic steroids?"

Dad's brows shot up. "They've been illegal twenty years now. That's what was hot when I did my exposé all those years ago. Designer steroids, they're called. Only way to get them now is through the black market."

"Online?"

"Sure, that's one way. Or if you know a dealer. A shady doctor."

I most definitely did not know a dealer, but I made a note to ask Leo if he did. Maybe he'd arrested one at one time.

Turning my attention back to the article, I scanned the comments. They numbered over three hundred. But Dad hadn't printed them all. I flipped through the pages. Only the first twenty-five comments were there.

I gave a low whistle. "Did you show this to the police?"

The fourth comment down was a death threat to me and my family. The sixth comment was a promise to burn the office of the paper to the ground.

I stopped reading and faced my dad. "I'm sorry. I never thought this would affect you all."

His eyes softened as he brushed a thumb over my brow, easing back the tension I was holding there. "Sammy, I've faced worse than this in all my years of reporting. Your mother and I have really thick skins. But you..."

"I've faced mean people before, Dad."

He smiled a bit sadly. "Yes, but these people are mean, angry, and motivated. That's a whole lot different from a teacher who thinks you're faking."

"But not so different from a playground bully."

"These bullies have means. This is going to get a lot worse before it gets better, and some people may never forgive you for being on AJ's side."

"Even if he's innocent?"

The fallout from this case was becoming evident. Maybe that's why I'd been frozen. Maybe I'd known not only that it would be hard, that I was out of my element, but that I was going to have to take a side. And that would make me an easy target for people to take out their anger on and, by extension, make my family a target also. Regardless of the outcome, the case would affect my livelihood, my friendships, and my own perspective.

I glanced at more comments, sucking in breaths of disbelief, then I panicked.

"If Rachel sees this, she's going to flip out." My sister's inability to control everything in her young daughter's vicinity would drive Rachel insane. Fear had a way of doing that to people.

"We have a phone call scheduled for tomorrow. You should come by and tell her. She'll see the comments soon enough. Might as well get ahead of this where you can."

"Okay."

But first, I needed to decide what to do. I glanced up at the ceiling and blinked back tears. I despised feeling inept, out of control, and bullied. My fear, though, was what might happen if I pushed through and something happened to my family.

I could never live with that.

This. This is what I've been afraid of. This was the bad feeling I'd had in my gut for weeks—a warning.

Trouble was here.

FRIDAY

I TOOK THE BACK STEPS UP TO MY APARTMENT. MY PARENTS used to rent it out with Airbnb, so the place was tastefully decorated and comfortable, with views of downtown and Windy River itself.

My apartment's layout was simple. When one entered from the back, one bedroom lay on either side, with a bathroom to the right past the bedroom, then the hallway opened up to a living room, galley kitchen, and the front door. A built-in bar with seating for two acted as my dining table. Inside, I tossed my backpack into my bedroom as I passed and moved toward the living room.

The sun was setting, and the apartment was cast in shadows. When I came into the living room, as I reached for the light switch, I noticed a man sitting on my couch. His legs were stretched out, his head back against the top of the couch. Shadows cloaked his identity.

I screamed and instinctively jumped back, ready to retrieve my backpack and the stun gun within.

The man jumped up from the couch, assuming a karate

position.

Awareness caught up with me and overrode my fight or flight. I hit the light switch, bringing light onto the scene.

"Jeez, Tyson. What are you doing here?"

Lockett dropped the fight stance then stretched, arms going high in the air. "I was getting in a catnap when you came in and screamed."

"I wasn't expecting anyone to be in my house."

"I need a place to stay while I'm in town." His glance shot to my spare room.

"Well, since you know the code to get in, you might as well stay." I went into the kitchen and opened the fridge.

My parents had installed a keypad lock on my front door. I'd given Lockett my code several months before, when I was questioned for the murder of a local principal.

"You want a beer?" I asked.

"Yeah, that would be great. Thanks for letting me crash."

"Already have your bags in the guest room, don't ya?" I took two IPAs from the fridge.

Lockett chuckled. "It's like we've been friends forever."

I joined him on the couch, handing him his beer.

He said, "I probably could use something stronger, but we'll be working late, so better keep it light."

I cut a side-eye to him. "Working late?"

Lockett rubbed a hand down his face and sighed. "How well do you know AJ, Sam?"

I echoed his sigh. "Not well enough to say definitively that he didn't kill McVay. But I think he's innocent. I can't picture him bashing someone in the head with a dumbbell."

Lockett said, "Heard about the prints, huh? And here I was worried about breaking it to you."

I chuckled bitterly. "Heard it from someone not even on

the case."

We sat in silence, drinking our beers, and I'm guessing he was contemplating like I was. Though I bet Lockett was contemplating his defense angle and I was contemplating... my role in this mess, perhaps—or whether I wanted to drag my family into it or not. *Yeah, all of the above.*

Lockett finished his beer and slid the empty bottle onto my coffee table. "I sure don't envy you."

"Why's that?"

"Because my job is to do the best job I can. I've defended people whose innocence I've questioned."

"Why do it if you think they might be guilty?"

Lockett retrieved two more beers even though I still had a quarter of mine left.

"Because my job is to create doubt if there's a place to create it. If a person confesses, then my job is to be their sound mind when looking at sentencing. In AJ's case, there's plenty of doubt. There's no smoking gun. There are a million possible scenarios for how McVay ended up dead."

I nodded in understanding. "And AJ doesn't have to be in any of them."

He clinked his bottle to mine. "Exactly. It's your job to find out which of those scenarios seems the most likely."

"What if I'm wrong about his innocence? What if my insistence ends up causing my family trouble?" I asked.

Lockett studied me before saying assuredly, "It's our job to show AJ could be innocent, not to decide it. If you've already made up your mind about him, then you need to tell me right now so I can decide if you stay on or not."

Honestly, I was shocked at Lockett's stern words and felt the need to defend myself. "My family is getting death threats. I've lost a client. This is already affecting my life."

Lockett held my gaze. "You never struck me as a woman who preferred the path of least resistance."

When Lockett and I first met, we were in his office, where he told me my husband was dead and also wasn't legally my husband. That might have been the first blow of that day, but it certainly wasn't the last. And I'd faced each of them with steely determination. In that situation, my life was the one on the line, but I considered whether I would do less if Precious were the one in jail.

No, I would not.

I said, "This is big. Bigger than I'm used to. I'm scared."

Lockett nodded. "Good. You should be. But this is it, Sam. Either you do this or resign yourself to finding missing cats and taking pictures of cheating husbands."

"I could never live with myself if I didn't help and AJ went to jail."

I stood, placed my empty on the coffee table, and picked up my second beer. From behind the couch, I slid out a giant pad, twenty by thirty, and propped it up against the wall. From the top, I ripped off the first page. The back was sticky, making the page a giant Post-it note. I stuck it on the wall then repeated that with three more sheets. Then from a drawer under my coffee table, I took out a fat, broad-tipped black marker and wrote "Keith McVay" across the first page. On the second, I wrote "AJ Gunn." On the third, I wrote "Brad Jenson," and the fourth I left blank.

Lockett stretched out on my couch, his upper body propped up. "We're going to need reinforcements."

I sipped the beer. "Food or people?"

"Food."

A knock on my front door immediately followed.

Lockett jerked his thumb behind his shoulder toward the

door. "People reinforcements are already here."

I gave him a puzzled look before opening the door. Precious stood outside, two large takeout bags in each hand.

She said, "Hold on to your titties, kitties. It's about to get real smart in here." She bumped me with her shoulder. "Move. These are heavy."

I stepped aside, and she hurried in. Toby followed, with Lady G peeking out from her new pouch, a large felt carrier shaped like an orange. I was about to close the door when footsteps pounding up my stairs stopped me. Leo came into sight, and I broke into a smile. I'd never thought I would be happy to see Leo Stillman, but I was. He was carrying two growlers. I pointed at them.

He held one up. "Hard cider for Toby and Precious."

"And IPA for the rest of us."

He winked. "You got it." He stopped in front of me and scanned my face. "You look tired."

"It's been the longest day ever."

"Everything okay with Paulie Bea?"

I shrugged. "It will be."

"Should I have not introduced you two?" His brow furrowed.

I smiled. "I'll let you know when this is all over. Or ten years from now, when I've learned all I can and he's annoyed me one too many times."

Leo chuckled and went inside, and I followed. Precious was setting out several Styrofoam containers. Toby was holding a handful of forks. The aroma of perfectly cooked beef and something slightly spicy filled the air.

I inhaled deeply and enjoyed. "Do I smell chicken wings?"

Precious looked at me and grinned. "Yes, buffalo, Hawaiian, and teriyaki." She popped open the tops to three containers then moved on to the rest. "And in this one is poutine. Here are mushroom-and-swiss beef sliders, and this one is nachos." She went down the line, opening containers. "And this one is spinach-artichoke dip."

She and I said simultaneously, "Because everyone should have at least one vegetable." Then we gave each other a high five.

I said, "This is a comfort food-a-palooza gold mine."

The room got quiet as if they knew something I didn't. I looked at each of them before coming back to Precious. I knew she wouldn't ever bullshit me.

At my questioning look, she said, "I saw the comments on *The Wind River Journal.* I was on the phone with Tyson when he found out about the dumbbell." Her gaze darted briefly to Lockett's. "And I lost a client today because of my association with AJ."

"I'm sorry," I said.

She gave a nonchalant shrug. "Me too, but I'd rather my clients be open-minded."

That made sense. Being a life and professional coach and helping people change their lives would be hard if they're shortsighted.

Toby sighed with delight as he surveyed the spread. "All this good stuff needs a little something special." He gave us a smile and wagged his brows.

Lockett tossed his bottle cap at him. "Weed is not an accessory to everything."

Toby dumped fries on his plate. "It should be."

Leo twisted the top off a second IPA and handed it to Lockett. "Only for you, Toby."

The conversation went from ribbing Toby to ribbing

each other. At some point, Lockett took off his tie and shoes and became more the surfer guy we knew and less the lawyer. Briefly, I wondered if that's how he did it, morphing into what his clients needed by putting on a power suit. Precious wore a coach's whistle and actively used it, and she was always dressed like the successful business owner she was.

After we were all fed and hydrated, I handed Precious the large marker then went into the kitchen to straighten up.

I said, "Let's start listing what we know."

We'd done this before, and it helped me later with recall. At the moment, everything was a jumbled mess in my head. After that night, I would easily be able to recall these giant Post-it notes and the information on them. As a dyslexic, reading and spelling were not my strong suits, though I'd gotten better over the years. But seeing the world through pictures was where I excelled.

I stacked the dishes in the small dishwasher as Precious kicked off her heels and took her coach's whistle from around her neck. The men sat around her.

Once done, I moved to a barstool and sat behind them all.

She pointed at the first giant notecard. "McVay. What do we know?"

I started the conversation. "He was a first-round draft pick. His rookie contract was up, so he stood to make big money getting a franchise contract. He's an All-Pro quarterback with a winning record. Current salaries are one hundred million plus. He's single. And recently, he was busted with performance-enhancing drugs in his system."

"An insanely large dose," Toby added. "Anabolic-androgenic steroids."

Lockett turned to Toby, mouth agape. "How do you know that? I'm still waiting for the judge to give us permission to access McVay's medical records."

Toby looked down at his nails then glanced from Leo to Lockett. "Do you really want to know how I know?"

Leo shook his head. "Not if it's illegal."

Toby snorted. "It's only illegal if you're caught, and I never leave a trace."

Precious and I looked at each other and smiled. She believed that bit about it being only illegal if caught no more than I did, but we knew Toby had a renegade side. He just expressed it online. Then he needed a sugar glider as an emotional-support animal to help him get over whatever he saw or did.

Getting us back on topic, I said, "And this was the first drug test McVay failed? Am I right?"

Toby nodded.

I put a few of the pieces together. "Drug testing is random. McVay got notice that day at the team meeting, from what I understand. And he can't leave without taking the test. If McVay was doing PEDs, he knows he's going to pop positive. Yet he does nothing to get out of the test. He even demands to redo the test and have an independent lab do one."

Lockett pointed at Precious to write that down.

I asked Toby, "How hard would it be to get anabolic-androgenic steroids online?"

Toby shrugged. "You ever heard of the Silk Road?"

"Wasn't that the dark-web black market?"

The Silk Road was known for selling all kinds of drugs to anyone across the globe. Then it branched out—human organs and likely more unthinkables.

Toby nodded and scratched Lady M's head. "Yeah, the FBI shut down the site in 2013, but that doesn't mean a handful of others didn't pop up afterward. Getting a steroid on the dark web takes no more than some Bitcoin, a VPN, and some clever packaging to fool the post office."

Leo asked, "Are you talking from experience?"

Toby picked up an empty vape-pen vial and held it to his lips. "No, man. I may hang out in dark alleys, but I'm not stupid. I wouldn't trust none of that crap coming off the dark web." He tapped the vial. "I gave up vape juice that I could buy right at a store by my house because it wasn't safe."

Leo nodded. "Good point."

I addressed Toby. "So finding out if anyone who works or plays for the Pioneers bought online steroids is impossible."

Toby shrugged one shoulder. "Maybe. I'll hang out in some rooms and see if anyone talks. But any shady doc could get it too."

"Look into the team doc, please." I looked at Precious. "Write this too: McVay had been in a car accident the weekend after Thanksgiving."

Toby shook his head sadly. "The last few weeks for McVay were really bad. Do we know if he was impaired when he was behind the wheel?"

Lockett laughed. "The only one in this room that would know would be the guy who saw the records that a lawyer hasn't been given yet."

Toby pulled out his phone and tapped away. "This is why it's important to have a designated time when you get high, and people know it, no one expects me to drive or do anything that could endanger others or myself."

Leo nodded. "You are a very responsible pot user."

Toby nodded with him. "Yes, I am."

Lockett got up and went into the kitchen. "By chance, was blood drawn while McVay was at the hospital after that accident?"

Toby shook his head. "Nope. You would think, if you were T-boned by a large delivery truck, you'd be jacked up. But he was in a Mercedes Defender. The police report was graphic, but McVay walked away with some cuts and bruises. They gave him a prescription for the aches and pains. Nothing addictive or illegal."

Leo closed his eyes and mumbled, "I'm gonna pretend like I didn't even hear that because I doubt the police report is accessible by the public yet."

Toby snickered. "Dude, you would be wrong. The report became available a few hours ago. Sorta."

"Sorta?" I asked.

He shrugged. "It was uploaded and set to publish at midnight. I just saw it a few hours earlier. Website plugins are like leaving the back door open. And as for the other stuff... well, I'm not the only hacker out there."

"You mean to say others are hacking this info and posting it online?" Lockett said.

Toby nodded. "Just need to know where to look."

"Wait, go back," Precious said. "The hospital gave him a prescription, but did they fill it? When I was discharged following my concussion, they gave me a prescription for superstrong ibuprofen. I had to go fill it."

Toby scanned his screen. "I can't tell from this. My guess is if you're Keith McVay, they make sure you leave with the prescription filled."

Lockett said, "I'll follow up on this." He scratched a note on his notepad.

Toby looked around the room for a sign that he should

continue. When he had everyone's attention, he said, "McVay graduated from Stanford over five years ago. Sam mentioned his draft in the NFL—I'll skip that. He owned his house on Lake Oswego, paid just over two mil for it. He wasn't married and wasn't dating anyone that I could find. McVay was the only child of Barb and Bob McVay, both schoolteachers in small town Minnestoa. That's where he grew up. His parents were killed in a car accident his first year in the league."

I said, "Leo mentioned that McVay went to college with the Pioneers' owner, Austin Strong."

Toby tapped on his phone some more. "Yeah, but Strong graduated a couple years ahead of McVay. Looking at this, I can't see where their paths might have crossed. Strong's course load was all business and computers. McVay studied communications. No excessive debt. Money in the bank. Nothing of concern. And you asked about Brad Jenson? He graduated University of Washington ten years ago. Lives in a town house near the training facility. He doesn't own it and doesn't have any money in the bank, has a maxed-out credit card." He looked around the room at us. "He likes to hang out at the casinos."

Lockett touched my shoulder, drawing my attention, and said quietly, "You still good with this?"

I met his gaze. "I can't walk away from this and live with myself."

He nodded. "I got your back."

I smiled. "And I got yours."

I looked around the room, wondering how I could cover all these people and my family. That's what scared me the most.

11

SATURDAY

AFTER A HEATED AND FRUSTRATING CONVERSATION WITH Rachel and my parents about everyone's safety, no one could come up with a solution we all liked, so we left the discussion open for more talks.

My plan for the day was to stake out Brad Jenson. I didn't believe for a moment he'd open his door to me, hence the stakeout. As I didn't see him as much of an outdoors enthusiast, I was banking on him leaving for food or something, and I could corner him for more conversation. In the worst-case scenario, I would don a food-delivery hat borrowed from Toby and knock on his door.

Brad's town house was nondescript, like him. Actually, the place reminded me of the one I used to live in with Carson. The row of conjoined two-story rentals was painted different colors lest somebody try to enter the wrong home. Brad's was a light green.

I idled in the corner spot of the lot, facing Brad's home. The blinds on the front were closed. No lights were on that I could tell. After a ten-minute wait, I decided to walk around to the back. I'd staked out someone before, only to find they'd fled the country. I didn't want to waste my day if Brad was already at the casinos even though his truck was parked out front.

A walking path at the end of the complex was where I started. I counted town houses, afraid I might peer into the window of the wrong one in case the back sides weren't painted to match the fronts, then started down the path. I wished I had Simon with me. Walking a dog would be the perfect disguise. I was picking him up that day, so if I needed to, I could come back with him.

The day was wet and gray, with wind occasionally stirring through the space and lifting some fallen ugly brown leaves. The path took me to a small park with two benches and a simple play structure with a rock wall and a slide. I slipped onto a bench. My butt instantly got wet from the seat as I looked toward Brad's place. I counted just to make sure.

No lights were on. The blinds were more open than in the front but turned down slightly, like people do when closing themselves in for the evening.

My watch said eleven o'clock. Brad was either a late sleeper or not home.

I pushed up from the bench and beelined for his back door, not caring if I looked suspicious. I should've been giving people pause—neighbors should've been questioning me. I stood on the small square concrete slab that served as his back patio and angled to try to see through the slats.

The interior felt still. I pounded on the sliding glass door. Nothing.

I pounded again with no response. Without reservation, I cupped my hands around my eyes and looked into the town house. Nothing.

"Food delivery!" I yelled while pulling Toby's hat from my back pocket and putting it on my head.

The sliding door next to Brad's opened. A lady in a bathrobe, with white hair, colored curlers on the sides, and a tiny dog tucked in the crook of her arm poked her head out. "He's not there. Left last night. I didn't hear him come back."

My expression probably showed my skepticism.

She continued, "He's the noisiest neighbor. Keeps his TV loud and is always screaming at it."

"Football?" I asked.

She hitched the little dog up to her chest, under her chin, and stroked its ears. "Mostly. Or hockey or horse racing—anything a person can bet on is my guess. I used to be married to a gambler, may he rot in hell, and if the curses my neighbor shouts are any indication, he's no good at it, like my Larry. Spent all our retirement, he did."

"I'm sorry—you think Brad's not around because there's no shouting at the TV?"

"That, and I watched him leave last night—late, after I went to bed. I know this because I was just about to drop off to sleep when I heard a door slam and some shouting. Pinkie here started barking like mad, trying to get at the window. I looked outside, and sure enough, this idiot is out there"—she jerked her chin toward Brad's place—"and someone is trying to get him into a car."

My interest was piqued. "They were forcing him into a car?"

Her lips thinned as she thought. "No, more like trying to help him in." She lowered her voice. "I think he might have been hitting the sauce. He looked a little wobbly."

"But did he seem like he wanted to get into the car?"

"He got in on his own."

"And what kind of car was it?"

"One of those big ones. Full sized."

"A sedan or town car?" I was thrown by the *full sized*. "Or an SUV like that Explorer?" I pointed across the way, where a few of the parking spots could be seen.

She nodded. "Yeah, like that but bigger."

Excursion or Suburban. "What color was it?"

"Dark, with dark windows. But silver running along the bottom, like a skirt."

She was very observant for someone who had been woken up. "Any chance you caught the plates? Washington or Oregon?"

"Oregon. And your friend got in the back."

I took a business card from my backpack and handed it to her. "My name's Samantha. You've been very helpful. I appreciate it. If Brad comes back, would it be too much to ask you to give me a call?"

She shook her head and stared at the card. "Private investigator, huh? Sounds exciting."

I scratched Pinkie's head. "Mostly, it's not." I tucked Toby's ball cap in my back pocket.

The neighbor's eyes widened. "I know you. I saw you on TV. You're helping that killer." She dropped my card then stepped on it.

I sighed wearily. "Actually, I'm trying to get to the truth. Did you know that AJ is raising his kid brother while his mom is getting treatment for cancer?"

I didn't know why I bothered to tell her that. But people blindly accusing AJ was wrong.

"The BTK killer was a Cub Scout leader," she retorted.

"Fair enough," I said. "Thanks for your time."

I returned to the path to make my exit and glanced back

once before turning the corner. Her door was closed, my card still on the ground. I had a choice—I could leave or stick around and hope that Jenson showed up. In today's tech world, a way had to exist to have my cake and eat it too. The trouble was that if I put a camera on Jenson's front door but he came in any other way, I'd miss it. Or if he came in to grab something then left right away, I'd miss my chance. I had to pick up Simon by dinner, so I had some time to contemplate my next move while I waited to see if he would show.

I got into LC and pulled a bag of popcorn from between the seats. Next, I dropped a quick text to Toby to see if he could find any activity on Jenson. I gave him Jenson's cell number, which I'd gotten from Lockett. The entire evolution took thirty minutes and ended with a text from Toby.

Toby: **Nothing. No activity. Used Find Friend App. Phone not on.**
   Me: **Poop.**

I made myself comfortable and settled in for the duration.

Two hours later, I was desperate to pee; the popcorn was all gone, and the rain was coming down. A cop car pulled into the complex lot and stopped in front of LC, blocking me in. A short, squat man got out of the car and pointed a flashlight into LC's window, right at me, which was kind of unnecessary as it was midday and overcast, not dark.

He strolled to the window and, light still pointed at me, signaled me to put my window down. I complied.

"What are you doing?" He lowered the beam, sweeping it around the inside of my Wagoneer. Rain dropped off his wide-brimmed hat. A clear plastic poncho covered his uniform.

"Waiting for someone," I said.

"For two hours?"

I didn't know whether to tip my hand and say I was a PI or act like a worried friend. I figured a 50 percent chance the lady with the curlers had tipped the cops to my job when she called in to report me. Nobody else would have known how long I'd been there.

"He left yesterday and hasn't come home. He didn't leave with a bag." I was guessing about that. "And he has information about a crime. I'm concerned for his safety and hoping I'm wrong. Only way I'll know he's okay is if he shows up here," I said, playing the public-safety aspect.

Cop guy shook his head. "Nope. No loitering. You're freaking the neighbor out." He wiped a line of waiting droplets from his hat's brim. "Listen, I don't want to be standing out here in the rain. And if I have to do it much longer, it's gonna make me grouchy. When I get grouchy, I tend to make other people's lives miserable. You can ask my wife if you don't believe me."

"I'll take your word for it."

"Move on. Move on now, or I'm gonna get grouchy and give you a ticket. Or worse, take you in. Understand?"

I nodded. "Understood."

We waited, glancing at each other.

He raised his eyebrows. "Start your car and get out of here. If I find you in another spot or loitering across the street, I'm not going to be happy."

I turned LC's engine over. "Can I cruise by at a respectable speed occasionally?"

The cop closed his eyes briefly. "Space it out so the neighbor doesn't call it in again, you hear me?"

"Yes, sir."

He gestured like I should get going.

I pointed at his car. "Um..."

He pointed the flashlight at me. "Don't get smart with me."

I shook my head.

The cop walked to his car and, once inside, backed it up. I pulled LC out of the spot and cruised through the lot at a slow speed before exiting, the cop behind me.

Not looking for any more trouble, I drove to AJ's to pick up Simon.

What a waste of a day.

On the way home, I got a text from Lockett: *Anything? Give me some good news.*

I didn't respond.

12

SATURDAY

SIMON AND I POPPED OVER TO THE DOG PARK ON THE WAY home to toss a ball and burn energy. I was the only one there. The rain was a fine, steady mist, which was likely what was keeping any others home. I wore a rain hat with a four-inch brim—I wasn't a fan of umbrellas—and a rain shell, but by the end of our hour there, my jeans-clad legs were soaked, and my mood was as wet and heavy as my pants.

"Hey," I asked Simon, who shook the water off his coat, "wanna trade lives?"

After he licked my hand, I scratched him behind the ears. "I bet you miss AJ. Don't you worry, buddy, we'll get through this together. This is me having a positive mindset." I tapped my temple.

Simon panted happily, likely hoping a treat would fall from the sky or my hand. He didn't care that I sounded like Precious, but having said I was going to be positive was already changing my mood. I couldn't dwell there—I had to be on to the next thing.

"Come on, handsome, let's go home."

He jumped into LC's front seat, and I lowered the window so that he could hang his head out. Parked outside my apartment were Precious's SUV and Leo's truck. Simon and I climbed the stairs and found no one waiting on my balcony. I assumed they were all inside.

"Does everyone know the passcode to my place?" I asked the dog.

He wagged his nub of a tail.

Inside, Leo, Lockett, Toby, and Precious were sitting in the living room. She was dressed in a slinky black T-shirt dress with thigh-high boots, her hair in a high ponytail. The men were in dark-washed jeans. Toby had on his typical ironic T-shirt; Lockett was in a Hawaiian-print shirt that was too summery for our winter season, and Leo had on his typical Henley.

"What's all this?" I went to the kitchen to set Simon up with food and water.

Precious stood, clasping her hands in excitement. "We're going to a disco. I'm meeting a potential client, and he'll be in downtown Portland at this outdoor disco."

"Sounds cold," I said, still in my wet jeans.

"It won't be. It's got lots of fires and stuff. Come on. Get changed. We have to leave in forty minutes."

Dinnertime hadn't come, and I wondered what kind of disco started so early. A geriatric one?

Precious must have read my expression because she said, "We're having dinner first. My treat. Hurry. Wear something cute." She grabbed me by the arm, dragged me to my bedroom, then pushed me through the door.

Sixty minutes later, we were in downtown Portland, eating at a Brazilian Steakhouse. I was dressed in black leggings and a thin, black, long-sleeve T-shirt patterned with a mass of white, yellow, blue, and green paisley. When stretched, the material was translucent, but the T-shirt was thin enough on its own that the pattern made my arms look tattooed. Over it, I wore a black puffy vest and had finished the outfit with mid-calf boots. Pinned to the inside of the waistband of my leggings was my secret pouch where I stored my handcuff keys. For good measure, I had tucked a small pocketknife in the small sack too. I'd seen it in my backpack, and something told me it would be better off hiding in the pocket, so I moved it. Slipped into one boot was mace, in the other a stun gun. Leo would've been proud of my preparedness.

Having put only a handful of buffet food on my plate, I sat next to Lockett and was caught off guard by his plate, heaped with food.

"How do you shut it off to enjoy yourself?" I asked. "To have an appetite?"

He was seconds from stuffing a bite of bacon-wrapped steak into his mouth. He paused to say, "It doesn't do me or them any good to be all moony because I'm free and they aren't. That could change in a second. But also, I need to be my whole self so that I can be my best for them. Relaxing is part of that." He crammed the steak in.

I nodded. He was right, of course, but actually relaxing was harder than not.

After dinner, we drove to Waterfront Park, off the Willamette River. In the open space, a large, football-field-length deck had been constructed. Lanterns swung from the riverside railing. Large firepits surrounded the dance floor and heated the space.

To enter, we were funneled between two folding tables lined with bulky, thick-armed men, likely bouncers. Taking

our money and handing out headphones were a handful of
women dressed as cats, each one's outfit a onesie. A Siamese
cat, thick pointy-eye makeup and all, was strapping yellow
wristbands onto patrons.

Precious stepped up to the table. "I'm on the guest list.
Erika Shurmann?"

A calico cat with one eye done up in black and the other
in silver flipped through some papers and tapped midway
down the page with a coffin-shaped black nail. "Yep, I see
you right here. Total five, right?"

Precious nodded. We were given bright-green wristbands
that said VIP along with our headsets.

Calico Cat Girl said, "There are two channels, one for
each DJ. Enjoy." She showed us how to change the channel
then was immediately done with us.

Ahead on the dance floor were clusters of people moving
to music no one but they could hear, along with anyone else
on the same channel. Some headphones were glowing blue
and others red. That corresponded to the different channels,
I assumed, because those with blue seemed to be dancing in
sync but not with those with red headphones. Looking into
the scene from the outside was kinda hysterical.

I elbowed Leo. "Look, there's a guy over to the right in
the white T-shirt with an alien on it. His headphones have
no color. You think he's not hearing any music and just
dancing to his own beat?"

Leo shook his head. "I'm not so sure about this."

I agreed. "I kinda feel ridiculous. Maybe we can bail and
head up to the Hyatt for drinks or something."

Precious grabbed me by the elbow. "I heard that. And no
one is bailing. Come on, let's get seen."

We followed her across the dance floor toward the DJs.

They were encased in separate booths, both apparently soundproof. I didn't recognize one of the DJs, but the other was Lil' Megalodon. His small dreads were sticking up, a jogging headband woven between them. He was wearing headphones, but only one was over an ear, leaving the other exposed. His body moved in tune to the record he was spinning. Blue light ran around the perimeter of his booth. Red light ran the perimeter of the other DJ's booth. Dressed in jeans, with holes at the knees, a Stanford sweatshirt, and Doc Martins, he glanced up, saw Precious, smiled, and gave her a chin nod.

I put my headphones on and clicked to the blue channel. "Mozart's the foundation. It's pretty good," I told the group.

The others put their headphones on. I stopped Precious before she could click hers on and moved one side off my ear.

"Is Lil' Megalodon your potential client?"

She smiled widely and stepped close to quietly say, "Yeah, he's had a rough few weeks and trouble with his agent. He said he was having trouble letting go of the anger and thought maybe I could help him get perspective, and he's looking to scale up, but he's unsure about decisions. He's had his agent since college but now doesn't trust him."

"He doesn't care that AJ is your client too?"

She shook her head. "You and I are going to dance and have a good time, and I'm going to get a sense of Lil' Megalodon the rapper, and when he and I meet tomorrow, we'll decide if we should combine our superpowers."

I laughed while scanning the crowd. "This silent thing is kinda weird. I'm even more self-conscious about dancing."

Precious pulled me toward the guys, who were standing

by the rail overlooking the river. "Let's dance," she called and dropped my hand to take Lockett's.

Toby clicked his headphones to blue and swayed with the music. "I should have brought Lady M!" he yelled then moonwalked, albeit poorly, away.

Leo flung an arm around my shoulder. "Shall we?"

I shrugged because dancing with Leo would be weird. Even though Leo had taught me how to shoot a gun, wiped away my tears, and even taken a bullet for me, dancing was like moving into a zone I wasn't sure I was ready for.

Leo paused. "You know how to dance, don't you?"

I rolled my eyes. "Of course. I've been out dancing with your brother hundreds of times."

Leo faced me, palms up and out, waiting for me to take them. "What's the hang-up? What's the difference between me and Hue?"

"Nothing," I said and put my hands in his.

But Hue's hands had never made me aware of my girly bits.

By the second song, I started to relax as the group danced together, laughing and switching our channels to see if we were in or out of sync with each other.

Lockett spun me around like the song suggested, right round round, and I ended my spin facing Lil' Megalodon, his gold-framed shark's tooth reflecting beams of colored light.

His sweatshirt was glowing in the dark, and I had to read it three times before something hit me.

I spun back and grabbed Toby by the arm. Removing one side of his headphones, I asked quietly, "What college did you say McVay went to?"

"Stanford."

MONDAY

Sunday was spent catching up on sleep, going over my notes from AJ's interview, waiting for Toby to finish his looksee into Lil' Megalodon, and wearing Simon out at the dog park.

The following morning, Precious texted and said she was taking on Lil' Megalodon—whom she referred to thereafter only by his real name, DeShawn Cook—and was very excited. Leo texted and asked me to meet him at the new coffeehouse, which coincidentally was having its grand opening that day.

Replacing How Ya Bean, a Wind River staple for the past six years, was Java Magic.

The former owner of How Ya Bean had gone to prison for an undetermined amount of time, pending her behavior. I couldn't help but think Java Magic was doomed simply because of its predecessor.

The coffee shop's sign was glittery and kitschy, with streamers of metallic colors cascading down.

I stood on the sidewalk and looked in through the large

plate-glass window. The crowd was a decent size, with none of the Mommy Mafia I'd had a run-in with at the beginning of the school year. Since their fair leader had been eighty-sixed to pursue crime in the afterlife, the hunter-boot-and-puffy-vest moms had probably gone somewhere else to practice their snark.

My mother rushed out the door with a medium cup wrapped in a cardboard protector.

"Hi," I said. "What do you have there?"

She kissed me on the cheek. "Tea. You look lovely."

I was wearing leggings, ankle-high winter boots, and a long tunic-style sweatshirt that looked more sporty than sloppy. My winter coat was thin but well insulated, so I had it open to stay cool.

"Why aren't you having tea in your office?"

Mom, a lawyer by trade, was the mayor of Wind River and very picky about her tea. If she did takeout, it was coffee.

She pointed at a cable utility van parked outside her office at the town hall. The garish Java Magic sign had distracted me so much that I wasn't noticing the obvious.

"We're having the lines upgraded to improve our internet speed."

My eyebrows went up. The internet speeds downtown did lag at times, for reasons we could only guess. Some people speculated the clouds were the reason. Others attributed the slow speed downtown to the lines being a million years old, before the lines were fiber optic.

"Will the entire downtown get this boost or just the mayor's office?" I asked.

Mom smiled. "This block, to start."

"Yes," I said and gave her a thumbs-up. Since I lived over

the newspaper, which was across the street from the town hall, I was getting an upgrade.

Mom smiled. "I'm glad I could make your day. But for now, the tech guy is in my space, so I'm going to go pester your dad. Want to come for dinner?"

"Can I bring Simon?"

She nodded.

"Okay. See you later."

After she crossed the street to Dad's, I turned back to the coffeehouse. I loved when someone else made my coffee, but the vibe that place was putting off didn't make me want to get coffee there, which was stupid, no doubt. But metallic streamers like the ones on the sign were also hanging from the ceiling inside, covering the walls with rainbows.

Leo came up beside me. "I'm sure it's harmless to go in. It's coffee."

I grunted in frustration. "I'm only drinking black coffee. Nothing fancy." I pointed at the sign. "If that's any indication, then I think black coffee might not even be on the list."

Leo chuckled. "We'll never know if we don't go in."

I gave him a push. "You first."

We entered, and the bell over the door made a jaunty little jingle, one that could get annoying quickly.

A lady my age, early thirties, wearing a green floral long-sleeve dress that nearly touched the floor, rushed to greet us. "Welcome, welcome. Let me take a look at you so I can get a sense of what you should be drinking."

Whoa. I was going to decide what I wanted, not some stranger with a French braid and no makeup, who smelled like patchouli oil and looked like she should be churning butter or something. I had a feeling that we didn't have the same sort of taste buds as I would never be caught dead in a green floral dress. She probably put lots of sugar in her black coffee.

"I like to read your aura. At Java Magic, we like to help you make your day the best. The food you eat, the drinks you consume... They can affect your day and your aura." She put a palm out toward me. "Yours looks to be straightforward—coffee, a mild roast with sweet notes and a healthy splash of half and half." She moved her hand toward Leo. "You're simple, black coffee for you too, but you want an exotic brew. I have a Peruvian blend that I think you'll just love. Bold, nutty, with a slight peppery taste."

Leo said, "Wow. Sounds good. I'll try it." Dressed in his uniform, he stuck out his hand. "Leo Stillman."

She dropped hers into his, all dainty like. "Lark Ogilvy. I'm the owner."

Leo asked, "What brings you to Wind River?"

Lark held her arms out wide. "This opportunity. I'm from Portland, but it's too expensive there."

I jumped into the conversation. "You had a shop there?"

She shook her head. "Worked for a shop and got lots of practice. I would try out a variety of concoctions. Used to give them away to the homeless, so I think I have a good sense of what works for people and not."

I guess I was being shortsighted by assuming that I had different food expectations from a homeless person's.

"We'll grab those drinks, Lark. And good luck. I hope you like Wind River," I said.

From a large pocket in the front of her dress, she took out a Post-it note and a Sharpie. She wrote Leo's coffee order on one sheet, peeled it off the top, and slapped it onto his chest, right over his badge. She did the same to me then gestured for us to continue to the counter.

"Let's take these to my balcony," I said after we got our coffees, the barista having snatched the sticky notes from our shirts and pressed them onto our takeout cups.

Minutes later, we were kicked back in deck chairs, looking down at the activity in town. The town was relatively quiet, the occasional person going into the newspaper or the corner market. The yoga studio was letting out, and those patrons were flocking to Java Magic. I got us two mugs to put our coffees in because coffee from a mug instead of a paper cup is better-tasting coffee. I kicked my feet up to rest on the deck railing.

"How's the case coming along?" Leo asked.

I gave a one-shoulder shrug. "Slow. I hit a dead end with the trainer. Toby's been tracking his cell phone and credit card, and there's been no activity for the last few days. That worries me. I called the training facility and asked for him, said I was the loan manager from his bank, and they said he wasn't in. I'll try again later."

Lockett came out of my apartment with a stack of papers in one hand and a smoothie in the other. He'd refused my invitation to join Leo and me for coffee. "Got the full medical examiner's report and the crime scene report," he said and pulled up a chair between Leo and me. He handed Leo a sheet.

I would go over the pages later, alone, when I had more time and could concentrate. For the time being, I waited patiently for them to share what they learned. While they scanned the papers, I surveyed the town. Wind River was growing. Its proximity to Portland and Olympia then Seattle made it appealing. The marina, to the left of my apartment, was at over 50 percent capacity, and many of the boats docked were expensive mini yachts. I wondered where those boaters went once they docked. Maybe our great hiking trails drew them in.

My attention got snagged by a guy sitting on the hull of his speedboat. He appeared to be looking right at us.

Something about him was familiar. He had a ball cap pulled low, so I couldn't make out his face. I looked away, not wanting to draw attention to the fact that I'd been staring. My heart beat wildly as my mind ran through all the scenarios of who the person might be because he couldn't possibly be who I thought he was. My not-legally-married husband had died when his car crashed into a tree and burst into flames earlier that year. He certainly wasn't sitting on the hull of a boat. Yet I couldn't shake that feeling.

"Tyson," I said, calling Lockett's attention away from the paper. "Keep looking down at your reports, but in a moment, look to your left at the marina. The middle pier, right side is a cruiser speedboat. White with blue and gold stripes. There's a guy sitting on the hull. Does he look familiar to you? He's looking this way. Hasn't looked away. I think he's watching us."

Leo stood and handed his papers to me. "Now you can look that way without it being suspicious."

I also thought that was a bit of posturing to let the boat guy know a cop was on the deck, not that I thought that mattered. The boat guy had likely seen Leo and I come up. I was thinking of him as the boat guy because he couldn't be Carson. *Right?*

Lockett looked toward Leo then sucked in a deep breath as if trying to cover a gasp. "Nah," he said under his breath. "Can't be."

I glanced back at the boat guy, trying to seem like I was looking at Leo. The boat guy stood. He was tall, about my height, with broad shoulders. He readjusted his cap, and the brief action gave both Lockett and me a flash of his face.

"It's not Carson, right?" I said.

Lockett shook his head. "Carson is dead."

My bigamist husband with two wives had also been Lockett's best friend since middle school. If either of us would know whether the boat guy was Carson, it would be Lockett.

"But it looks like him, doesn't it?" I asked.

Lockett looked down at the papers and wiped a hand over his face. "Yeah, he moves like Carson, has the same build."

"And last spring, we saw a guy in a speedboat who we thought reminded us of Carson then, remember?"

Lockett nodded.

Leo put his hands on his hips. "You two are nuts, seeing ghosts. Carson is dead."

"Is he?" Lockett and I asked in unison.

Leo pointed at Lockett. "You're no better than her. Seeing ghosts where there aren't any. People can have similar builds. Similar mannerisms." Leo moved his pointed finger to me. "And you, thinking a flasher in the park was Carson. Maybe you should ask yourself why you want him to still be alive."

I sat back, indignant. "I don't want him dead." I held up a hand. "Make no mistake—I'm not saying I want him alive so I can be with him. I just would prefer people to live out their lives. Carson was young when he died. I know he wasn't the best, most ethical of men, but to be glad he's dead... to prefer that..." I shook my head. "No."

Lockett said, "He's leaving. I think he knows we're watching him too."

I looked at the marina, and Leo turned as well. The boat

guy jumped into his speedboat and backed it out, not appearing to be in any rush.

Leo sighed. "Carson or not, you two have bigger issues." He turned back toward me. "That report you're holding says there's a video with a timestamp that shows AJ arrived at McVay's at seven in the evening and left at nine-thirty. And McVay's time of death is between eight p.m. and midnight."

14

TUESDAY

BREAKING AND ENTERING WAS DUMB. BREAKING AND ENTERING in broad daylight was dumber. And since I was about to do both, I suppose that made me the dumbest dummy in Dumbville. But whatever.

I parked LC on the road between McVay's house and the neighbor's and checked LC's undercarriage to make sure he wasn't leaving a trail.

Keith McVay lived in Lake Oswego, on the lake. People who lived in that neighborhood had lots of money. From the front, the modern-art cement house was L-shaped. A three-car garage sat on one end with plain, heavy doors, black with no details. The living-quarters portion was a white slab of concrete, and a large glass-block window ran from ground to roof and sat next to heavy black wooden doors with glass-block inserts. Chrome handrails on stairs leading down to the front door shone in the morning sun.

The house had been built into a hill. I was facing the top floor and knew from an online search that McVay's residence was four stories. The top floor held the main living space and kitchen, the master bedroom and home office were directly below that, the second-to-bottom floor was more bedrooms, and the bottom floor was the basement. The entire back of the house was a wall of glass.

I hung my camera from my neck and moved across the street to take shots of the house from various angles. I didn't need photos but just wanted to have a purpose in case anyone stopped me.

My cell phone rang.

"Hello," I said after touching my earbuds as I kept looking through my viewfinder.

"Where are you?" Leo asked.

"Good morning to you too. I'm fine. How are you?" I asked.

He chuckled. "Sorry. Good morning. I'm calling because your speedboat is back."

I lowered my camera. "Really?"

"Yep. I sent Officer Gee down to the marina to get the hull number. He did and ran it for me."

From the background sounds, I could tell Leo was driving. "And?"

"And it's registered to a dummy corp called Phoenix Rising."

Remembering my ruse, I lifted the camera, took a few more shots, and started down the long driveway to McVay's house. Running along the driveway was a metal stairway that led to the lake and the back of the house, and I headed down. Along my descent, I took pictures of any entries and cameras placed around the property.

Each level had its own balcony and access to a small garden. I continued down the stairs to the basement level.

There, the yard was bigger and had access to a dock, the lake, and a boat garage.

"If you're asking if that sounds familiar, or something Carson might have named a company, I can't say. No, he never used Phoenix for anything, but also, he was married to another woman and didn't tell me that."

Leo grunted. "And where did you say you were?"

"I didn't."

What I needed to locate was the name of the security system so that Toby could determine if it was engaged.

Leo asked, "Why do I feel like you're being purposefully evasive?"

"Because you don't really want to know where I am and what I'm doing, so let's leave it at that."

From my back pocket I took out a small notebook and drafted a diagram of camera placements. Cameras sat on each corner of the back of the house, top and middle, some pointing toward the sliding glass doors, others toward the water. Three over the garage pointed toward the driveway, the front door, and the back of the house.

"How will I know if you need to be rescued?" Leo mumbled.

"Ha ha," I said. "I think I'm okay today. You can stand down." After tucking my notebook back into my pocket, I pulled a chair over to a camera near me and stretched as long as I could make my body to see if a company sticker was on the frame.

Nothing.

"Hmm. That's weird," I mumbled.

"What's weird?"

"There's no company name on these cameras. There's no sticker of any security company on the doors. What I did learn from Carson, who owned a security company, is that companies put their names on these things for several reasons."

"Please tell me you aren't at McVay's house."

I scoffed. "Why would I be there?" I almost said *here*. That would've been bad.

"Because yesterday, we read about AJ being caught on camera at McVay's, and you said something about checking things out, seeing for yourself."

"Even if I had come to McVay's, it's not like I could enter the house. I don't have the keys." I moved the deck chair back to where I'd gotten it then stepped back to scan the house for an entry point. Chances were one of the sliders might be unlocked. From a security standpoint, the house was a nightmare—too many ways to enter. One of them had to be open.

Leo said, "So you're not at McVay's?"

"Why are you so stuck on this?"

Two doors were on that floor. I tried the first—locked. I tried the second—open.

"Because trouble seems to find you, and I have this uneasy feeling that you might be getting yourself in trouble. And if you're doing a B and E, you're just asking for trouble."

"You should rest assured that I am not breaking and entering into anyone's house. The door was unlocked." I let it swing open into the dark, windowless basement, whose air was musty and smelled like the lake, a tad fishy and like algae with a mix of gasoline. "I need to go. I need my phone for a flashlight." I discontinued the call but not before Leo let out a swear word that would have made his mother box his ears.

I called Toby.

"What you got? My fingers are poised to do some online snooping."

"I got nothing. No sticker. Nothing." After pulling my phone from my other back pocket, I turned on the flashlight and scanned the room. Empty. Stairs led to another door directly across from me.

"Did you check all the cameras?"

Crap. I had not. Maybe the sticker had fallen off the one I'd checked. "I'm in the basement right now" was my non-answer.

I fast-walked across the room, leaving the door to the outside open. I jogged up the stairs, stopping at the door at the top. I held my breath when I turned the knob, remembering at the last moment to use my shirt so as to not leave my fingerprints. That door was unlocked as well. It swung open into a butler's pantry.

"I'm in the house," I said breathless, as though someone might hear me.

"Do you have your phone set up to look for Wi-Fi?" Toby asked.

"Yeah, I think so."

"Open a web page like you're going to search, and tell me what names pop up as Wi-Fi options."

I did as Toby requested and took a snapshot of the pop-up and texted it to him. Then I stepped into the butler's pantry and closed the door quietly behind me. "Did you get my text?"

"Yeah, dudette. McVay was a tool. Did you see his Wi-Fi name was number one QB star?"

I glanced at the screen, which read #1QB*.

"Jeez," I said. "How do you explain that when people ask

to get on your Wi-Fi?" I stuffed the phone back into my pocket.

Toby snort laughed. "I've seen some that say Zombie Response Team."

"And FBI Surveillance Van," I added.

"You should use that one." He laughed. "Hang on. I'm seeing who his provider is. If we're lucky, they might also be the security company."

I moved slowly through the house, starting in the kitchen. Beer bottles sat on the counter, dishes in the sink. Black fingerprinting dust remained on the light-gray marble counters, the stainless-steel appliances, and everywhere else. The cabinets were maple and looked high end. The kitchen ran the length of the house and had a large sliding glass door that opened to the deck. I looked from the kitchen into the open-concept living space: a living room, a large dining room, and an entertainment space with a grand piano, all decorated in white cabinets with beveled glass.

I gasped.

"What?" Toby asked, his voice raspy with concern.

"I see where he died. No one has cleaned this place up. There's a large stain on the wooden floor. It's huge and from blood." I swallowed convulsively to hold back my queasiness.

"I'm glad it's you there and not me." He paused. "Crap waffles."

I took pictures of the stain and the area around it. "What?"

"McVay used the local internet provider for his internet services, but his security is Strong Code Security. I can't hack that."

My shoulders sagged. "That's not a positive attitude. Precious would say to visualize—"

"I've tried. Lots. Austin Strong is the master of code and blocking his back doors. You know, a few months back, some guy put on the dark web that he'd pay a hacker one million bucks if they could get into Strong's system. As far as I know, no one did it."

A large indentation was in the floor at the edge of the stain. I hadn't noticed it before because the blood had made the missing chunk dark like the walnut floors. The missing piece was three inches in length and longer than wider. I snapped a few pics from various angles, wondering what had made it. The dumbbell was my guess, used to bash McVay upside the head before the killer dropped it or let it fall to the ground. I wondered if that meant the killer hadn't been planning to use the dumbbell as a weapon or if it meant the opposite, that once the deed was done, the killer dropped the dumbbell and walked away, mission accomplished.

I backed away from the stain and looked around for the gym equipment. "Toby, who was the one that found McVay?" I felt foolish for not knowing.

Over the line, the clicking of keys was the only sound for several moments. "Hmm, the police did."

I stepped into McVay's office. "What? Why were they here first?"

"Got a call from McVay's mom saying she couldn't reach her son and could they do a wellness check. Said she was worried because he was on medicine and depressed. They did and found him."

I stopped in front of a wall of pictures. "Wait. Didn't you say his parents had been killed in a car accident?"

More clicking of keys. "Yup."

"So who really called the police?"

"I'll see what I can find out," Toby said. "You want me to stay on the line while you do the walkthrough?"

"No, I won't be staying long. Especially if we can't tell if I'm on camera right now." Although the thought gave me the willies, I figured nobody was going to press charges. "Hey, Tob, can you find out who inherits McVay's estate?"

"On it. Text me when you're free and clear."

"Okay." Staring at the pictures in front of me, I clicked my earbud to discontinue the call.

I scanned the room, looking for more photos, but what was out in small frames were the same as what was on the wall: Keith with Austin Strong, Keith at the NFL draft, and Keith with other prominent quarterbacks. I saw no pictures of Keith with women and no pictures of a personal life or vacations in foreign lands. I lifted my camera to take a picture of Keith McVay, Lil' Megalodon, and some dude in the middle. The guy in the middle had his arms around McVay's and Megalodon's shoulders.

Scrawled across the photo in gold ink were the words "My number ones. A power team that can never be destroyed."

The initials scrawled below were RS.

15

TUESDAY

SIMON WAS RUNNING ACROSS THE DOG PARK, IN HIS MOUTH a large ball with rope hanging off each side. Rocket trailed behind him, trying to catch up, in a simple game of keep-away.

Paulie snorted then spat. "How many cameras did you say?"

"Sixteen total. That sounds excessive, right? And only three caught AJ coming and going. One in the driveway, one at the front door, and one when they stepped out on the back deck. Most of the cameras were on the back deck, so why did only one catch AJ?"

That had been bugging me since I read the report and saw McVay's house.

"Place sounds like a prison." Paulie side-eyed me. "And you just walked into the house in broad daylight?"

We'd gone over that before. I hadn't wanted to tell him what I'd done but eventually came clean. Paulie didn't seem to believe me.

I shot him an irritated look.

He held up both hands. "It's just that what you did took cojones. I wasn't sure you had them. I'm impressed."

I rolled my eyes. "Whatever. You strike me as the type to underestimate women anyway, so you're easy to impress."

Paulie chuckled. "True. But it's progress that I gave you props, right?"

I smiled. "Yeah, that's progress. You know where else progress would be good? This case. Can we get back to it?"

Paulie and I had fallen into this weird passive-aggressive relationship that worked. He made me earn nuggets of golden advice from him, and I made him feel like a heel for it. I think he secretly liked me giving him a hard time.

"Sixteen, huh?" he said.

I nodded. The number bugged me. I didn't think a home-owner needed that many cameras to thwart break-ins or theft.

"I looked through crime blotters, and there are no reported break-ins or such at McVay's house. So why was he so paranoid about what was outside?"

Paulie scratched his chin. "Rethink it. Maybe it's not about what's outside but what's inside."

I narrowed my eyes, pondering what he was implying. But the cameras being focused on what was inside would imply McVay was a prisoner in his own home. I had a hard time wrapping my mind around that.

Paulie did a chin nod in the direction of the dogs. "Heads-up."

I turned to find Simon in the poop position, but before I could even dig a poop bag out of my pocket or take a step, the Dog Park Mafia had their Q-Beam flashlight on Simon's poo.

"Hello, dog owner," the one without the light said. "Pay attention."

I gritted my teeth and walked across the park to scoop the poop. After dumping the tied bag into the garbage, I went back to Paulie. "You really should come at a different time."

He shook his head. "I'm not going to change my routine because of those two bossy battle-axes. You mentioned the wall of photos. I agree—it's weird no pics were of family or a girlfriend. Dig around, but the answer might be something simple, like a bad breakup, and he recently scrubbed the house of her image."

True.

Paulie continued, "And this Sweezy? What do you know about him?"

RS was Rich Sweezy. "He used to be McVay's agent. But McVay dropped him a few months ago and took on a different agent, a Nick Hutton. My dad said when this happened, the papers went nuts. Lots of speculation on social media, and not a lot good about Sweezy. Apparently, an unnamed source said McVay dropped Sweezy because he didn't feel like Sweezy was representing him as much as he did the franchise. You know how people like to vilify on social media. Rumors of kickbacks and such floated around Sweezy."

Paulie nodded. "What do you know about the new agent?"

"I researched him, and he's the agent for a few other quarterbacks who were recently in contract negotiations, and he gets his clients fat cash."

"And—"

I knew the next question before he asked because it had

been the question I asked too. "Yes, McVay dropped his first agent in the middle of contract talks, and no, Sweezy doesn't have another QB on his roster. Other NFL players, some baseball guys, and a few musicians."

Paulie gave me a quizzical look.

"Yeah, I thought it odd about the musicians too. One is Lil' Megalodon. So I looked into that." I'd had Toby do it. "And Sweezy signed Lil' Megalodon while he was in college around the same time he signed McVay. The way it looks on paper, Sweezy was building his roster any which way he could."

Paulie pointed a bony, crooked finger at me. "Don't assume."

"I'm hypothesizing. I'll only know for sure when I talk to him." I'd gone over that with Lockett, and he agreed I should talk to Sweezy and gave me some questions to ask.

Paulie said, "When you meet this guy, you have to know that he's likely going to lie to you. He'll give you just enough truth to pacify you."

"Why lie? It's not like I'll be accusing him of anything. Yet."

Paulie shrugged. "People can't help themselves, and typically, they've got some skeletons in their closets they don't want people to know about. You need to go through this world assuming everyone is lying. Even your client didn't tell you the truth. I can promise you that."

Paulie's words gave me a stomachache. I pressed a hand to my belly, hoping if I pushed against the queasiness, it would stop hurting. Thinking about AJ and lies and going through life suspicious of everyone didn't sound fun or stress free. I blew out a breath.

"Okay, I'm going to talk to the agent. I'm having my guy look into who stands to inherit McVay's estate. What else?"

"What about the coaches and the franchise owner?"

I made like I was checking off a list. "Lockett's talked to all the coaches and met with Austin Strong a few days ago. Strong is helping pay AJ's defense bill."

"Has he actually sent the money, or is it all lip service?"

I shrugged, unsure. "I don't think we've got any money yet."

Paulie's lip curled, and he spat on the ground. "These rich ones like to offer and never come through with it. Wanna make a bet? I'll take lip service. You can have genuinely wants to help."

I waved my hand, passing on the bet. "Any other pearls of wisdom you have for me?"

"Look at the neighbor. Sometimes, the path to the answer is the easiest and most obvious one."

I tried not to let my confusion show. "The neighbor?"

Paulie shook his head at me in disgust. "I used to make a list of all the possible scenarios I could come up with for why a person was murdered, harassed, stalked, or what have you. I always started with the spouse or girlfriend. You're already working on that. Then I'd add coworkers and such. But what I hate to admit is that in more than one case, my bad guy was the neighbor." He shook his head sadly. "You'd be amazed at what pushes people over the edge. But start with an ex. They always have the best motives and means."

"The dumbbell weighed twenty-five-pounds. I can't see a woman swinging that upward unless she was crazy strong and as tall as McVay."

Paulie chewed his gum and looked at me hard. "A possibility, right?"

"Sure."

"Then put it on the list. I can see you're already dismissing my idea of the neighbor."

"I'm not. I'm not sure I'm sold on it, though."

Paulie's lips thinned in frustration. "Maybe they've had beefs with each other over time. Maybe McVay drives his speedboat late at night or blasts workout music or something. You won't know until you talk to the neighbor."

"You're saying McVay coached AJ, ate some Indian food, then AJ left, and McVay had a lot of beers, started working out—"

"Maybe he stood on his deck and pissed in the neighbor's yard. Who knows? But the neighbor comes over, pounds on the door, McVay answers, they get in an altercation, the neighbor picks up the dumbbell, and boom! Bashed McVay in the back of the head. Hell, the neighbor's not even a Pioneers fan. So good riddance."

Crap. Paulie was making sense.

I continued the story. "Horrified, he drops the dumbbell and leaves a gouge in the wood floor." I'd uploaded the pictures from McVay's house to a file on my phone, and I showed Paulie.

He nodded. "Yeah, but there are a ton of other reasons that gouge could be there. Don't forget that. You know what they say about cops who follow the evidence and cops who assume and see how the evidence fits?"

I nodded. In Wind River, our police chief was the come-up-with-a-theory-and-see-how-that-evidence-fits kind of guy. Leo was a follow-the-evidence-trail kind of guy. Leo's method had been my saving grace when I was a person of interest a few months earlier in the murder of a charter school principal.

Paulie continued, "PIs are the same. Which one do you want to be?"

"The open-minded kind."

Then make a list. Make lots of lists. How did that gouge get there? Scenarios of what happened that night. And let the people and clues tell you the story."

For all his crass mannerisms, Paulie was all right.

He slapped me on the arm with the back of his hand. "Look, Lady Laser Light's dog is dropping a turd bomb in the corner, and she's too busy gabbing to see it. Man, I wish I had her light."

I grinned and said, "I came prepared for this moment. Watch this." From my pocket, I took out a coach's whistle I'd gotten from Precious.

I gave a good blow, and the shrill, long shriek caused both dogs and people to look my way. When I had the owner's attention, I used her words and said, "Pay attention. Your dog just emptied his bowels over there."

Paulie lifted a hand and pointed. "Just walk in that direction. I'm sure you'll find it. It's large. I can see it from here."

She glared at us. Then she huffed and tromped off toward the pile.

I said, "That felt good."

He chuckled. "Yeah, it did."

I handed him the whistle. "For next time."

"She looked ticked."

I shrugged.

He said, "Oh, I don't care either. But let's not turn our back on her as she might brain us with her flashlight. Never can tell with people."

Point taken. I added the neighbor to my interview list.

16

TUESDAY

I DROPPED SIMON OFF AT THE APARTMENT AND DECIDED TO give Java Magic another try. My first visit had been a success, but talk around town was that the place was hit or miss. That made me curious, and besides, I liked getting coffee made by other people and considered it a luxury. But if the coffee wasn't palatable, that was enough to put me in a bad mood. And I was currently teetering between a good or bad mood every day because of the case.

Java Magic was unusually quiet. In the past, the coffee shop had been hopping, so much so that June, the previous owner, had kept a chalkboard of which groups were scheduled to use the tables in the shop at different times.

But Java Magic was devoid of patrons. No writers were on their laptops. No moms were in workout gear, having just finished a yoga class next door.

The owner, Lark Ogilvy, was leaning against the counter, her head resting on her hands and a frown on her face. One table was taken, and I was surprised to find Precious there

with a man. His back was to me, so I didn't recognize him—
likely a business meeting for her. That didn't stop me from
approaching, but first I stopped near Lark to place an order.

"Black coffee, please."

She shook her head. "Your aura is all out of whack. You
need something calming to help it. How about a chamomile
tea?"

"How about a black coffee?"

She narrowed her eyes. "Didn't you hear what I said
about your aura? To not realign it—"

"I'll take my chances. I like living on the edge." I tapped
the counter twice to signal we were done then approached
Precious.

She glanced up at me, smiled, and sat straighter. "Sam,
come here." She waved me over and gestured at the man.
"You remember Austin Strong. We met him—"

"At the Pioneers game. Right. You're the owner." I held
out my hand, and we shook.

Precious gestured to Strong. "Austin's considering hiring
me to do some work with his company."

I nodded. They were having a business meeting.

Strong was dressed in jeans and a V-neck sweater. An
unwrapped scarf hung around his neck. He stood and pulled
a chair over from another table. "Erika's been telling me a
little about the case. I've had a few conversations with AJ's
lawyer, Mr. Lockett, as well. If there's anything I can do to
help with the investigation, please let me know."

Precious said, "Austin's offered to contribute to AJ's
defense fund."

I raised my eyebrows and glanced at Strong. "That's very
nice. So you think AJ is innocent, then?"

Strong glanced at Precious then back at me. "I was just

telling Erika here that it's not for me to say if he's innocent or not. That's for the courts to decide. But I've met AJ a few times. He's a nice kid. Squeaky clean. It's hard for me to imagine he'd do something this horrific. Regardless, I want him to have a fair trial, and if contributing to his defense means you get to follow all the leads so that if he is convicted, it's done so without a doubt, that's money well spent, to me."

Squeaky clean and *if convicted*—the two phrases were at odds with each other. As I'd grown up with a newspaper man and a lawyer, words meant a lot to my family. I'd learned the definition of semantics at an early age. Strong was being generous, but I would've preferred the offer come with a firm belief that AJ was innocent. And, of course, Paulie's words played back in my mind—offering to contribute and actually giving were not the same.

I said, "I'm going to see AJ's lawyer in a bit. I can take your donation if you want."

Strong patted his shirt and pants pockets. "Sorry. No checkbook on me. But I'll call my secretary and have her send it today."

I would wait a few days to pass judgment.

Strong studied me. "Erika says you're going to talk to Keith's old agent tomorrow."

I cut my eyes to Precious, hoping she'd read my confusion regarding why she was sharing anything with Strong. But she smiled at me as if she didn't see the problem.

I said, "Following all the trails. Even if they're dead ends." I took the opportunity to do some more trail following. "I know McVay wanted to sign a big contract. I know you weren't crazy about it. Care to share why?"

Strong gave a closed mouth smile. "I think—well, I

thought—we could win the Super Bowl. And if we didn't this year, I believed we could next year. But had I given Keith a big contract, I wouldn't have had the money to pay the other top-notch players, and I'd lose them. And with them my Super Bowl hopes."

"But if you lost McVay, there went your chances as well."

Strong crossed his arms and leaned back in his chair. "I wasn't going to lose McVay. He was bluffing."

Bluffs were only that when the people making them had nothing to back them up. Being a sports writer's daughter, I found it hard to believe McVay didn't have any other offers on the table.

I suppose my skepticism showed because Strong said, "The situation with Keith wasn't as cut and dried as you think. There's more to football than playing the game and contract negotiations."

I didn't want to cross my arms in case that look too combative. Instead, I folded them on the table and leaned onto them as if we were just friends talking sports. "Is there really? When boiled down, isn't the end result a bigger contract from playing high-level football? Bring the wins, get paid."

"Everything can be boiled down. That doesn't mean it's as simplistic as you just made it."

"True."

Strong smiled again, this time a sincere grin. "What else you got for me? Any questions I can answer?"

"Yeah, can you tell me if Brad Jenson, the trainer, is missing or away due to a family emergency? He's been off the grid for a few days, and when I call the facility, they won't answer my questions. They put me through to his voice mail, which is now full and not taking any more messages."

Strong's eyebrows went up. "I don't know everyone who works for the Pioneers, and I haven't heard anything about a missing trainer, but I'll look into it. Can you give me a few days?"

I nodded. "Sure."

He put out a hand. "Give me your phone, and I'll put my information in. Give me a call in a few days, and I'll know more."

Handing over my phone made me nervous, mostly because I was suspicious by nature. But I figured that since I was right there, he wasn't going to steal my personal information. And also, he had endless money, so I probably didn't have anything he could want.

I slid the phone across the table to him.

Lark called from behind me, "One black big mistake of a coffee without the ability to adjust an aura."

I turned to her. "I think that's mine."

She nodded. "I did a slow brew because at least the fact that the coffee wasn't made in a rush will give some good energy. A slow and steady energy."

I rose and went to the counter. "Slow and steady? I'll take it because apparently, that means I can win the race."

Apparently, Lark didn't find me funny. "You'll need all the help can get."

I smiled. "I've heard that all my life."

I went back to Precious and Strong, coffee in hand. My phone was sitting on the table near my chair, and I scooped it up and stuck it in my back pocket.

"Thanks," I said.

He nodded.

I pointed at Precious. "See you tonight?"

She smiled. "Of course."

I waved to them and exited the coffee shop, my mind already going over my notes and making a list of what would come after my visit with McVay's former agent.

17

WEDNESDAY

McVay's agent had a Seattle office. Requesting an appointment on behalf of Tyson Lockett, defense attorney for AJ Gunn, got me on Sweezy's calendar, and I didn't even have to threaten him with a subpoena like Lockett cautioned I might have to do. Sweezy's willingness to meet helped me remain open about him.

The drizzly rain and gray skies didn't inspire skirt wearing, so I went with black trousers, black Klogs, a lime-green button-down shirt, and a black corduroy, tailored jacket. I pulled my hair into a clip at the base of my neck and kept my makeup simple.

Sweezy's office was on the third floor of a six-story building in downtown Seattle. But nothing of interest was nearby—not Pike's Market, not The Crumpet Shop, just a row of chain shopping stores and a head shop.

His receptionist walked me to his office and opened the door for me.

Rich Sweezy came from behind his desk with a hand extended.

"Samantha True." I shook his hand firmly. "I appreciate you seeing me on short notice."

If McVay had traded up in agents, I couldn't image the snazziness of the new guy's office. Rich's was all glass and chrome with a black leather couch and two black leather club chairs. One wall was lined with pictures of him and several public figures, actors, athletes, and musicians.

"Well," he said, "I'll admit that it's awkward for me as I want to see Keith's murderer go to prison for a long time."

"As do I. And if AJ's the guy, then we'll let the justice system do its job."

He gestured for me to take a seat in one of the club chairs. Once seated, I faced his desk and the window behind him, which showed a decent view of the buildings across the street.

He said, "But you don't think Gunn's the guy, do you?"

I pulled from Paulie's words. "I wouldn't be doing a good job if I came at this with preconceived beliefs. Is AJ my friend? Yes. Have I had friends kill people before? Yes."

Dear Lord. The fact that was true disturbed even me.

"You need better friends," he said.

"Maybe." I laughed nervously.

Sweezy was my height, with dark-brown hair and brown eyes. He wore a scruff of facial hair that looked to be more than a five-o'clock shadow but not yet a scraggy early beard. I figured that was the look he was going for, trendy and cool. From his shirt pocket hung black-rimmed glasses. I suppose he used those to add "smart" to the look. He was dressed in black slacks and a dark-gray button-down. Whatever message he was trying to convey with his look, I wasn't getting it. Unless "trying too hard" was the message.

"Do you mind telling me how you became Keith McVay's agent?"

Sweezy leaned back in his chair and tucked his arms behind his head. A smile pulled at his lips. "College. I'd gone to Stanford too. Though a few years ahead of Keith. I was a young agent, trying to build my roster, and I was with a firm that had offices on both the East and West Coasts. I used to go back for the games, scout the talent. Keith was just moving into a starting position on the team, and I saw the potential."

I quirked an eyebrow. "*The* potential?" *Not Keith's potential.*

Sweezy looked sheepish. "Yeah, the potential for both of us. Word spreads slower on West Coast players. Stanford is Pac-12, but the Big Ten and SEC teams always draw the attention first. I had the cred of a well-known firm behind me at the time." He gestured at the space around us. "As you can tell, I've since started my own firm."

"You were McVay's agent for what... seven years?"

Sweezy looked at the ceiling as if calculating then back at me. "Yeah, that sounds right."

"Until McVay decided to fire you? Why was that?"

Paulie had explained to me that I could ask questions that were buttheaded in nature then backtrack as a way to seem apologetic.

Sweezy waved a hand, dismissing my apparent rudeness. "We had a disagreement about how he should go about contract negotiations." He folded his arms onto his desk and leaned into them. He continued in a hushed voice, "Listen, I don't want to speak ill of the dead. Keith was my friend, not just a client. We had a disagreement, and he refused to see reason. He only saw money. We came to an agreement that splitting would be best for both of us."

"You're saying the split was amicable? Because the media did not spin it that way."

Sweezy rolled his eyes. "Clickbait. That's all they were looking for. Not facts. Keith was headed down a dark path. I don't know what had changed in his life. New friends? Bad influences? But my gut told me Keith was about to self-destruct and that if I ventured down this path with him, he was going to drag my company with him. Sometimes, you can make the PR spin in your favor. But what makes a squeaky-clean guy like Keith McVay suddenly do perfor-mance-enhancing drugs? What was the trigger?"

I offered, "Relationship gone wrong?"

Sweezy shook his head. "No sudden relationship breakup because there wasn't any relationship. I don't think he'd been on a date in more than a year. And his parents died several years ago, so that's not the trigger. This shift in behaviors was alarming. The media would have eaten him alive, said he'd been this way all along and had tricked everyone. I'm good with PR, but I'm not good enough to combat that."

"You said there's no girlfriend or significant other in the picture. Maybe he was lonely. Or maybe he was gay and afraid to come out. For as progressive as we are today, I imagine a gay man in the locker room isn't warmly embraced just yet."

Arms still folded on his desk, Sweezy pointed at me. The small gesture made the conversation feel more intimate, honest. I'd had many conversations like this with my dad.

Sweezy said, "I had those same thoughts. I even confronted Keith about it. Tried to be a safe space for him.

But he laughed in my face." Sweezy opened his mouth as if to say more then shut it.

The unspoken words hung in the air between us disguised as a long pause.

"So you and McVay split because he wanted more money in his new contract?" I asked. "Forgive my ignorance, but isn't that what you're supposed to be doing for him?"

Sweezy grinned, his head bobbing in agreement. "Totally, but sometimes more money isn't the best move up front. Sometimes, you have to give a little to get a lot."

I shook my head. "I don't understand." I sort of did, but I needed him to be more transparent.

"Keith wanted a three-digit-million-dollar deal. Currently, one hundred and forty million is the benchmark. For a ten-year contract. But the problem with those deals is salary cap. Are you familiar with that?"

I nodded. The salary cap was the limit a team could spend on players' total. "If you spend a lot on the quarterback, then you have less for the other players. In the past, teams have found themselves with a record-breaking player yet unable to pay that player what he wants because of a salary cap. Then they lose that player to another team, and now time and effort goes into trying to get a replacement player up to speed. And time and effort in that area means less chance of a payoff or Super Bowl opportunity."

Sweezy's grin spread wider. "Wow, I'm impressed."

"I like football. And my dad's a sportswriter."

Sweezy nodded. "That concept was something Keith couldn't grasp. Austin Strong wanted to keep Keith with the Pioneers. Desperately. And he wasn't opposed to paying him. He just wanted to do it in bonuses and other ways. Austin wanted to have enough money to pay some of his other players. Austin believed—we all believed—this was the team's year to make the playoffs and maybe even the Super Bowl. And if they didn't get there this year, they would be even stronger and better next year if they kept their players. But they couldn't keep them if they couldn't pay them. Keith didn't care that he might get a Super Bowl ring, that adding this to his résumé would likely make him a Hall of Fame candidate. Keith only saw the money."

How Sweezy was describing McVay was in direct opposition to the goals of any professional player. *Who walks away from the ultimate win? Who doesn't prioritize that?*

"Can you tell me if any other team was interested?" Maybe McVay thought he could make a lateral move, not that such a thing existed outside of theory.

"Yeah, a few teams showed interest. But I don't know how far that got because we parted ways. You'd have to ask his new agent about all that." Sweezy leaned closer, stretching across his desk. "But I'll say this: there was lots of speculation that teams were pulling back once he failed that drug test."

"Which is stupid to me because troublemaker players are signed all the time. Why would McVay be different?"

Sweezy shrugged. "Goes back to social media and the PR spin. Those other troublemaker guys already have that reputation. Keith didn't. His positive test was a stunner. And talk was 'What else was he hiding?'"

"And? What else *was* he hiding?"

Sweezy shook his head. "Sadly, I don't know. We weren't close enough for him to bear his soul to me."

Sweezy wasn't much of a friend, then, even though he'd said they were, even though his note on the picture called them a team, a power team.

I let out a sigh. "Thanks for your time." I stood.

Sweezy did too. "I hope I helped. Though I'm not sure how I could have."

"Oh, I almost forgot. You're also Lil' Megalodon's agent too, right?"

Sweezy's brows shot up. "Yeah. Why do you ask?"

"I saw a picture of you three. McVay and Lil' Megalodon."

"DeShawn went to Stanford as well. I met him through Keith."

"And signed him back then too?"

Sweezy nodded.

"I didn't realize he and McVay were close."

Sweezy laughed. "So close they're neighbors."

"Seriously?"

Paulie's words echoed through my head. I guessed I should check out the neighbor.

"And do you mind me asking how things are between you and DeShawn?" I asked. "If he and Keith were tight and all, and you and Keith had a falling out, I'm guessing that would affect your relationship too. If nothing else, it would make it awkward."

Sweezy stood and wiped his hands down his pants then straightened his untucked shirt. "Nah, DeShawn and I are good. Solid."

"I see." I did see. I just saw a man lie with ease, just like Paulie said he would. I happened to know DeShawn was hiring Precious because of his anger at his agent.

I held up one finger. "One more. Where were you the night McVay died?"

Sweezy's eyebrows arched. "I was waiting for that question. I was here. Working. Security keeps a log of who comes and goes twenty-four hours. And they have video." He lifted a folder from his desk and handed it to me. "I worked late and ended up sleeping here."

Opening the folder, I saw video images with timestamps of Sweezy entering the building at eight in the morning and exiting the next day at seven, dressed in the same clothes. That wasn't proof yet, but it might be. I would have to look more into the images and video.

I extended a hand. "Thanks for your time."

"It was a pleasure to meet you. I'm sorry it was under these circumstances."

I smiled then let myself out of his office.

Sitting in LC, parked in the garage next to Sweezy's building, I called Lockett and relayed everything Sweezy had told me. Then I called Precious and told her I'd met with Lil' Megalodon's agent, didn't trust him, and was requesting a formal meeting with her client.

I was about to pull out of my spot when an unknown number popped up on my screen. Typically, I ignored those, but since I joined the PI business, unknown numbers could mean clients.

"Hello, Samantha True speaking."

"This the lady who had her face pressed up against my neighbor's sliding glass door?" The voice belonged to an older woman.

"Um..." I wracked my brain for the moment she was referring to, and I suppose my pause was too long.

"You know, the sports guy: Mr. Loud and yells at the TV."

"Yes, Brad Jenson." I remembered his neighbor with the curlers in her hair and the dog tucked under her arm. "I thought you weren't going to help me."

She huffed. "I'm not. At least, I don't want to. But the idiot is back with his TV blaring, and I can't call the cops. There's nothing they can do about it. Maybe since you wanted to see him and all, you could get him to turn it down when you talk to him."

I smiled. "I'm on my way. But I'm a few hours out. You think you can make it?"

She let loose a colorful word. "If I have to."

"I'll drive fast," I promised.

"You'd better." She ended the call.

18

WEDNESDAY

ON THE DRIVE DOWN, THE TRAFFIC WAS LIGHT AS I'D TIMED IT at midday, fortunately. And the path from Seattle to Brad Jenson's was all interstate except for the last twenty minutes, which required me to go through town.

I stopped once for food, a potty break, and a check on LC's oil. Once we both were topped off, I pushed the gas pedal down, scanning nonstop for highway patrol.

Rush hour was starting as I crossed into Oregon. I called Lockett on my hands-free and told him what was up. Afterward, I called Toby.

"What up, dudette?" Toby said.

"Are you at home, or do you have a drive to do?"

Toby was also a private driver for the popular companies that people were using.

"Home. I didn't feel like going out today. I've got my chip-eating pants on, a show I'm gonna binge on Netflix, and four bags of chips calling my name."

"I hate to bother you," I said with fake sarcasm, but actually, I was envious. "But can you see if there's been any activity on Jenson's cards?"

Toby did some clacking on his keyboard then said, "Nope, nothing. No use of his debit or credit. And no activity on his cell phone either. It's not pinging."

I had no reason to think anything was amiss except for Jenson's sudden absence, the absence of activity on his cards and phone, and his sudden reappearance.

"His neighbor just called and said he's home. I'm on my way now. I just think the no activity is weird."

The sound of a cellophane bag opening was followed by the crunch of a chip. Then Toby said, "The dude's a gambler. Maybe all this business at work was too stressful, and he had a line or something at a casino and he went and played it. Maybe he's been binge gambling."

"But not show up anywhere?"

"Sure. Not unheard of if the house was sponsoring him."

"Okay, that's reasonable," I said.

"Call me if you want someone on the line when you talk to him. I know you're, like, in super-cautious mode these days."

"Thanks, I will. In the meantime, also look into Lil' Megalodon and his agent, Sweezy, and see if you can pick up why Precious said Megalodon was angry with him."

"You could ask her," Toby said, his voice heavy with sarcasm.

"I could, but then I'd be asking her to break the coach-client privilege that Precious holds so dear."

In other words, that wasn't going to happen.

A smacking sound came across the line. Then the familiar sound that made me think of locusts swarming followed. Lady M was crabbing, making her displeasure known.

"What happened?"

Toby sighed. "I just slapped myself on the dome because I shoulda known that about Precious, and now Lady M is upset."

"I'll let you go deal with that."

We disconnected, and I pulled into Jenson's complex, grabbing a spot next to his truck. His neighbor opened her front door and stepped out, dressed in the same robe and curlers as the last time we'd meet.

"About time," she said.

I said, "I told you I was a few hours out. I wasn't twenty minutes away."

"I got tired of the TV and banged on his door. He's not answering."

Anxiety at having missed him again made me tense. "He didn't leave, did he?"

She shrugged and readjusted the little dog under her arm.

"What time did he come home?"

She shrugged again. "What do I look like, his mother? All I know is that TV started blasting sports at five this morning."

That was too early for most people to be leaving for work. But maybe someone saw him come home. I could only hope.

"So he woke you up by blaring his TV?"

She nodded.

Wow, that must be really loud. I walked to Jenson's door and listened. The TV came through muffled but not blaring. I cut my eyes to the neighbor.

"From inside my apartment, it's absurdly loud." She cracked open her front door so that I could see inside her living room as she gestured for me to step over and listen.

Jenson's TV was coming through much more clearly.

"Wow, those walls are paper-thin," I said.

"You're telling me."

"Is it always this loud? Haven't you complained to the complex?"

She set her dog inside then closed her door. "It's never been this loud. And the complex doesn't care."

I went back to Jenson's door. I said to the neighbor, "I can take it from here."

"Not gonna happen. When he opens that door, I'm gonna give him a piece of my mind. Can't even take a nap in my place. And I love a good nap."

As a fellow lover of naps, I could relate to her frustration. "Fair enough." I raised a hand to knock but paused and turned back to her. "Mind me asking your name? I'll introduce you to him and point out how inconsiderate he is."

She huffed and stuck her hands on her hips. "*Inconsiderate* is being too kind. I'm Carol, Carol Norton."

I nodded then turned back to the door. I rapped hard, knowing he needed to hear it over the TV.

We waited. Nothing.

I pounded on the door then pressed the doorbell several times in succession.

Mrs. Norton snorted. "I did that too."

The blinds on the front windows were pulled closed. "Let's take this around to the back."

She nodded and went into her house, not inviting me in to follow. Instead, I had to walk around the row of buildings and make my way back to Jenson's, which was in the middle.

I stepped up to the sliding door and pounded on it with a flat palm as I looked inside. No lights were on even though the sun was dipping lower in the sky. I glanced around the complex and verified that others were turning on their lights.

The sliding door looked in on the kitchen-dining combination. That room was divided by a wall, and on the other side was the living room. From where I was standing, the opening into the living room showed the TV, which was the only light on inside. I pressed my face close, cupping my hands around my eyes to see inside better. A bright commercial came on and cast a light through the living room, and I caught sight of a foot. The tip of a shoe was extended as if someone were sitting in a chair and had their legs kicked out in front of them, in a stretch.

Maybe he was sleeping. But then all the banging should have woken him. I pressed my forehead against the glass, thinking.

"Is he coming?" Mrs. Norton asked.

With one hand, I pushed off the glass. "No, but I think I see him. He's in there."

Her eyes narrowed. "I bet he's drunk or passed out."

"Did he do that often?"

"You have a better explanation?"

I shook my head and tried the sliding door's handle. It was unlocked.

"Whoa, wasn't that locked last time?" I don't know why I expected it to be locked.

Mrs. Norton nodded. "What are you waiting for? Let's go in there and give him what for." She pushed me aside and slid the door open.

A wave of something not so fresh burst out the door and pushed us backward.

"Barf," Mrs. Norton said. "That trash needs to be taken out."

"I agree." Sour milk and meat gone bad made me think of smells around dumpsters. I lifted my shirt and covered my nose, as if that would make it better.

Mrs. Norton gestured for me to precede her. "After you."

I rolled my eyes. "Gee, thanks."

The TV volume seemed to triple when I stepped inside.

"Hey, Brad!" I yelled over the din as I stepped cautiously into the space.

Mrs. Norton came in behind me, grabbing the back of my shirt like I was a line leader.

I cut her a do-you-mind look. She didn't get it, instead jerking her chin up to tell me to keep going. We slowly shuffled toward the living room.

"Brad, wake up, dude!" I yelled, ignoring the cramping in my stomach, a warning sign if there ever was one. Something was off, and my instincts were screaming at me.

Yet I continued to walk toward the unknown. I rounded the corner first and gasped, bile rising up my throat. I spun and pushed Mrs. Norton back into the kitchen, toward the door.

"What the..." she said, fighting to get around me.

I didn't let up. "You don't want to see that. He's dead. Can you go to your place and call the police?" I needed to find a bush to upchuck in.

We made it outside and sucked in a deep, cleansing breath, an automatic response to the fresh air.

"He's dead?" She looked around me but made no move to go back inside.

I nodded and scanned the property. Seeing no bush, I instead headed for a hose and spigot and lost my dinner there. With one hand on the brick wall and the other on my stomach, I focused on keeping my eyes open because whenever I closed them, I saw Brad Jenson in his chair, bloated, discolored, eyes wide open, dried foam coating his mouth.

"I'll call the police," Mrs. Norton said. Her back door slid open.

I leaned my head against the cold brick wall and turned on the spigot. From the hose, I splashed cold water on my face.

A few minutes later, Mrs. Norton came back and stood beside me.

I turned off the hose and rolled my head sideways against the brick so that I could see her better. She held out two glasses.

"The cops are on their way." She moved a glass of amber liquid toward me. "This is whisky. It'll help with the shock." Then she held another glass out, with clear liquid. "This is water because you'll need it to chase away the bad taste."

I grabbed the whisky and tossed it back, letting the liquid burn down my throat in a single swallow. I chased it with the water.

"We should go around front," I said, albeit hoarsely.

"I told them to come around back." She closed Jenson's door then took the glasses from me. "Come on. Come sit while we wait."

She gestured for me to follow her to her patio with outdoor furniture, a table and two armchairs with faded cushions.

She set the glasses on the table before sitting in a chair. "Thanks for stopping me from seeing him."

I nodded. "A couple months ago, I watched a man die. I didn't know was dying. I thought he was choking or something. Anyway, I thought that was the worst thing a person could see, but this was right up there with it." I picked at my already chewed-down nail.

Mrs. Norton shook her head. "How'd he die? Gun? 'Cause I never heard anything like that."

I shook my head. "The TV would have muffled it. But I don't think a gun was involved."

She shuddered. "How?"

"Overdose, maybe?" But I was guessing. Maybe he choked on something he was eating. But even as I thought that, I recalled the scene, and no food was nearby.

The police arrived and took our statements. The coroner followed. We watched from our chairs; though, even that felt too close.

The cop—his name tag read Burns—asked, "Did you touch anything inside?"

I shook my head but glanced at Mrs. Norton. "Did I touch the wall?" I couldn't remember.

The moments leading up and right afterward were a blur, leaving only the crisp, clear image of Brad in a chair, his arms back almost like they were tucked behind the chair, his chest forward, his head upward like he'd been looking toward something.

"No, I don't think so. And I didn't touch anything either. I was holding on to her."

I nodded.

"And why were you there?" the cop asked.

Mrs. Norton said, "I was there to get him to turn down the blasted TV. She was there because she's a PI and wanted to talk to him about her friend who's been charged with murder. She works for that guy who killed the Pioneer quarterback."

The cop studied me.

"I can take out my license if you want."

He put his hand out. From my back pocket, I pulled out my PI license and placed it on his palm.

He said, "And it's just a coincidence that you came here and you two connected?"

I shook my head and told him about my first visit and Mrs. Norton's call that afternoon. "I've been looking for Mr. Jenson for a few days now." I couldn't tell him that Brad's cards had been unused and he'd basically been off the grid since Saturday.

"Do you think he overdosed?" I asked.

That was possible, yet something felt off, something about how Brad was sitting or the expression of surprise on his face. However, I'd never seen anything like that before, so my barometer for what's to be expected didn't exist.

"The detective will check all angles."

Following that remark, another guy, mid-forties, with a buzz cut, graying temples, and the beginning of a spare tire, wearing jeans and T-shirt and a gun in a shoulder holster, stepped out of Brad's apartment. He looked familiar, but my brain was too foggy to place him.

"I'm Detective Daniels," he said. "I know Officer Burns has taken your statement, but I'm going to need you to tell it to me. I apologize for making you repeat it."

A crime-scene tech stood at the sliding door and brushed fingerprint powder across the handle and glass.

I said, "You're going to find my prints on that glass. I was trying to look into the apartment earlier."

Detective Daniels moved our glasses off the outdoor

table, placing them on the ground, then sat on it. "Start at the beginning. What's your name?" He held a small, palm-sized notebook in his hand, his pen at the ready.

"Samantha True."

He glanced up at me. "You're the PI working the Gunn case, right?"

Then his name and face clicked in my mind. He'd been one of the arresting officers in AJ's case.

I nodded and jerked my thumb toward Brad's place. "And that guy in there. He was a trainer for the Pioneers. I spoke to him a few days ago, and he warned me about this case. Said he was sorry AJ got roped into this. What does that mean? Guess I'll never know because now he's dead, and AJ wasn't the one who killed him either."

19

THURSDAY

LATE THE PREVIOUS NIGHT, THE PORTLAND COPS HAD GIVEN ME the okay to go home, calling Jenson's death a likely suicide. Thankfully, Lockett was staying with me and took care of Simon.

Detective Daniels cleverly skirted any questions I asked about McVay's case, but contact was contact, and I felt maybe he would meet with me, should I put my name in with the front- desk warden at the police department.

Exhausted from the night's events, I spent part of the morning lying in bed, going through the articles Toby had sent about Lil' Megalodon and his agent falling out. The sounds of Lockett banging around in my kitchen forced me out of bed.

"What's your plan?" Lockett asked over home-brewed coffee. My mood was ugly, so going down to Java Magic didn't seem like a good idea. I didn't need Lark Ogilvy to tell me my aura was black.

"I want to talk with DeShawn Cook. Apparently, he's McVay's neighbor."

Lockett, about to take a sip, paused. "You're kidding."

I filled him in on my visit with Rich Sweezy and how he'd lied about his relationship with Lil' Megalodon and who knew what else. I showed him the folder with the photos Sweezy had handed over as his alibi. I also shared what I'd learned that morning.

I added two scoops of sugar to my coffee in hopes of sweetening my mood.

Lockett said, "I had a conversation with McVay's new agent, Nick Hutton."

I arched my eyebrows in interest. While I'd been assigned the old agent, Lockett had taken on the new one, Nick Hutton.

"And?" I said.

"It looked like McVay was going to go elsewhere. Hutton and McVay had an offer on the table from an East Coast team that McVay liked. The Pioneers refused to match it. The deal was contingent on McVay getting his team to the playoffs. A likely probability."

"Did the fact that he sat out a few games matter?" I thought McVay had a lot on the line when bad luck chased him down.

"Not as much as the PEDs did. The team started to waffle some, Hutton said. Another team stepped in and offered less —not much less, mind you. They didn't care about the PEDs."

"Was McVay interested?"

Lockett smiled. "Here's where it gets interesting. McVay wasn't interested the first time they made an offer. But he was after he popped positive and the other team started to balk."

I picked up my mug and moved to the couch, settling

myself in a corner and propping my feet up on my coffee table. "What makes an All-Pro quarterback with a fantastic record want to walk away from his winning team? Everyone says they were playoff bound and had a good chance to go to the Super Bowl. Who gives that up?"

Lockett shook his head. "I can't find anything in McVay's life or past to answer that question. He didn't have a life. Only football."

I said, "Maybe that's the answer. Maybe he was lonely out here or something? He had no family. No significant other. He broke up with his 'friend' and agent." I made air quotes around friend because Sweezy didn't strike me as the sort to be a good one. "Maybe he wanted a fresh start."

Lockett put a palm out to gesture his disbelief. "From what? Nothing here was stopping him from having a full life."

Our gazes met and locked.

"That we know of," I said. "He's got cameras all around his house. Is he paranoid? If so, what of? He's got no personal life. He wants to leave a winning team, sure, for more money, but he's set up for becoming one of the greats, and he's gonna trade that on for cash? Why not have both? He's got a good reputation except, all of a sudden, he pops positive on a drug test. It's not lining up."

"I agree." Lockett stood. "You said you're going to talk to the neighbor and friend?"

I nodded.

"I'm off to talk to AJ again. We need to talk to some more players that were close to McVay. Once you talk to the shark rapper, call me."

I laughed. "You got it. Over the fridge is a travel mug for your coffee."

He gave me a thumbs-up and busied himself with preparing to leave. I dictated a text to Precious.

Me: Meet with Lil' Megalodon today?

But the text didn't say "Lil'," autocorrecting to "leal," which forced me to send a second text with the shark and record emojis.

Precious: **No. Maybe tmrw.**

Well, that won't do.

I gave up the comfort of my couch and went into my room to change, putting my hair in a braid then donning jeans, a pullover tunic-style sweatshirt, and my puffy jacket. I left five minutes after Lockett, stopping to wave to Stella through the window at the newspaper.

The rain was a drizzle, and the temps were low and not expected to rise, mimicking my mood. I crossed in front of the market and had stepped into the road to cross to where LC was parked when I heard my name.

I turned to find Leo coming out of the market, a bag of oranges in his hand.

He caught up with me. "I heard about you finding the trainer's body. Sorry."

He was dressed in jeans, a flannel shirt in shades of green, a white T-shirt underneath, and a thick outdoor working jacket. He touched my arm, and I wanted to melt against him for comfort. But the friendship between Leo and me was still new. Even though his kid brother was one of my best friends, Leo and I hadn't been in each other's lives until Carson died. Prior to that, we hadn't seen each other in ten years. So instead, I leaned against LC but gave his hand a squeeze of appreciation.

"I don't think I ever want to see something like that again." I pressed my palms to my temples because closing my eyes made me recall the image vividly.

"Suicides are tough."

I dropped my hands and stared at him. "That's the thing. I overheard Daniels say something to the photographer last night, something that struck me too."

Leo raised his eyebrows, waiting.

"He wanted shots of the positions of Jenson's arms."

"Because?"

"They were like this." I mimicked how Jenson had been in his chair: chest slightly out, head thrown back with his chin up, his arms back as if they had been trapped behind him.

"Easily explained, I'm sure. But your creative mind is saying what?" He gave me a crooked grin.

"Remember when I was in school for crime-scene photography?"

Leo nodded. "I remember your first assignment, when you threw up all over the—"

"I had the flu!" I punched him on the shoulder.

He chuckled, rubbing his shoulder. "That story never gets old."

I thrust my key into LC's lock. "I'm out of here."

Time was supposed to make embarrassing moments easier, but that one wasn't any more tolerable than it had been back then, maybe because that event, my first assignment, was a turning point in my life. I did, after all, go into stupid, soul-eating studio photography for ten years.

Leo placed his hand over mine, stopping me from getting

into LC. "Come on. Don't be mad. Tell me what you saw that made you think of that night ten years ago."

"It's not so much what I saw but a gut feeling that something about this wasn't right, and the more I think about it, the more I think it had to do with his position. If he committed suicide by popping too many pills, why didn't he slump in his seat?"

Leo shrugged. "It would depend on what he popped."

I nodded. "I suppose. But it looks almost like his hands were tied behind him."

Leo arched an eyebrow. "Or he'd been convulsing. Where you headed?"

"To see a shark rapper about his friendship with a dead quarterback and maybe trip him up into confessing he murdered him." I unlocked LC and opened the door.

Leo closed it. "You think this rapper might have killed McVay?" He kept a hand on the door, keeping it closed.

"I think it could be anyone. So why not a rapper he went to college with? A guy he shared an agent with. This same agent that Precious said he was mad at because the agent jacked something up."

"And what was that?"

"From what I read in the few articles Toby sent me, it would seem that there's this insanely hot podcast, *The Morning Rap*, and it's a big deal to be on it. Lil' Megalodon was asked to be on it. Only he no-showed. And let me tell you, the fans of the show are eating him alive on social media."

"What was the reason he didn't show up?" Leo leaned his shoulder against LC, still keeping me from leaving.

"Communication error with his agent." I jerked a thumb to one side, telling him to move.

"The agent might have messed up this deal?" Leo didn't budge.

I nodded. "Yeah, the timing of it appears to coincide with McVay drop-kicking his agent to the curb. I'm just gonna go by and see if my new rapper friend might want to get all this off his chest."

Leo shook his head. "Sounds like motive. I'm going with you." He pushed off LC and pointed at his pickup, parked two spots away from mine. "I'll drive."

I feigned indignation. "You got a problem with my vehicle?"

He chuckled. "Nope, and that's what makes you mad? I thought you'd tell me to butt out. That you got this."

I shook my head. "Nope. I love a sidekick. Why do you think I was so freaked out about Toby and Precious being able to protect themselves? Because I like having them along with me. You packing heat?"

Leo, who'd been leading me to his truck, paused. "You think we're gonna need it?"

"You never know with me," I said and pushed past him.

"This is true," he said and met me at the passenger door, opening it for me.

We splurged on drive-through coffee and pastries from one of the many coffee shacks scattered throughout Washington. Then we crossed into Oregon and headed to Lake Oswego.

Leo gave a low whistle as we pulled up outside McVay's house. "Nice."

"Not nice enough to keep McVay in town. He was trying to get out of here."

"Was his house for sale?"

I put up a finger to signal he should wait then pulled out

my phone. "I didn't see anything inside his house that indicated that."

Leo groaned. "Please don't tell me about your breaking and entering."

As I typed in McVay's address, I asked, "Is it a B and E if the doors are unlocked?" I scrolled through the sites. "According to the World Wide Web, his house wasn't listed."

"Doesn't mean he couldn't have been talking to someone about it but never got it finalized before he was murdered."

"Yep." I pushed the door open then stood at the front of Leo's truck and looked at the houses to either side of McVay's. "Either one look more like a rapper's house?" I wasn't above knocking on both doors but hoped to get it right the first go.

Leo said. "I'm sure Toby could find out."

I gave a mock gasp. "Are you saying I should hack a system to get the info?"

Leo shook his head. "You three are a bad influence on me."

I laughed then slapped him lightly on the shoulder with the back of my hand. "Look, the one on the left's garage door is opening."

A black minivan backed out. A woman was at the wheel with two kids in car seats in the back.

"The house on the right it is." I headed for that driveway.

A dark SUV was parked two houses up, facing us, and movement inside the SUV caught my attention. I'd noticed it coming in but thought the vehicle was empty.

"Is there someone in that car?" I asked Leo.

Leo's response was quick. "Hard to say, but I think so. Have you seen it before?"

I shook my head. "I don't think so. But aren't black SUVs

suspicious by default? Besides, I'm just trying to pay more attention to my surroundings. I'm not sure if you remember, but I've had some trouble with people catching me off guard. Never turns out well for me."

Leo's steps faltered. "Not my favorite phone call either." He pretended to hold a phone up to his ear. "Hello, Leo. Listen, I was just jumped by a lunatic with two different-colored eyes. He flung me around like a rag doll then took my lunch. Oh no. Oh no. Oh no. Oh, look, a quilt shop."

I rolled my eyes. "I did not say that."

"Close enough. I have to admit, you have the cutest goofy loop ever. And I've seen lots of goofy loop in my time."

Goofy loop was essentially when a victim would get stuck on one element of a situation. They sounded like a broken record.

"Next time, I'll call someone else."

Leo stopped and faced me. "Let's not have a next time."

I shrugged. "That would be my preference too, but I'm a realist."

His eyes flicked toward the SUV parked up the hill. "And this car bothers you?"

I grabbed his elbow and steered him toward the rapper's front door. "Only because Mrs. Norton—she was Brad Jenson's neighbor—said he left in a black SUV with silver trim."

"Of which there are hundreds in this state and ours."

I nodded. "Yep, but doesn't hurt to make note of these things."

"No, it does not."

We reached the door. Classical piano could be heard coming from inside.

I said, "Well, he does use classical music as a foundation to his raps."

Leo pointed at the door. "Shall I, or do you want the honors?"

I gestured for him to go ahead.

He pounded strongly on the door. We waited. Leo pounded a second time.

Moments later, Lil' Megalodon jerked open the door and frowned at us. He was dressed in a white T-shirt and loose lounging pants with sharks on them. He wore slippers with one shark embroidered on each slipper. His head of short dreadlocks was covered by a beanie. The area on his arm that had been covered with a large bandage was now exposed and showed a large scratch far into the healing stage.

"Nice," I said without thinking. "You take branding all the way."

"Maybe I'm just a superfan of sharks. Now, who are you, and what do you want?"

I moved in closer to stick a foot against the doorjamb and leaned against it. "My name is Samantha. I'm a PI, and I'm working the McVay case." From my back pocket, I took out my identification and showed it. "We met two weeks ago at the Pioneers game."

He took it and stared at the picture. "Are you laughing in this picture?"

"Yeah, so what?" I snatched the ID back. I'd felt so ridiculous that day, getting my photo for my PI's license—like a poser.

Lil' Megalodon squinted at me. "You're Erika's friend. I told her no, I wasn't ready to talk to you." He looked at Leo. "What's with the cop?"

I smiled at Leo. "It just radiates off you," I told him. To the rapper, I said, "Yeah, she told me you said no, but I came anyway. Sorry." I jerked a thumb toward Leo. "This is Leo Stillman. He's not here as a cop. He's here as a friend because he thinks trouble has a way of finding me and creating problems."

Lil' Megalodon studied Leo then me, cleaning his teeth with his tongue while doing so. "And he thinks maybe he can stop it?" The rapper looked over my shoulder. "Did you bring any trouble here? Because that would be not cool. Not cool at all."

I shrugged. "I hope not. And I'll leave in a few minutes. I had a few questions about McVay that I think only you can answer, and I wanted to know what you thought of your agent, Rich Sweezy. I saw online what happened with you not going on that podcast." I grimaced. "Yikes."

Lil' Megalodon crossed his arms. He didn't invite us in and stood dead center, blocking me from pushing inside. "He's lucky I don't kick him to the curb like Keith did. And you know what sucks about all this? Rich came out and admitted he forgot to tell me the date I was supposed to show up, and no one believes him. They think I blew it off because I think I'm bigger than I am. Man, people online are mean."

"They are," I said, recalling the comments my dad had showed me.

Lil' Megalodon was on a roll. "You know who else I blame?"

I shook my head.

He pointed at McVay's house. "Keith. I blame Keith and his selfishness. He dumped Rich a week before all this happened. Rich was so worked up he forgot all his clients and focused on one thing, getting Keith the cash cow back."

I stuck my hands in my pockets. "Wow. I would have been mad too. I don't know what I would have done."

Without hesitation, Lil' Megalodon said, "I wanted to kill him. Shoot, I wanted to kill them both."

20

THURSDAY

HYPERBOLE. OR MAYBE NOT. MAYBE MEGALODON CAUGHT McVay after AJ left, and they had an altercation then. In a fit of anger, he swung the dumbbell AJ and McVay had used to work out and bashed McVay in the head, killing him. I thought it would be awesome if that were the case, if the rapper was ready to confess, the burden of what he'd done too heavy to continue to carry around. I crossed my fingers.

"Did you confront Keith? Tell him how you felt?"

Lil' Megalodon put his hands on his hips. "Of course I did. Nothing can be resolved without a conversation. Communication is essential in difficult times, which is why I'm struggling with my agent. He failed that core duty."

"Wow, that's very..." I searched for the right word. I'd come to the house with a preconceived idea of how I expected the rapper to behave, expecting a little more street attitude.

"What? Mature? Insightful? My dad is a cop. My mom's a schoolteacher who taught piano on the side. I wasn't raised by wolves on the streets. I was raised in a three-bedroom house with a chore chart and three other siblings."

"My apologies. Your dad's a cop? I bet he has lots of interesting cautionary tales to tell. My mom's a lawyer. I bet, like me, you know a little bit more about the ins and outs of law than the average person."

Megalodon's hackles were rising. Soon the conversation was going to devolve.

I asked, "You went to Stanford, right?" I couldn't recall what the rapper had studied at college.

Lil' Megalodon curled his lip. "Yeah, what of it?"

Leo picked up on my direction and asked, "What did you study?"

Maybe Megalodon had studied something in criminal science.

Lil' Megalodon gave Leo the you-crazy look. "Music, duh."

"You have a degree in music?" I asked.

His lip curled again. "Yeah. Full ride on a music scholarship. You have problem with that?"

I shook my head. "You said you confronted McVay? When was that?"

Megalodon narrowed his gaze. "I know what you're implying, and we're done here." He tried to close the door, which bounced off my foot as I pushed with my hands.

"Thursday, right. You had a fight with him the day he died." My heartbeat quickened.

Megalodon threw up his hands in disgust. "Yeah, but during the day. Before lunch, even. Caught him down on his dock and roughed him up a bit." The rapper rubbed his jaw. "He roughed me up some too," he said quietly, touching the scratch on his arm.

I straightened, putting pieces together.

Leo said, "You two got into a fistfight on the dock?"

Megalodon's cheeks pinkened. "Keith was always worried about hurting his hand, and I wear an Invisalign." He bared his teeth and popped the retainer slightly so that we could see it. "He knew how important straight teeth were to me, and I knew his hand was his life, so imagine less a fistfight and more a tussle."

"Okay," I said. "I'm trying to picture you and McVay fighting. You what... slap each other?" The scene in my mind was a comedic picture of the two men engaged in a half-hearted fight.

He glared at me. "We just shoved each other some, pushed each other in the water, and then took turns holding each other's head under."

I said, "I bet the water was cold."

"Darn right it was. Knocked some sense into us. We climbed out and went into his place to warm up."

"Is that how you got that?" I pointed at his scratched arm.

"Yeah. Caught on a nail on his deck when I was climbing out. I caught Keith across the nose when I was flailing in the water, trying to get out."

That explained the cut across Keith's nose.

"And all was forgiven?" I asked.

I wondered what Lil Megalodon's lie in this story was. His first claim, at the game, was that he'd been knifed. But did he really catch himself on a nail? Was this version true or another fabrication?

"Nope, but what was I gonna do? Rich had already screwed me with *The Morning Rap* podcast. Keith kept telling me to fire him, that doing so would tell the press that Rich was the one who jacked this gig up for me."

"And why didn't you?" Leo asked.

"I still might. Haven't decided yet. I have some other agents who've offered to rep me. But, man, I've been with Rich for years. We have history. He gets me. I'm not sure I want to start over."

I nodded. "But Keith didn't consider any of that. And from what you said, his dropping Rich was unexpected? Even though Rich says the split was amicable."

Lil' Megalodon's lip curled in disgust. "Rich said that? Nah, Keith threatened Rich with leaving, but Rich didn't take it seriously. Wrecked him when Keith dropped him and signed with Nick Hutton. Rich used to work for Nick, back when he was starting out. Nick fired him. Rich doesn't know I know that, but that's what Nick told Keith."

So McVay dumped his agent for his nemesis.

I brought the conversation full circle. "And after getting dumped, Rich gets so distraught he forgets your big gig."

"Yep." Lil' Megalodon made a gun hand and pulled the trigger. "Bang. You got it, girl."

"Why did Keith want out of here so badly? From the outside looking in, he was about to hit the pinnacle of pro football."

Lil' Megalodon shifted awkwardly. "I'd tell you to ask Keith, but, well... dead men don't tell tales." His gaze met mine.

"What tale would Keith tell?"

Megalodon blew out a heavy sigh. "Man, I don't know. Maybe Keith didn't like the front office of the Pioneers."

I asked, "But you went to college with Austin Strong, right? He should have known it then if he wanted to work for him or not."

He nodded. "Strong was a few years ahead of us. People

change. Maybe Keith got sick of it here. He was always complaining about having no privacy."

I looked from Leo to Megalodon. "That doesn't make sense. Am I to assume he'd have more privacy elsewhere?"

Leo asked, "Were the Pioneers the controlling type?" He looked at me. "When I played ball in college, I had to sign this contract that said if I had conduct unbecoming, I could lose parts of my scholarship. Maybe McVay's contract had similar clauses."

I looked at Megalodon.

He shrugged. "All I know is Keith kept saying he felt stuck. Said he never would bring a person into his life and subject her to this madness."

"Madness? I wonder what that means?"

Megalodon shook his head. "Dunno. But that's what he said. He was stoked to have other offers on the table. He said he'd play for anyone just to get out."

"Why didn't he just quit football, then, if he hated it so much?" I asked.

"Because he didn't hate football. Just the Pioneers."

"And Thursday night? Where did you say you were?"

Megalodon's nostrils flared. "I didn't. Now, listen. This is time-consuming, and I'm tired of talking with you both. I've got songs to write and decisions to make. I have to visualize what I want for my future, and you all are bringing me down. So go away." He flicked a hand to shoo us.

I stepped back, and Megalodon slammed the door.

"Thanks for your time!" I yelled at the wooden door.

We headed toward Leo's truck, the rapper's words running through my head.

I stopped at McVay's driveway. "I want to see this nail that scraped up Megalodon's arm. Notice how he didn't give us an alibi?"

Leo's phone rang, and he pulled it from his pocket and glanced at the screen. "It's Tupi, likely something from the tribal council. I'll wait here for you. No going inside, hear me?"

"Whatever." I made my way to the back of McVay's house and looked around at the dock. Everything looked like it had when I was there last.

The dock also acted as a deck. It attached on one side to the yard and at one end to the boat garage. The rest was open to the lake. Four deck chairs and two planters with wilting plants made the dock an outdoor lounging space. A ladder was attached to its side, allowing people to climb out of the lake with ease. *So how did Megalodon get scraped by a nail?* The only answer was that he didn't use the ladder. I got to my knees and felt along the edge of the deck, close to the water, searching for a nail.

I found the nail toward the end of the deck, opposite the ladder. It stuck out a good two inches, jutting just below the water's surface. I could see how Megalodon wouldn't have seen it and could've caught himself on it while climbing out.

A light splashing sound pulled my attention toward Megalodon's house. His deck was vacant. I looked back at the nail while reaching for my phone. I wanted to get a picture.

Suddenly a smooth black head popped out of the water directly in front of me. My first thought was I was looking at a seal. But a man's face stared back at me. With a scuba tank register in his mouth, he sounded like Darth Vader breathing. My brain couldn't register why a diver would be in the water, which dulled my reactions.

He grabbed me by my sweatshirt and pulled me into the

water, pushing my head down below the surface, and held me there.

Oh no. I had no way to call Leo for help. I'd dropped my phone when the masked man pulled me in.

Oh no!

I clawed at the man's arms, fighting his hold on me. My lungs burned, screaming for oxygen.

Oh no. Oh no. Oh no.

21

THURSDAY

SOMETHING INSIDE ME CLICKED. MAYBE THAT WAS THE moment my brain consciously realized I really could die. Maybe that's what survivors mean when they say their lives flashed in front of them. Scenes didn't actually flash in front of me, but one second, I was confused but expecting to get to the surface, and the next, I clearly realized that any moment following could be my last.

My lungs screamed for air. My vision dimmed. The water was cold and seeping into my bones.

Fight! Don't give up!

But to fight this man would be an effort in futility.

Logically, I knew I needed to resist my fight-or-flight instincts. But doing so took every ounce of willpower I had.

I went limp, pretending I had passed out or, worse, died.

Instinct screamed at me to resist. My arms twitched to reach for the surface.

Instead, I forced my body to relax, to let my arms float at my sides.

The flow of the lake began to move me away as the man's

grip lessened. My brain screamed at me, *Get air! Get air now!* Yet I couldn't.

Scuba Man gave me a shove on the shoulders, pushing me farther into the bowels of the lake.

The lake was murky and dark, thick with algae, but keeping my eyes open was necessary for survival. I could make out the form of the scuba diver as he pushed me down and away. As I let my arms float, they brushed across his face. In the soft coldness of the water, the contact with his hard mask came as a surprise and triggered a reaction.

I jerked unexpectedly and grabbed at him, aiming for the face. With his arms off me, he was now stretching toward me, trying control me again, like he had moments before. I flailed, trying to avoid his grasp while also trying to grab his regulator.

My first attempt pulled the mask from his face. I no longer had any air to breathe out and was fighting the urge to open my mouth and take in a breath of air. The pain in my lungs was searing, nearly debilitating.

Focus. His regulator.

I had one chance left to get his regulator. I needed only a few seconds, but those few seconds lay between life and death.

I needed only enough time to get one breath. One breath would give me one more swing at staying alive.

I flailed again and came up against his regulator, and with what little energy I had left, I tugged it from his mouth, cutting off his oxygen and drawing his immediate attention to that problem. Any diver worth their weight would recover in seconds, but that's all I needed, enough time for one gulp of air.

Without the bottom of the lake to push off and with little

strength and air left, I struggled to move away and up, desperate to get to the surface and the air. Though my eyes were open, starbursts were occluding my vision, which I knew was due to oxygen deprivation.

"Please. Please. Please." That was the chant in my head as I closed in on the surface.

I broke the surface and sucked in a desperate breath, only to be tugged under once more by a leg.

The air wasn't enough. I needed more and fought against the downward pull, wanting to sob as the surface tipped sideways and farther away.

A splash nearby disoriented me. Above me was the light and air, and I opened my mouth to take in the lifesaving air, but all I got was a mouthful of water.

Instantly, I was in a worse situation than a second before. *What do I do with the mouthful of water?*

In desperation, I kicked and reached for the light and rose toward it, surprised to find nothing holding me back.

Dread consumed me as I waited for the pull I knew would be coming any moment. Being so close to air was the worst sort of torture. And my brain's oxygen deprivation was making me consider calling it quits. To let go and stop fighting would be much easier.

When my head broke the surface, I coughed out the water, sputtering as I tried to take in air as well. I took in a second breath, then a third, and air filled my body.

With air came awareness, and survival once more became my priority.

More splashing at my side pulled my attention, and I scanned the lake around myself, searching for the diver. A struggle appeared to be going on below the surface, and though everything in me screamed to get out of the water and run, a tiny niggling of uncertainty, of wondering why the diver hadn't pulled me under again, pushed me to dive under to learn why.

Another person was struggling with the diver—Leo.

I pushed to the surface to take in three deep breaths, bracing for a fight. Nothing was on the deck that I could use against the diver. I was two arm's lengths away from the dock, so I swam to it. Having gone without oxygen, I was depleted of energy. I would need a boost.

I pushed off the deck with my feet, projecting me toward Leo and the diver. As I closed in, I thrust my arms downward, trying to come down against the diver in a striking motion. But the water slowed everything.

I realized I was getting nowhere, and he and Leo were in a power struggle, each holding on to the other. But like me, Leo didn't have air, while the diver had an unlimited supply.

The tank.

The diver had his back to me as he fought Leo, which gave me an advantage. I started yanking at hoses, pulling them from the tank.

The diver let go of Leo to reach over his shoulder. Again, a skilled diver would have solutions. We needed to get out of the water.

Leo was swimming to the surface, and I followed. We broke through seconds apart.

"Get out of the water," he said and moved toward the dock.

We pulled ourselves up onto the wooden platform, and I scurried back, away from the water, like a crab on the run. I glanced at Leo, who was holding a shoulder. Red-stained water seeped between his fingers.

"What happened?" I crawled on my hands and knees to him.

"He had a knife. Just nicked me." He looked over my shoulder. "My phone is here somewhere. We need to call the police."

I scanned the deck for our phones. I'd dropped mine when I was pulled in, so it likely went into the water.

From next door, Lil' Megalodon yelled, "What are you two lunatics doing? That's private property."

"Call the police!" I yelled back. But my voice was raspy from the water, dimming my volume.

I spotted Leo's phone lying next to a planter, under a deck chair.

"Just get out of there," Megalodon said. "No one wants any trouble."

"I'm serious! Call the police!" I scrambled to the phone, snatched it up, and handed it to Leo. Then I saw mine near the edge of the dock, where I'd pulled myself up and out of the water. I went over to find the face cracked and wet.

"Don't threaten me! Because I just might!" Megalodon shouted.

"I got it," Leo said, pressing his phone to his ear.

A winter breeze came off the lake, and I shivered. With one look at Leo, I knew he was cold too. His lips were pressed tight, and goose bumps covered his arms.

He stood and held out a hand to me while talking to the local force's dispatcher on the phone. He pulled me up and guided me to the stairs. When he hung up, he said, "We have to get out of these clothes. It's forty degrees out here."

We shuffled to the front of the house and Leo's truck, shock and cold settling in.

"Stay with me, Sam," he said.

I nodded again.

"Tell me what happened."

My teeth chattered as I told him about finding the nail before the head popped out of the water and the man pulled me in.

Inside Leo's truck, we stripped out of our wet clothes. He had a change in the back, and while he donned the jeans, I slipped on his oversized sweatshirt. He wrapped one scratchy wool blanket around my shoulders and another around his.

"You're prepared," I said in admiration. I kept a spare set of clothes, water, and granola bars in LC as well.

Leo stared at me then came to stand in front of me.

I touched his blanket where a red stain was slowly growing larger. He lifted a strand of hair from my forehead.

He said, "All I keep thinking is what would have happened if you'd come here alone."

I'd had the same thought. "But I didn't."

He dropped a kiss on my forehead. "Thankfully."

I closed my eyes, leaned into him, and gave thanks that he'd once again come to my rescue.

The police took our reports and description of the diver and my thoughts on the possible connection to the black SUV with the silver detail skirt. But no diver was found, and the SUV was gone as well. Nothing would come of the assault unless the diver decided to surface or attack again. I hoped he would try.

The EMTs had been called and had bandaged Leo at the scene.

Lil' Megalodon joined us and listened to our report, sighing and shaking his head throughout. While the EMTs were stitching Leo's upper arm, he told me, "I'm sorry. I thought you were joking when you said to call the police."

"Can you think of anyone who might want to kill Keith McVay?" I asked. "Because the trainer is dead, and now someone has come after me, I assume to stop me from continuing my investigation." I had nothing to lose by asking; though, I wasn't sure the rapper had a hitman on call to do work on short notice.

He pressed his lips together and shook his head. "I'm beginning to think nothing was like it seemed."

"Watch your back," I told him. I was still going to find out what his lie was.

Leo and I rode halfway home in silence, the heat blasting.

"The one thing I wish LC had was heated seats," I said, curled up with my legs under myself.

"Weird question, but I'm starving. Do you want anything to eat?" He gave me a sheepish grin.

Still numb from the shock of the day and the cold water, I said, "Does a bear poop in the woods?"

I was always ravenously hungry after an attack. How terrible that I had experienced such things enough to know that.

We drove through a popular burger joint and got large everything.

"I'm so glad my phone didn't get ruined," I said, texting Lockett and asking him to walk Simon.

I'd cleaned it the best I could, and though the screen was jacked, the phone was working. I didn't dare remove the case as I believed that its compression was holding everything in place. By habit, I scrolled through my emails as I stuffed fries into my face.

"Yeah, getting a new one is a pain. At least all you need is a new face."

I stopped on an email with the sender name Samantha True and the subject "We see you, but you don't see us." The subject line reminded me of one from way back, when all those college students found spyware on their computers, and videos of them were splashed all over the internet. Clicking on such an email was likely asking for virus trouble, but I did it anyway.

A video popped up. The first scene was my mom working in her office, doing the everyday tasks of her job, then the scene switched to a short clip of her and Cora walking down the street to her office. The next clip was of Dad and Stella at the paper. Then Dad was at home, working in his home office, Cora riding a broomstick horse around him. The last was my apartment, showing Lockett playing with Simon and us talking about the case. The video ended after the words "We see everything" scrolled across the page. The cracks in the screen distorted the video, which made it even creepier.

"Dear Lord," I said and began to tremble all over again.

22

FRIDAY

BOTH MY DAD AND MOM ALSO GOT THE THREATENING VIDEO. More than anything, Cora was the one we worried the most about. The fact that whoever had done this made sure to include her scared me to my very core, and I was unable to sleep.

Early the next morning, I drove out to Mrs. Wright's house. She was my go-to gadget lady. Her husband was a retired cop, and she'd picked up a few things from him.

I knocked on the door with trepidation, afraid she might be a late riser.

She flung open the door and surveyed me. Wearing a Led Zeppelin shirt and jeans, Mrs. Wright looked fresh and ready for the day. Her blue eyeshadow was heavy and glittery.

"What'd ya do now?" she asked in the Jersey accent I'd come to love. She took a bite of the toast she had in one hand and waved me inside the house with the other.

The house was silent.

I looked at her, wide eyed. Her husband usually had the TV blaring so loud that a person couldn't hear herself think.

"Where's Marv?" I reared back slightly. "Did you have him taken out?"

Mrs. Wright laughed. "Nah, he went to the VFW," pronouncing it *vee-eff-dub*. "What kinda trouble you in now?"

From my bag, I pulled out a handheld bug scanner. When my husband died, I'd discovered his home security business had also done PI work... with my name on the PI license. And I'd been totally clueless. Apparently, he did the PI work to get the goods on locals, which he could use later in a land grab. That produced a shame that was taking me a long time to live down.

But one bonus to inheriting the business was inheriting Toby too, and I'd found a secret room full of gadgets. I'd taken a few home, like the bug detector I was holding, a stun gun, and a hot spot. The rest had been destroyed in a fire.

"I need to know how to use this. It can't be as easy as sweep the room and let it beep."

She waved for me to follow her into the kitchen and gestured at a mug. "Coffee?"

"Yes, please." I sat at her table.

She poured me a cup then sat across from me. "It is that easy. Here's what you need to know. Detectors come in all shapes and sizes, like men's ding-dongs. And like men's ding-dongs, they do the same thing. Only some do it a little better and are a little more skilled."

I didn't dare ask which she was specifically referring to, the devices or the ding-dongs.

"The one you got there is decent. What happened?"

"I was sent a video of us being filmed unknowingly."

"And you don't think a man was doing it from afar?"

I shook my head. "No, the videos were of my dad working at his desk. He doesn't have a window in his office. Or me in my house, after the blinds were closed. But more than that, they filmed my niece. She's only six. I have my IT guy scanning my stuff for spyware, but I need to know if there are bugs in my house and in my parents' home and offices. I turned this on this morning, and it started beeping like mad."

She nodded knowingly. "And you got scared and freaked out and came here."

"Yeah, my friend is being charged with murder. My other friend is his lawyer. If they've recorded our conversations, they know exactly where we are in the defense process and have been one step ahead of me the entire time." That would explain a lot.

"There are camera bugs, mic bugs, and motion bugs." She pointed at my device. "This handy guy uses wideband radio frequencies, infrared probes, line-drive probes, and microwave RF probes. Only thing you're not scanning is for GMS. That's 'global systems for mobile communication.' It'll scan all cellular devices and look for Bluetooth spying. I got one in my closet. I'll get it for ya."

She was back in a flash and showed me how to use both gadgets.

"Listen to me, Sam. Wear the headphones when you're scanning. Know where the bugs are first. Take note and map them. Do not take them out because this is your chance to strike back, using their tech against them."

I hadn't thought of that, and feigning ignorance might be a moot point as I'd called Toby on my cell phone on the way over and already told him what had happened. I told

Mrs. Wright that if my phone was bugged, then I'd blown it.

"Gimme your phone."

I handed it over. She put on the headset and moved so that I could look over her shoulder and watch the screen on the scanner. Nothing.

"Can I take this off?" She pointed at the case.

I saw no point in keeping the phone together if it was being used to spy on me, so I nodded.

She took off the case and gently turned the phone over in her hand then pressed the home button. She scrolled through my apps. Following a heavy sigh, she set my phone on the table.

"They know you know. This app here is how they've been listening in on your phone."

"But it's a weather app."

"You ever pull it up to look at the weather?"

I shook my head. "I like a different one."

"Then why don't you delete it?"

I paused. "I thought I had."

"And yet here it is." She attempted to open the app, but it did nothing but spin in a perpetual state of not opening. "You need to factory reset your phone."

"Will it still act as a bug if it's turned off?"

She shook her head. Her eyes were narrow, her lips pressed into a thin line. "This makes me damn mad, Sam. You go home. Find all the bugs and strip them out. And you sweep every day. You hear me? From now on, you move forward as if there are ears everywhere unless you've checked and double-checked."

"How did they get access to all this?" I'd asked myself that a million times since seeing the video.

Mrs. Wright shrugged. "They break into your house while you're gone. You put your phone down for a second, and they add the app. They tap into the cameras on city streets or use an email with your IP address to tap into your computer camera."

Toby had said essentially the same thing. I was hoping Mrs. Wright could give me something I could fight. Toby said that sort of expertise was readily available for hire on the dark web.

I left her house, having replaced my fear with anger—a deep, vibrating anger that gave me a taste for revenge. I just needed a target.

My first sweep was at my parents'.

After I removed all the bugs we could find, the family went out into the yard for a discussion... just in case.

Mom gave me a hug. "I don't want you to take this wrong, but your dad and I decided that we're going to take Cora on a trip."

I said, "That's a good idea. Why would I take that wrong?"

Dad said, "Because we don't want you to come. Rachel's ship will be in Greece over Christmas. We're going to meet her there so she can spend Christmas with Cora."

Mom rushed to say, "It's not that we don't want you there or that we don't want to spend Christmas with you, but in light of the videos and the spying, we thought maybe it would be good to get away from all this."

"And trouble follows me," I mumbled.

Dad squeezed my shoulder. "Maybe more that this will give you time to get to the bottom of this without having to worry about us."

I asked what had been nagging at me since having watched the video. "What if I never get to the bottom of it?"

My mother rolled her eyes. "As if that would ever happen. We have faith in you, Samantha. And if there's one thing I know about my daughters, no one messes with their family. I see doubt in your eyes, but that's because you're scared. More than the doubt, I see determination. I saw that same look when they said you'd need learn to read and we knew you'd been trying but couldn't." She put an arm around my shoulders and gave me a side hug.

"I'd never bet against you." Dad joined us and folded me into a hug with my mom.

"Just be careful," Mom said, running a hand down my hair.

Dad squeezed us both and sighed.

"When do you leave?" I let them be the ones to pull away as I needed the hug far more than I'd thought.

"Tomorrow," Dad said. "Call it an extended vacation."

"And you'll be back?"

Mom said, "The twenty-seventh. We'll do Christmas with you then."

I nodded. I wanted them to leave. Doing that felt like a safe move. And they were right—I would worry less. But I was bummed about not spending Christmas with my family. *Perspective, right?* If they stayed and something happened to one of them, I would never forgive myself.

We decided I would check the house and be sure to bring all the packages in and wrap them so that they would be ready for Cora when they returned home.

Then I drove to my apartment and did a sweep there. Lockett was in Portland. I left him a note about checking his phone for the spyware app I'd had. Then I loaded my stun gun, the bug detector, a bottle of water, and my lock-picking kit into my backpack. I needed to replace my phone's face, but I had another errand I wanted to run first.

I drove by the police station and caught Leo clocking out after ending his shift. He was dressed in his typical jeans, Henley, and Carhart coat.

I pointed at his shoulder. "How is it?"

He rolled it a few times. "A little tight but good."

"Want to go back to McVay's house with me?"

He looked at me like I'd lost my mind. "What could you possibly want to go back there for?"

I told him about the bugs at my parents' and my house. "I want to sweep his house too."

"And what's that going to tell you?" he asked as he reached for LC's passenger door.

"It'll explain the privacy stuff he was freaked out about. I think McVay knew someone was listening in on him. If I can figure out who, then I might just have caught my killer. I think it's the same person who's spying on me."

Leo hopped in, and I peeled away. We talked about the case on the drive over.

"You don't think it's Lil' Megalodon?" he asked.

"Could be," I said. "Maybe he's been playing us all along. I asked Toby to look into him, and yeah, he went to Stanford on a music scholarship, but he also minored in sound engineering. I know that's a stretch into being a tech wizard, but maybe it's not all that hard."

At McVay's, I told Leo to wait outside because he was a cop and I was about to trespass.

"Nope," he said. "I'm sticking to you like glue."

"Are you sure? I wanted you along to keep an eye out for me. Watch my back, so to speak. I know asking you look away while I enter McVay's house is an issue for you. Going in... Well, Leo, if we get caught, you'll be in more trouble than me."

He shook his head. "Last time I left you alone here, a man tried to drown you and stabbed me. I'll take my chances. Your safety is more important."

"Good," I said. "The basement gives me the creeps."

Like before, the doors were unlocked. We had maybe an hour of daylight left. From my backpack I took out a notepad and pencil. I needed to log any bugs like Mrs. Wright said, so I quickly drew a layout of the first floor then donned the headphones and started scanning. Leo signaled that he was going to look around.

The bug detector began beeping seconds later. A camera was connected to his TV. So whoever had planted it was likely getting a notification that someone was in McVay's house right then and was watching me sweep it.

Anger coursed through me. I wondered if the person watching me right then was the one who'd watched my family and niece and used that to intimidate me. I walked close to the TV and stared directly at the black screen. I lifted a hand and extended my middle finger and held it there for several beats, not blinking, not wavering. That was the only thing I could think of to do to a nameless, faceless voyeur.

I lifted my nose, turned my back to the camera, and continued to log the numerous audio and video bugs.

No wonder McVay had been complaining of lack of privacy. I had to believe he knew his life had been invaded. I wondered if he'd known the extent of it. *Questionable.* But that was very likely, given his strong desire to get out of town. That made me think McVay believed the privacy invasion wouldn't follow him, that it was isolated to his home. With the right spin, that could be used against AJ. The prosecution could say he was trying to spook McVay to get him off the team so that AJ could take his spot.

I stood in the kitchen and was looking at my drawing with all the bugs when Leo joined me. I showed him a note telling him we were likely being watched and listened to.

He leaned in and whispered in my ear. "I noticed something strange about the butler's pantry. If you stand in the living room, it looks longer than it is. I checked all around it, and there's no closet or anything to explain the size difference."

I gave him a puzzled look. He nodded for me to go stand in the living room and look toward the kitchen.

From there, I could see what he meant. The end of the kitchen opened to the butler's pantry, our entry point into the house. From my viewpoint, the wall ran over ten feet. But inside the pantry, that wall looked no longer than six feet.

I walked around like Leo had and found no other room or closet that could explain what that four feet of space was. When I returned to the kitchen, Leo was standing in the pantry, looking at the ceiling. He pointed at the far wall, which was floor-to-ceiling shelves, and moved his finger toward the ceiling.

In my ear, he said, "It looks like a poor fit, where the top of the shelving meets the ceiling. See the large gap?"

I nodded and cut my eyes to him, knowing he could read my mind. My husband had had a secret room at his security business. Toby had shown it to me and Leo when I'd gone out there because the business had been burglarized.

I looked under the shelves and moved appliances, looking for a secret handle or switch or something. I found it tucked under the fold of the middle shelf, right at waist level, a tiny one no bigger than a light switch. I gave it a click. Leo tugged at my elbow and gestured for me to step aside, which I did. He then tugged at one end of the shelving unit, which popped away from the wall.

Behind the shelving unit was a steel door. Leo grasped its handle and turned. I held my breath, scared of what we might find.

23

FRIDAY

"It's a panic room," Leo said. "A panic room with a secret exit."

One wall had several monitors and a control panel. A second door was on the other side of the room. Leo opened it to reveal a dark landing.

"Dare we explore?" he asked.

I didn't want to but nodded instead. I stepped inside the panic room and pulled the shelving unit closed. Then Leo closed the steel door.

Claustrophobia slammed into me, and I took several breaths, trying to act all cool like I wasn't worried. I wasn't a fan of small spaces even if they had monitors.

Leo gestured toward the other door and the dark landing. He used his phone's flashlight and led the way into the darkness. A balcony ran from the door along the right side of the house. We were above the basement yet in the in-between. The air was damp, and the musty smell of poorly circulated stale air mixed with the lack of light was a disturbing sensation. That was probably what being buried alive felt like. Or maybe that was my claustrophobia kicking in.

The space between the walls had been expanded to allow an average-size person to move between them. Behind the wall on my left and below me was the basement, where we'd come in. To my right was the kitchen wall. The narrow balcony ended at a stairwell on our right. Leo had to turn at a slight angle to fit down the corridor. We were moving away from the backyard and going toward the front of the house. As we descended, I guessed at our position and believed us to be tucked between the exterior garage wall and interior of the garage. Like rats moving inside the walls, we scurried to the bottom of the stairs, which ended at a larger opening.

I put my hand on Leo's shoulder to ground myself. "Is that a hallway?"

"My best guess is it runs the length of the property and comes out across the street. This hallway runs under the driveway, but I'm not sure where it ends. Considering it's an escape room, I can't see it depositing the people who are trying to escape in the driveway. Likely somewhere off the property."

"Do you think McVay had this built?"

Leo shrugged. "Hard to say." He took my hand and led me down the long hallway. Standing water made the concrete slippery, and the walls were damp. I learned that when I accidentally put out a hand to keep myself from bumping one. My hand came away wet and grimy. At the end of the tunnel was a ladder up.

"You want to go first?" Leo offered.

"No, you go ahead. I'll be right behind you."

He climbed, and I let him get a few rungs ahead before I began my ascent.

"There's a door like you'd find to an attic. It's locked."

I groaned. "Please tell me we don't have to go back the way we came." I was done with this adventure.

"No, it's a dead bolt. The turn assembly is on this side, but to enter from the other side, a person would need a key."

At that point, I didn't care. The lock clicked, and Leo pushed against the trapdoor, which opened easily.

"That's odd," he said, sweeping his phone light around the area.

"What's odd?"

"I think this has been used recently. It's dusty up here but not around the opening." He shined the light near himself. "I do think we need to go back. What if we're disrupting evidence?"

I rested my head against the rung and closed my eyes.

"Sam?"

"Give me a second. I'm working up my courage. I have the heebie-jeebies something awful, and I'm ready to go home."

Leo chuckled. "Yeah, it is kinda creepy. But preferable to being held underwater in the lake."

"True." I climbed down and stood as close to the wall as possible without touching it to allow him room.

He closed the trap, jumped down next to me, and took my hand. "Come on, it'll be much faster going back."

And he was right. Getting back into the pantry took only minutes. When we exited the escape room, the house was dark as the sun was almost gone. We exited through the basement door and were back at LC in less than five minutes.

Leo stood outside LC and looked around. Without pointing, he said, "See that green utility box across the street?"

I glanced in that direction then back to Leo. "Yeah."

"I think that's where we would have come out."

I gestured for him to get into LC. Once in the driver's seat, I asked, "Where does a person go once they get out to here? If someone's inside your house and looking for you, they're bound to look outside too."

"Maybe you run to a neighbor for help. Or maybe you hope they never find you in the panic room. Maybe the exit is the last resort."

I looked at McVay's house. "If someone entered from the utility box, that would explain why no one else was caught on the cameras. No camera points in this direction." I looked at the neighboring houses, but from where we were sitting in LC, my view was limited. "I'll come back tomorrow and see if anyone has cameras pointed in that direction." I turned LC's engine over and let him idle. "What makes a man put in an panic room with a secret escape?"

"Paranoia?" Leo said. "But is he paranoid because that's his mental state or paranoid because he has a reason to be? That's the question."

"Meaning someone's come at him before. Or maybe he knows things about people?" I picked up my phone, ignored fourteen missed text messages, and went to Toby's contact information. "Where did McVay keep his secrets? His house is almost minimalist in personal touches. I think about Carson and the secrets he was keeping. When it came to safeguarding them he had stored his secrets in one place. Where's that place for McVay? Because it's not here."

I pressed Call and put the phone on speaker.

"Superspy, what's up?" Toby said into the phone.

A glance at the clock told me this was his private-driver time.

"You out on a call, or are you free?" I asked.

"Free. Lady M and I had a playdate with another sugar glider earlier, and now we're chilling. Wasn't feeling the car today."

"I need you to dig more into Keith McVay. See if he has a safety deposit box somewhere. Or rents a storage unit or something. Maybe he has property elsewhere. Let your imagination go nuts. Find anything and everything you can on McVay. Please."

"Sorry, I'm eating Doritos," he said, crunching in my ear. "You should be stoked. I've been hopping down a McVay rabbit hole all day. I found some smack talk between him and a linebacker named Roman Castillo."

Leo said, "Castillo plays for New York. They're out here this weekend to play the Seahawks."

"Yep," Toby said. "You know this Castillo guy, Sam. He's the long-haired player who does the shampoo commercials."

"Oh yeah. He's very pretty."

Precious and I had admired his shining locks and physique for quite some time. The commercial did show him in the shower after all—waist up, of course.

Leo cleared his throat.

Toby continued, "Apparently, Castillo went to Stanford for two years. Then transferred to Wisconsin and stayed three. He entered the draft a year after McVay."

I looked at Leo. "That's odd. Most of the time, players leave earlier."

Toby said, "I asked your dad about it because I couldn't find many articles about it. Your dad said that rumor has it the Pioneers were looking to take a quarterback and a linebacker, and Castillo was on their list. He waited a year because he didn't want to go to the Pioneers."

I raised my eyebrows in surprise. "What was the trash talk about?"

"I'd call it a Twitter fight. Someone called out McVay for his intention to leave after the season was over. McVay tweeted that while he'd loved his time in Portland, he thought it would be best if he started a new season with a different team. He got razzed by fans, and he promised them a good and honest run for the Super Bowl, pledging that he was dedicated to the Pioneers until the season was over; however, that season may end."

"Which is stupid," I interjected. "Who's going to believe that?"

Toby crunched some more. "Fans told him to go now. They were lining up to hate him."

I gave Leo a look, wondering if that could've contributed to McVay's paranoia. A new question came to mind. "And how did word get out that McVay wanted to leave? That hurts him and the team." To Toby I said, "Tobe, see if you can find the first article to mention McVay considering other contracts. Let's see if we can find out who leaked it."

Leo asked, "What did Castillo say?"

Toby chuckled. "He said, 'You don't deserve a fat payout. You deserve a fat lip.'"

I said, "That's not too threatening."

"He amps up the smack talk. Says McVay's a dirtbag who should be in jail, not on a football field. Said being with the Pioneers is exactly where McVay should be. Said he's not surprised McVay failed his drug test and that he probably did it to tank the team. Said it wouldn't be the first time McVay threw a game."

"Wait, what? I never heard about this," I said, totally caught off guard.

Toby continued, "I asked your dad about that too. He said a rumor that McVay threw a game back in his second year at college floated around for a while. But there wasn't any proof, and the source was someone from the other team, so in your pop's words, 'It was unsubstantiated.'"

I said, "But it might explain why Castillo left. Maybe he didn't want to take the risk of being on a team with a bad rep."

Leo asked, "Has Castillo tweeted since McVay was killed?"

Crunch, crunch. "Only to say he'd contribute to AJ's defense fund if needed."

"Thanks, Toby. Where would I be without you?"

"Dunno. But it's a good question."

I laughed and hung up then opened my messages. I'd prioritized Toby because I wanted to not get distracted from what was right in front of me. All but three were from Lockett. The remainder were from Precious.

Lockett: **Where are you?**
    Precious: **I'll save U a seat**
    Lockett: **AJ's asking for you**
    Lockett: **Hello**
    Lockett: **Hello**
    Lockett: **I'm getting worried**

They continued in this vein.

"Is today Friday?" I asked, slapping a hand against my forehead.

Leo nodded.

"Poop. AJ was arraigned today." I dialed Lockett's number.

He answered, saying, "I was getting worried."

"I'm sorry. I'll explain when I see you. Where is AJ now? Did he get bail?"

"You bet your sweet butt he did. I'm awesome at what I do."

"I know you are." I laughed.

He said, "Precious is taking us both to your place. The press were swarming his house."

"Okay, we'll meet you there. I'll grab takeout."

"Deal," Lockett said.

I was relieved to have AJ out of jail. However, I wasn't under any illusion that the case would become easier or life safer. The contrary was more likely.

We picked up Italian food, foregoing our traditional preference for Indian or Thai, afraid to remind AJ of the night McVay had died.

At my place, AJ was sitting on the couch, Simon at his feet. Lockett was in the chair next to him.

I rushed in and gave AJ a hug, nearly flinging myself onto the couch next to him in the process. "I'll be honest," I said. "I was worried you were gonna get shivved or something while behind bars."

Lockett sighed. "You watch too much crime TV."

"Maybe." I squeezed AJ's hand.

He looked tired, bags under his eyes, his mouth pulled down. "I was worried about the same thing. I barely slept while I was in there."

"There's a duffel with some of your clothes in the guest room," I said. "I packed it when I picked up Simon."

AJ closed his eyes and sighed. "You're the best, Sam."

Precious said, "We decided AJ would stay with me, and you can keep Simon for the time being. Sound good?"

I gave her a thumbs-up and returned my focus to AJ. "I'm sorry, but I need to ask you a few questions."

AJ opened his eyes and gave me a wary look.

Precious groaned. "Can we just celebrate tonight?"

I shook my head. "No, this is important." I glanced at Leo, who nodded for me to continue. "What do you know about McVay potentially throwing a game? Is it even possible that McVay spiked his own drink?"

AJ reared back and swiped a hand down his face before answering. "Keith wouldn't throw a game. He was a competitor. He wanted to win."

"You don't think he'd make himself sick to get out of playing?"

AJ looked at me like I was crazy. "To do that would sabotage any chance Keith had at getting a contract from any other team aside from the Pioneers. Because he didn't make himself sick. He popped positive for an illegal substance. There's no way he'd tarnish his reputation that way or ding his star power."

"And can you think of anyone who might want McVay to fail, to not get a contract, or maybe they were mad because he wanted to leave?"

AJ shook his head. "Outside of the Pioneers? No. And even then, front office was overheard saying they should let him go if he didn't want to stay. It would make for a tense locker room."

"What about Brad Jenson? Could he have wanted McVay dead?" I hated not knowing how all the dots connected.

"I don't know anything about Brad," AJ said. "He wasn't the head trainer, and he was quiet and kept to himself. He worked the workout room mostly, setting guys up with reps and helping them adjust when they needed it."

I sighed heavily, frustrated.

Leo put a hand on my shoulder. "Let it sit. You need some distance."

"And noodles," Precious said and handed me a plate.

Leo was right. My dad always said that if a person was stuck on a problem, they sometimes had to walk away from it to see it better.

But that nagging gut ache, the bad feeling I'd had when we went to the mountains, had begun to burn, its intensity increasing. Whoever was behind everything was stepping up their game. We would have to as well.

24

SATURDAY

TOBY, PRECIOUS, AND I MADE A ROAD TRIP TO SEATTLE. Precious drove. Toby had found out where the New York team was staying, and we had a solid plan.

Actually, we had no plan. We were going to crash the hotel and hope for the best.

The team had arrived earlier that day, and AJ said they'd been in meetings, reviewing plays. Our best hope of getting time with Roman Castillo was in the evening, between the end of the meetings and bedtime. The game was scheduled for ten on Sunday morning. AJ said the team likely had a suggested curfew policy of ten in the evening.

Paulie having called Precious my honeypot had given her the idea to be bait if she had to. Just in case, she'd worn a clingy T-shirt, leggings, and knee-high boots. I wore jeans, a T-shirt with a long cardigan, and knee-high boots as well—casual but not too much.

"Hold on to your titties, kitties. We're gonna go get us some crime-solving information tonight." Precious pressed on the gas, and we sped up Interstate 5 to Seattle.

Toby said. "I'm here because the risk of getting shot is low, and I want to meet Roman Castillo. I hear he uses a hemp shampoo on his hair."

I said, "You maybe just jinxed yourself."

He responded by rolling his eyes.

The rest of the ride was not making a plan but teasing each other.

At the hotel, Precious left her SUV with the valet, and the three of us headed for the hotel bar. Toby had his laptop in a messenger bag strapped around him, with Lady M snug in her felt orange.

I pointed at the messenger bag. "You gonna need that?"

He cut me a look. "You never know. I don't ask you to leave your tools of the trade at home, do I?"

I tapped my forehead. "That's because I travel every-where with mine."

Toby laughed. "Whatever, dudette. You gonna tell me you don't have handcuff keys pinned to the inside of your pants?"

I shoved his shoulder, sending him stumbling slightly to the side.

"Don't ask me to share my Doritos with you." He laughed.

We entered the lobby and paused a few feet inside.

"What now?" Toby asked.

I nodded toward the bar restaurant. "We can go in there. Maybe he'll be eating there or something."

Precious said, "We can ride the elevators and walk the floors."

I cut her a side-eye. "And do what? Call out his name as we walk down the hallway?"

She crossed her arms and frowned at me. "We had a two-hour drive, and we didn't come up with a plan. Don't knock mine."

"Point taken." I turned to Toby. "Can you hack into the hotel computer and find out his hotel room?"

Toby reared back, horrified. "It's one thing to get po-po records and other deets that'll become public. But what you're asking me to do is illegal."

I grimaced. "Sorry. The line is kinda blurry for me."

He reached into his messenger bag and pulled out a snack-size bag of Doritos.

I surveyed the hotel. The décor was dark-brown leather furniture with navy-and-gold accessories, yet somehow the scheme wasn't gaudy.

I pitched an idea. "What if I just ask the guy at the front desk to call his room and ask him if he wants to talk with me?"

Precious nodded in agreement. I balled up my courage and went to the front desk.

"Hi, could you please call Mr. Castillo's room and tell him Samantha True is here and would like to speak with him." I flashed my PI license.

The front desk attendant, a twentysomething guy with a man bun, ear gauges bigger than my thumb, and winged eyebrows, gave my ID barely a glance then lifted his chin.

"Sorry. You either have access to Mr. Castillo or not. And by coming to me, I'm going with not."

He looked down at whatever was hidden by the tall counter he stood behind and moved stuff around. Or maybe he started typing.

"I'm investigating a murder that he has an interest in. I'm almost certain he'd like to know I was here."

Without looking at me, the attendant said, "Almost is not the same as certain."

He scooped something off his area, papers, and walked away.

I turned to my friends and put my hands up, asking what next because I'd just failed. At a loss for words, I walked over to them.

Toby said, "I've a good mind to give them a bad review for their unfriendliness. Bash them on social media."

Precious huffed. "Yeah, how dare they protect the privacy of a customer?"

Toby glared at her.

I snapped my fingers. "That's it. Toby, you're brilliant."

He puffed out his chest. "Duh. But just so we can all be on the same page, what have I done that's so amazing?"

"Social media," I said. "I'm going to send Castillo a tweet. One problem. I don't have a Twitter account." And I liked it that way.

Precious put up a hand. "I do." She whipped out her phone and tapped on it. "Okay, what do you want me to say?"

I looked around for a place to meet. "Say this: Working McVay case. Would love to talk. In hotel bar. Will wait for two hours."

That put us at the ten o'clock curfew.

Precious's thumbs moved like the wind. "Sent," she said while tucking her phone away.

"We might as well go into the bar and order food," I said.

Toby pulled down a fist. "Yes."

Inside the bar, the hotel's main color scheme carried over —brown, blue, and gold. The lights were low and cast golden halos over the tables. We found a table where we could watch people enter and see most of the space.

"Did he respond?" I asked.

Precious checked her phone and shook her head.

Toby picked at the bowl of bar snacks on the table. He flicked a nut up into the air and caught it in his mouth. "Have faith."

We ordered an assortment of plates to share and waited. The waitress was removing our plates when Precious hit me on the shoulder. She nodded toward the bar entrance.

Roman Castillo was standing there, looking around. I jerked Precious's hand up and made her wave. After all, her picture was associated with the tweet.

Roman Castillo surveyed us from where he stood, likely debating whether talking to us was a good idea. He had to know that I considered him a suspect and that I'd seen his tweets because that's how I'd reached out. I wondered if his hesitation meant anything.

He was a tall man, though not as tall as McVay, maybe three or four inches shorter. His shoulders were insanely broad and thick with muscles. His T-shirt was stretched across his body like a second skin. And his hair was just as nice in real life as in the commercials—long, blond, and wavy, with a shine most women would envy.

"I hate him," Precious said under her breath. "I've used that shampoo he pushes, and my hair doesn't have a fraction of the silkiness his does." She ran a hand through her own blond locks.

I said, "He probably has a team he uses every day to make it look that good."

Toby said, "Or he just has better genes. Better hair."

Precious threw a nut at him.

Castillo came to our table and looked down at me. "You're Samantha True. I saw you on TV." He glanced at Precious.

I said, "I don't have a Twitter account, so I used my friend's." I introduced them and offered Castillo a seat.

He took it and looked like a giant in a toddler chair he was so large and broad.

"Thanks for meeting with us," I said. "You said in a tweet that you'd contribute to AJ's defense fund—"

Castillo interrupted with a loud sigh and a shake of his head. "Is that what this is about? You want money? Fine, how much?"

I shook my head. "No, we don't want money. I brought it up because your tweets didn't really say you believed AJ was innocent but more that McVay got what he deserved."

Castillo's eyes narrowed. "He did. Almost eight years too late, but karma is a bitch, and it got Keith good."

Castillo's hatred for McVay was palpable. His hands were clenched on his knees, fingers digging in. His blue eyes appeared to be made of steel. He wasn't the same as the guy in the shampoo commercials, who came off friendly and slightly goofy.

Precious folded her arms on the table and leaned onto them. "Wow, I bet you have lots of stories to tell about McVay."

I picked up where she left off. "And it's weird. It's like no one knows him to tell any stories. It's almost like you're the only one. His parents are gone. He didn't have a girlfriend or anything. I've talked to his teammates, and they only know him from their time at work."

Castillo crossed his arms. "When you lie with dogs, your only friends are fleas."

I didn't remark on the inaccuracy of his saying because the point was made. Instead, I said, "You played ball with McVay, then you transferred to a smaller school. Was it because of McVay? Because that's what I assume."

Castillo's cold unwavering stare remained fixated on me.

I continued, "Listen, AJ Gunn is my friend. He didn't kill Keith McVay, and he shouldn't take the fall for it. I don't know who killed McVay. I don't know much because the few people that know anything don't talk. I know McVay popped positive on PEDs, which was out of character for him particularly because he was trying to negotiate a big contract. I know he didn't want to be with the Pioneers anymore." I shrugged. "I don't know why. But I do know there were rumors about McVay throwing games—once in college—and speculation that his behavior before his death was another one of those attempts. I know you said he deserved to be in jail. But what I don't know is the why to any of that, and you're the one who can help me understand. You may not care if McVay's case gets solved, but a personal trainer who appears knee-deep in this committed suicide—or so they think—a few days ago. His family cares."

Something flickered in Castillo's eyes. "Another innocent victim in the wake of Keith McVay and Austin Strong."

I tried not to react. "Tell me about McVay's relationship with Austin Strong."

Castillo wiped a hand down his face then recrossed his arms. "Strong was a few years ahead of us in college. Little pencil-neck dweeb he was and still is, if you ask me. Always lurking in the background. I didn't trust him back then, and I don't now."

"How come?" I leaned in, giving him my full attention.

He tapped his gut. "Just this."

I smiled slightly. "Not that I don't believe in gut intuition —because I have it too—but I was hoping for something more, something I could dig around in."

Banging my head against a concrete wall would be easier and less painful than getting information from this guy.

I said, "You know, if McVay is a dirtbag like you say—"

"He is!" he nearly shouted.

"Then I can bring all this to light. Why not tell the world? Why not let it be a cautionary tale to remind us that things aren't always as they seem?"

Castillo frowned. "Because the story isn't mine to tell."

"Whose story is it?" Precious asked. "Do you think they'd be willing to share?"

He shook his head. "She's put her life back together. She wouldn't want it to be torn apart again, and I won't be the reason for it."

Toby pulled Lady M out from her pouch. She blinked big, dark eyes at us. "I think you need to pet my emotional-support animal. This is Lady M. She's a sugar glider. Dude, you're hanging on to a lot of anger toward a guy who took a dumbbell to the back of the head. Whatever happened in the past is there now." He handed Lady M to Castillo.

Instantly, the man's features softened as he held the tiny ball of fur in his hands.

Castillo said, "Only it's not. Everything lives on the internet forever."

Toby tapped his temple. "You're talking about the video that went viral of the girl doing a striptease for her boyfriend, aren't you? That girl was a student at Stanford, right?" He squinted as though trying to remember.

Castillo stopped stroking Lady M. "He was not her boyfriend."

Toby turned to me and Precious. "You know that video, the one of the girl dancing? That video invasion into her privacy was the reason Strong invented StrongWatch anti-virus ware. The girl attempted suicide and then dropped out of school. Reports say that she was harassed and heckled incessantly because of the video."

I'd seen the video. I turned to Castillo. "How do you know it wasn't her boyfriend in the video?" The video never showed the guy. He could only be heard saying a few words in the background.

Castillo rubbed Lady M with his chin, snuggling her. "Because I was her boyfriend at the time, and I wasn't in the video. McVay was."

25

SATURDAY

THEREAFTER, THE WORDS FLOWED FREELY FROM CASTILLO. Maybe Lady M was working her magic. Or maybe having a captive audience appealed to him.

Castillo said, "The team had a party after winning our homecoming game. Kami and I went to the party—that's her name, the girl in the video. Anyway, Kami wasn't a drinker, so she'd brought her own. A few times in the past, the nonalcoholic drinks had been spiked. She said she went to the restroom and took her soft drink with her but forgot it when she left the bathroom. When she remembered and went back for it, the drink was right where she'd left it. She didn't think anyone had messed with it. Only a few minutes had passed since she left the bathroom."

"But it had been spiked?" Precious asked.

Castillo nodded. "Next thing I know, she's telling me she's going home—she doesn't feel good. I walk her back to her place, make sure she gets in safely, and I go back to the party. The next day, I wake up to a video of her doing a striptease for McVay. I recognized his voice in the background."

"How? What?" I had a million questions.

"Kami didn't remember a thing. Still doesn't. Only that shortly after I left, McVay came to her door. She said she thought she'd dreamt it all at first. Until she saw the video. Man, she got harassed. People would throw fake dollar bills at her. Called her a slut. Her life during that time was awful." He closed his eyes as if trying to unsee what the conversation had dredged up.

"What happened then?" Precious asked.

He continued, "Kami hit rock bottom, and we, her family and I, convinced her to transfer to a different school."

"Is that why you transferred?" I asked.

He nodded. "Mostly, but there was the time McVay 'got sick' before a big game that we should have won, hands down. Magically, he was better the next day. Claimed food poisoning. We lost, and word on the street was that's how Austin Strong got his start-up cash to develop and produce StrongWatch."

"He bet against you all?" I asked.

In doing so, the odds would be great and the payout greater.

Castillo shrugged. "You have to ask him. But with that rumor and what Kami was going through, I needed to get out too."

"This is why you said McVay needed to be in jail," I said. "You think he spiked Kami's drink and caused the fallout in her life."

He nodded. "And I think Strong was in on it and used the video to launch his product and make a shit ton of money."

I shook my head. "I don't get it—the connection between Strong and McVay—other than they went to school together."

Castillo's brow shot up. "They were roommates. Strong even stayed an extra two years to do his master's work, which he never finished, but I think it's because those two were running some kinda con."

Using a Chuckit, a long-handled device for chucking a ball across a field, much like a lacrosse stick, I let the ball soar, and Simon raced across the dog park to retrieve it. The two bossy ladies with their four dogs, the two small ones and the two Labs, were on the other side of the park. We were watching them like hawks, waiting to call them out as they were so famous for doing to others. Joining Paulie and I were two other dog parents, Diane and Brian. Diane had an Australian shepherd and Brian a coonhound. Paulie had cleared them, saying they could listen to our conversation. I wasn't so sure but getting mentored while not disclosing all the information was tough.

Paulie said, "Strong have an alibi for the night McVay died?"

I nodded. "He was in his office at the Pioneers' training facility. The video shows him there from six in the evening until two in the morning. His car never left the car park. All timestamps prove it. His secretary was there until eight forty-five. The car park guard was night shift. Said Strong's car never left."

Toby and I had done more digging into Strong, but he kept coming up squeaky clean. Even Precious went to bat for him, saying she'd had a handful of meetings with him and he was genuinely a nice guy.

Paulie asked, "You think Strong and McVay were lovers?" He was dressed in dark joggers, a dark long-sleeve

T-shirt, and stark-white running shoes. Though the sky was drizzling, he wore only a waterproof vest to keep his chest dry.

I shook my head. "I don't know what to think because after we left, Toby ran some checks on what Castillo told us. Because, like you said, I can't assume everything he said was the truth."

After leaving the hotel the night before, we'd driven home and talked over what Castillo had said. His anger toward McVay was understandable, but it was also motive.

Diane asked, "Whatever happened to this football player and the girl?"

I said, "Eventually, they broke up. He's engaged to an underwear model now."

Paulie asked, "What's his alibi?"

"He says he was at his team's facility the night McVay died, which is all the way across the country. But Castillo must have thought I was clueless about football because his team was on a bye."

A bye was a week off from playing. Typically, players went on mini vacations for some rest and relaxation.

"I had Toby check flights, and sure enough, Roman Castillo flew into Seattle the day McVay was murdered. He flew out on the red-eye that night."

I'd done the math. McVay was killed after nine in the evening, after AJ left. That left little time for Castillo to do the deed then drive the three hours north to the airport to catch a 12:53 a.m. flight out of Sea-Tac—a tight time line but not impossible. And if Castillo had taken a private flight from Oregon to Seattle, that would've made killing McVay even easier. *But why? Why wait almost a decade to off McVay? Was it the large payout McVay was about to get?* For the time being, all I could do was speculate while Toby did more digging.

Brian said, "So the pretty boy lied."

"I'm not buying that shampoo he touts anymore," Diane said. "Nope. No, sir."

I told Paulie, "Lockett's going to call him as a character witness. Maybe we'll get to the bottom of it then. But for now, I'm taking what he says about Strong and McVay with a grain of salt. I should also add that the woman in the video, Kami Bartell, has a restraining order against Castillo."

Diane and Brian "Oohed" simultaneously.

I continued, "Apparently the breakup was hard on him. Three years after, Kami Bartell was granted the restraining order. And she's renewed it every two years."

Paulie told Brian and Diane, "In order to renew, the person filing the order has to have reasonable fear of the defendant."

They "Ohhed" in response.

We all nodded. I then chucked the ball again for Simon. He raced Paulie's dog, Rocket, to get it.

In the far corner, the Lab was dropping a load.

Brian said, "I hope Mean Lady doesn't see it."

Diane said, "Please let me blow the whistle this time."

We waited in anticipation, but much to our dismay, she saw her dog and immediately went to clean up the poop.

We sighed with disappointment. Then a car pulled up, and a guy with a large Great Pyrenees got out. From his trunk, he took out a toddler balance bike.

Brian said, "I can't wait to see the dog ride that."

We all laughed.

A kid no more than three climbed out of the car and

pushed the bike to the gate. The dad let his dog and the kid in.

Diane said, "Well, that's not a good idea."

We all shook our heads. Too many big dogs. Too much that could go wrong. We turned our attention to the bossy ladies.

Paulie said, "Three, two, one..."

On cue, the Q-Beam went on, directed at the kid, who was balanced precariously on the bike.

"Hey!" the one with the Lab shouted to the dad. "Is that a good idea? Let me answer that for you. It's not. This is a dog park. Dogs run here and get rough. You okay if they take your kid out and run him down?" She was holding her dog by the collar.

The dad said, "Uh..."

Lab Lady directed her beam to the large sign that greeted dog lovers when they came into the park.

"Nowhere on there does it say to bring your kids to play. Out you go." She pointed her light at the gate. When the dad didn't move, she pointed at the kid then the gate.

"This is gold," I said. "Though I hate admitting she's kinda right."

Brian said, "Yeah, but she doesn't have to be so bossy about it."

Diane said, "I'd hate to see the kid get hurt."

We all nodded as we watched the dad wrangle his dog and kid, constantly checking over his shoulder at the Q-Beam ladies.

Paulie said, "She's an ass, and the man can be responsible for his dog and kid. It's not her place to manage the people who come into the park. People do stupid stuff every day. We ain't the park police."

He turned to me. "And you—no stone unturned. You gotta talk to the broad who filed the restraining order."

"You think using the word *broad* will upset me, don't you?" I smiled.

He smiled back. "Does it?" An eyebrow shot up with his query.

"Nope."

He said, "But talking to her bothers you, and you can't let it."

"I hate to dredge up bad memories for her."

He smacked his lips with distaste as if I had disappointed him moments after proving myself. "I bet your pal AJ will understand when he's behind bars—"

I held up a hand to stop him. "Yeah, yeah. I'll talk to her." I knew I needed to though I dreaded it.

He narrowed his gaze at me. "Listen to me. I know you think this list of suspects isn't all that intimidating. You got a pastry chef, a linebacker, a rapper, and a dead trainer. But what you don't see is that everyone but the trainer has money behind them. And money can buy all sorts of imaginable outcomes. And these people... they make money for other people, and those people have a vested interest in keeping that money coming in. You get what I'm saying?"

"I think so. I mean, I'm taking this very seriously. My family has left town as a protective measure. I sweep my house and car two to three times a day. I'm making sure I'm not being followed."

Paulie scratched above his right ear. "All good things. But people with money can make you disappear, never to be found. They can make killing in a car crash look like an accident. And if you do find out who did this to McVay and that person is arrested, that don't mean this is over. Crime bosses have run businesses from behind bars. You seeing the bigger picture?"

I nodded and swallowed the lump of fear in my throat.

"You need to tuck a gun in that backpack of yours—better yet, on your body—a gun that shoots bullets. And I hope you won't be afraid to use it."

26

SUNDAY

Kami Bartell was a baker, a professional pastry maker who apparently worked under several well-known pastry chefs and had made a name for herself with her creative confections. But she was known as K. Bartell now, and everyone called her Kay.

Kay was the head pastry chef on a popular TV show where people tried to recreate her food art and often failed. Though Kay wasn't on the screen, her work was recognizable by amateur pastry chefs across the country.

When Precious learned I was hopping a flight to California to try to meet up with Kay Bartell, she'd included herself.

"Just in case," she said.

Just in case of what, I wasn't sure.

"Ironic, really," Precious pointed out. "The woman who became the poster child for why we should put anti-virus ware on our computers is once again familiar in millions of households everywhere."

I'd done a Google search to learn more. "She rarely

makes public appearances, and there aren't any good pictures of her. The show's website shows her wearing the white chef's hat, but her face is down. There's no way I'd recognize her."

I continued, "She did judge a show in Seattle a few weeks ago. She was the keynote speaker. And not one mention in the paper or on the competition's website about her past."

Precious nodded with appreciation. "That's good. These days, I wouldn't be surprised if something like what she went through was used to get more people watching. Clickbait and all that."

"How it looks to me is like she's really hiding from her past."

"Can you blame her?" Precious asked.

I shook my head. As a woman whose husband wasn't legally hers, I understood embarrassment and humiliation —on a smaller scale, admittedly.

"According to this press release, Kay will be a judge at a San Francisco Holiday Bake-Off. The grand prize is a cool one hundred thousand." I shot Precious a look. "I'm in the wrong business."

She shook her head. "I've had your cookies. You didn't miss your calling."

I sat back, indignant. "Hey, I make good cookies."

She nodded. "You do. Right out of the package. But when's the last time you just dreamt up a cookie recipe or added to one to make it better?"

I gave it some thought. "Never. No reason why. The one from the tube is already perfect."

"Bingo," she said. "No pun intended, but cookie creation isn't your jam."

"Fair point."

The plane landed two hours after we took off from Portland. We Ubered to the convention hall where the contest was going down. While I was doing that, Lockett was working with Toby on verifying who'd leaked the fact that McVay was looking for a contract elsewhere. From what Toby had found in articles, we believed the leak came from the new agent, Nick Hutton. After my chat with Kay Bartell, I would have to tackle Castillo's lie of an alibi and try to trace his whereabouts while he'd been in Seattle.

One hurdle at a time.

We paid the entrance fee and spent an obscene amount of time trying to figure out how to breach security to the backstage area where the judges were sequestered. We caught a break when the security guard stationed outside the backstage doors got called away to run interference with a scuffle over a giveaway down at the KitchenAid booth.

I jerked Precious by the arm—she was watching the two ladies scream it out over a mixer—and pulled her through the door seconds after the guard turned his back.

Behind the scenes was a maze of hallways and empty rooms. We wandered around until we found a row of rooms set up as waiting spaces for the judges. Some doors were open and some closed. That was going to make things awkward if we had to knock and see who was behind the door.

But we got lucky. When I peeked into the third open door, Kami Bartell and another woman were sitting at a table talking, papers between them.

I cleared my throat to announce us. When they both looked my way, I said, "Hi, my name is Samantha True. This is my friend Erika Shurmann. You're Kami Bartell, aren't you?"

The color drained from Bartell's face. "My name is Kay."

I put a hand over my heart, horrified by my mistake—not the best foot to start out on. "I'm so sorry. Of course you are. Again, I apologize for approaching you this way. I tried calling the show and your agent, but I have some questions for you, and time is of importance."

Her silence prompted me to continue.

"I work for the defense of AJ Gunn. You may know his name. He is currently being charged with murdering Keith McVay."

Kay began shaking her head.

The lady across from her reached across the table and took her hand. "Breathe, sis. Breathe." She shot us a look of panic.

Kay mumbled, "Nope, no, nope, no way. Make them leave. Make them leave."

I felt more than saw Precious back away, and I knew why. The distress on Kay's face was nothing but pure terror and anguish.

That's what I feared and instantly hated about my job. No way was this woman faking her reaction to get out of talking to us. If she was, she was awesome at it. Her distress was so thick and consuming, I couldn't help but check over my shoulder for McVay or, worse, his killer.

I put my hand up. "I'm sorry. We'll leave. I'm so sorry."

By that point, Kay had her head between her legs and was sucking in large gulps of air. The other woman was coaching her through what sounded like coping strategies.

Precious was ahead of me as we backed away and turned to leave.

She whispered, "I feel terrible."

"Me too. There's no way I'm going to ask her anything,

and I'm okay with that. Maybe Toby can find out more for us, or we can find a friend who might know more."

We were several doors away when a woman called out, "Excuse me."

I turned, and the other woman from Kay's room was rushing toward us. I met her halfway.

"I'm so sorry," I said.

She waved off my apology. "It's okay. You just caught us off guard. Not that you should have. When we saw that Keith had been murdered, we expected to be approached. Oddly, no one has until you."

Precious asked, "Is she going to be okay?"

The woman nodded then stuck out her hand. "I'm Kallie, Kay's sister. I'm also her personal assistant." Kallie, like her sister, was petite, with wavy blond hair and cornflower-blue eyes.

Precious and I reintroduced ourselves.

Kallie said, "You came here to ask questions. I'm not sure I can answer them, but I can try."

I glanced at Precious, reading her body language, uncertain if I should push forward.

Precious said, "We don't want to make today any more awful than we already have."

Kallie shook her head. "Actually, you proved to my sister how well she can handle this."

I tried to hide my skepticism.

Kallie smiled warmly. "In the past, she would've totally lost it. She'd need a sedative. She won't need one today, and she'll be able to judge. That's huge."

I nodded. "Okay. If you're sure."

She shrugged. "I am, but I can't promise anything."

I pulled in a steadying breath and asked, "Roman Castillo... Why does she continue with the restraining order against him?"

Kallie's smile wavered. "Roman's a good guy. Well-meaning. And he loves my sister. But every time she sees him, she's back in college, and she relives what happened to her all over again. She's built a life by blocking out the past. Is it the healthiest? Probably not. But it's what she can live with. And when Roman comes around, he brings all his hatred for Keith and everyone involved. And as you can see, she's coping, but there's still work to do. This is why she keeps the restraining order. But Roman has a hard time taking no for an answer."

Precious asked, "Isn't he engaged, though?"

Kallie nodded. "That doesn't stop him. And I'm not trying to paint a bad picture of him. When all this happened, he stood by my sister but couldn't do anything. He couldn't stop the harassment, online or in person. I think that he's still trying to make it up to her... that he feels like he let her down."

I could see that. When I found out that Carson was dead and we weren't legally married, I'd seen something similar in Leo's eyes—the need to rescue me while not being sure how. I'd also seen it in Lockett's face and even Precious's.

I asked, "When all this was happening, what did the police do about it?"

The hackers who invented the spyware were never caught. Per Toby, some speculation went around online that they were Russian, Chinese, or even American because right after the spyware crisis, a group of American college students were caught running an online con. They hacked into and stole emails from several top banks and brokerage firms, only to send the clients of those firms emails about investment opportunities and collected broker's fees. This online con raked in hundreds of millions of dollars. And even though they were caught, many speculated that the mastermind wasn't, that he lived abroad and the students had been lackeys. Many believed that use of spyware to invade others' privacy was a test run performed by that team of hackers.

Kallie shook her head. "The police are limited in what they could do. We don't have strong privacy laws in this country that protect victims online. And the question becomes whether the issue is a civil matter or a crime. In my sister's case, the harassment continued and even got stronger as she fought back. The more she tried to find out who was behind it, the more she was stalked."

"How so?"

"Before she put the anti-virus on her computer, she'd get creepy videos of her studying or eating lunch at her desk. The message attached was 'We see you.'"

Chills ran down my arms. That was the same message I'd received.

"What happened after she put the anti-virus on her computer?" I asked.

Kallie nodded. "Yeah, that stopped the Computer Peeping Tom. But then she'd get emails with videos attached: Kay getting in her car. Kay and Roman together. That's when she tried to, you know"—Kallie gulped—"hurt herself. After that, we moved her far away from the scene of the crime. Tried to get a fresh start. Funny, right? Moving away but taking the internet with you. A person can never truly get away from it."

Precious asked. "Did it stop then?"

Kallie nodded. "Yeah, I think because we stopped pursuing it." She pointed down the hallway behind her. "Every day, my sister lives with no justice. Every day, she's a victim without a voice. That's why she reacts the way she does."

"Who of us would be any different, having to live through what your sister did?" In typical Precious fashion, she grabbed Kallie and pulled her into a hug. "This story breaks my heart. I want you to give this hug to your sister."

Kallie smiled, tears in her eyes. "Thank you."

I said, "Maybe when all this is done, your sister will get some peace."

Kallie nodded. "Maybe."

"Last question," I said. "Do you think Roman is capable of killing Keith McVay?" After hearing that story, I wasn't sure why Roman waited as long as he did if he, in fact, did do it.

Kallie's eyebrows went up in thought. "Yeah, I can see Roman doing it. Heck, I can see myself doing it. But the night Keith McVay died, Roman couldn't have done it."

"Why not?"

She looked over her shoulder before answering. "Because he was in Seattle, where my sister was judging a contest. I saw him hiding among the crowd, watching her. And I later saw him at the hotel. Like he was making sure we got back okay."

"What time was that?"

"Well, the judging happened at eight in the evening. The awards were handed out forty-five minutes later. We stayed for the celebration. We were back at the hotel by ten."

"And Castillo was there the whole time?"

She nodded. "I kept track of him, just in case. I didn't want Kay to see him. We had a drink at the hotel bar, and he stayed in the lobby until we got in the elevator to go to our rooms. That was slightly after ten-thirty."

Dang it. There goes that suspect.

27

MONDAY

"Unless Castillo has a secret way to teleport, there was no way he could watch Kallie and Kay get into an elevator then rush to an airport—the closest from the hotel was twenty minutes—fly to Oregon, get a car to McVay's to kill him, and get back to Sea-Tac in time for his red-eye," I told Lockett.

He said, "I depose Castillo in a few days. Until then, we're looking at video from the event to back up what Kallie Bartell told you."

"And Lil' Megalodon's alibi?" I asked. "How's that panning out?"

We were in my dad's newspaper building, using an extra office. Dad, Mom, and Cora had landed safely in Greece, and Dad had given Stella the time off as well. But she refused and was sitting at the front desk, a large canister of bear spray at her side—for use on "the lost and confused," she'd said and dared them to wander into her territory.

I'd done a sweep for bugs when I arrived. The place was clean.

In true Dad fashion, he was turning their trip into a working vacation and was sending articles and the like to Stella while away.

Lockett flipped through some pages on his notepad and said, "Lil' Megalodon, also known as DeShawn Cook, was home alone. He says he has Facebook Live videos and tweets to prove it."

I curled up my lip. "Everyone in the world knows there are services that can post those for you at scheduled times. His alibi is weak."

Lockett nodded in agreement.

Stella knocked at the open door. She held out a small three-by-five, padded envelope. "Messenger delivered this for you, Sam, just now."

I cut Lockett a worried glance. "I guess I shouldn't worry too much. It's too small to be a severed head or anything."

Lockett shook his head. "Not too small to be severed finger. Or a picture of a severed head."

I let the disgust show on my face. "You have a way of ruining things, you know that?"

He shrugged one shoulder. "It's called being prepared."

Stella laughed. "I'll just go back to my desk. In case there's a tiny bomb in there."

"Ha ha!" I yelled at her retreating back. "Neither of you are very funny."

Just in case, I put my ear to the package to listen for ticking. Lockett chuckled and handed me a letter opener. I eased it between the flaps and gently cut the package open then tipped the package upside down and let the contents fall out —a thumb drive.

I groaned. "This can't be good. I don't want to see anyone get beheaded either."

I glanced at the package. It had no return address, but the postage stamp showed it had come from Seattle.

Lockett handed me a ziplock bag. "Here, put it in this bag in case we need to look for fingerprints."

I glanced inside the envelope before putting it in the plastic bag. A small folded piece of paper was stuck at the bottom. I pulled it out using the smallest pinch of my thumb and index finger possible, hoping to keep the paper intact.

I placed the note on the table, and Lockett used the tip of a pencil to open it.

On the page was a computer-printed message: "Surrounded by liars."

I glanced at the thumb drive. "Hey, Stella," I called. "You don't have any—"

She came into the room and slapped a plastic bag on the desk, the kind for produce at the grocery store. "No, but you can use this. I went to Chuck's just now to get it."

Chuck's was the local market in town and happened to be adjacent to Dad's newspaper.

Using the bag in place of a glove, I picked up the thumb drive and inserted it into my laptop. Two video files popped up.

I hovered the cursor over the file names. "Eenie, meenie, miney, mo."

"Either one could really blow," Lockett finished.

"I have a bad feeling about this."

I clicked the first file. McVay's house was the opening shot. The sky was black, the neighborhood quiet. AJ's car was in the driveway. Another car was parked at the end of the drive, a Honda Civic. When AJ came out of McVay's house, the guy in the Civic jumped out and jogged up to him. AJ put a hand up, keeping the guy at arm's length.

I said, "Reporter, I think."

"Likely."

We watched AJ back out and drive away. The camera followed him. On one side of McVay's house was the lake. Across the street were other houses and the empty lot with the escape room exit. Behind those houses was the exit out of the neighborhood.

AJ drove out of sight, presumably leaving the neighborhood. The camera panned from McVay's house and swung left to the houses across from it. The camera zoomed in on the space between two houses. A car just like AJ's cruised across the screen then came to a stop and idled.

From behind the camera, coming from McVay's house—or the escape room exit, if I were to guess—a man jogged across the screen toward the car.

"Is that McVay?" I asked, stunned, as I leaned toward the screen.

Lockett bowed his head and rested it on the table. "What were they doing?"

My mind could not compute the fact that AJ had lied to me, to us. I rewound the video and watched it in slow motion. "Look, based the angle the guy enters the screen, I think it's likely he came from the escape room exit. Leo said the dirt had been disturbed there. I thought it meant someone went in that way, but now I think someone came out from there."

I pointed at a dark spot on the screen where a person suddenly appeared, a backpack over his shoulder. The moonlight showed us only his silhouette. He jogged to AJ's car and got in and they drove away.

"We can't clearly say it's McVay or that's AJ's car," I said.

"We need to talk to AJ," Lockett said. "It's not going to be hard to convince a jury it's them. Look how quickly you and I jumped to the conclusion that it was them."

"Who do you think is filming this?"

"Good question."

"Well, whoever they are, they now know of McVay's secret entrance."

Lockett leaned back in his chair and stared at the ceiling. "Why are they filming McVay? Or are they filming AJ?"

"Maybe the next video will answer all those questions," I said hopefully.

"We're not that lucky." The look on his face was utter disgust.

I could totally relate. I'd gone out on a limb for AJ, and he'd lied to me.

I clicked on the second video, and Brad Jenson appeared on the screen. He was sitting in a chair facing the camera. The shot was from slightly below the shoulders on up. Behind him were a bed and end table. He was in a hotel room. The room was sterile, no clothes out, the bed made. The video gave us no more information.

A light went on, and Jenson squinted, looking away. He hadn't moved and seemed startled by the light, and I got the sense that he wasn't alone. But the other person wasn't making a sound and hadn't come into the frame.

Jenson spoke. "My name is Brad Jenson. I'm a trainer for the Portland Pioneers. I have worked there for twelve years. I am addicted to gambling." Brad's throat convulsed, and he looked to the right of the camera for the briefest of moments.

I paused the video and touched the screen. "Look, there's a shadow. Half of it's been cut off by the frame."

Lockett leaned in. "That's not a shadow. That's the texture from the wallpaper. Or a stain."

I shook my head. Photography had been my livelihood for over a decade. I knew shadows. "No, let's go back a frame. Jenson hasn't moved." I clicked the video back two frames to when the light went on. "See, he's still in the same position, and the area is lighter. Now, watch." I clicked one frame. "A stain appears, directly behind him." I clicked to the second frame. "Now, the dark pattern has moved to the edge of the frame. Someone clicked on the light then walked from left to right. They're now standing to Jenson's left. Almost diagonally."

Lockett nodded. "I see it. Good eye."

I sighed. "In today's world, though, with deep fakes so easily made, I can't say any part of this video is real, from the background to the shadow. This could have been filmed in Jenson's house the day he died and superimposed over this background."

"Then the same could be said for the other video."

I nodded. "Yeah." I'd forgotten to consider that, having jumped to a bad conclusion. "We'll have to ask AJ and see what he says. In the meantime, let's finish this, and I'll send them to Toby and see if he can look at the code or whatever magic he does."

I clicked Play.

Jenson cleared his throat. "It's because of my addition to gambling that I agreed to help AJ Gunn murder Keith McVay. AJ got Keith out of the house, and I snuck in and waited for him. I'm also the person responsible for Keith having performance-enhancing drugs in his system. Following his car accident, he was given a shot pregame to help with pain. I obtained a shot that was labeled as the painkiller but had the PEDs in it. AJ was paying me half a million dollars to do it. His motivation was the starting position. I am confessing this because the guilt is too much, and I'm too chicken to go to the police. This is my final confession."

I paused the video, afraid we were about to see something graphic. I advanced it frame by frame. Jenson looked toward his left and followed someone or something back across to the center. I rewound and watched again.

"Look. The shadow is moving," I said.

We watched it forward and in reverse several times. I'd found that watching things in reverse sometimes showed details that got lost in forward play.

The light clicked off, and the room dimmed. Jenson ducked his head, then the camera went off.

I shook my head. "Nothing about the video feels right." I pointed at the screen. "Why didn't he stand to turn the video off? Why is he already sitting when the recording starts? Maybe I've seen too many movies, and my expectations are skewed by that, but this doesn't feel right. And who makes a suicide video someplace else then leaves and goes home to do the deed?"

I picked up my phone and called Toby, putting him on speaker.

"At your service, dudette," he said.

"I have a few videos I need you to look at and see if you can dig into them or whatever. I need to know if they're real."

Toby grunted. "I'm not an expert on deep fakes. I can look at the code, but if the person's good, then I'll miss it. But I got an online buddy who might be able to help."

I glanced at Lockett, who shrugged. "Do you trust him?" I asked.

Toby snort laughed. "Can you trust anyone online? But that's the only solution I have. I'll look first and then let you know if I need to bring him in."

Lockett nodded.

"Deal," I said. "I'm at my dad's office."

Typically, I would've let Toby in using screen-sharing software, but after getting hacked, I wasn't taking any chances.

"On my way," he said then disconnected.

I dialed AJ next. He answered on the second ring.

"You need to get down to my dad's newspaper right now," I said, not too friendly.

"What's going on?"

"You can tell me when you get here." I disconnected.

"What if he goes in the wind?" Lockett asked.

The thought had occurred to me. If my call spooked AJ enough, he might run, especially if he was guilty. I'd had flashes of doubt and was having one then. But I'd come that far, trusting and believing in him.

"He won't. But if he does, then we have our answer, don't we?"

"Are you sure about him?" Lockett side-eyed me.

I nodded and crossed my fingers under the table, hoping I was right.

28

MONDAY

BEFORE AJ REACHED THE END OF THE VIDEO, HE CONFESSED.

"Okay, I omitted some parts from that night." He looked at Lockett and me. "But I didn't think it was pertinent."

Overcome with anger, frustration, and disappointment, I looked for an outlet to vent the mass of feelings consuming me. I kicked him hard in the shin, twice.

He doubled over. "Yow! That hurt."

I leaned in close. "You're lucky I didn't punch you in the face or use my stun gun on you. Which, come to think of it, is a pretty good idea." I turned to Lockett. "Grab my back-pack, please."

AJ pushed back in his seat. "Sam, I'm sorry."

I held up a finger. "My family's privacy was violated. My six-year-old niece was used to threaten me. I've lost clients."

"You were almost killed," Lockett said.

I stared at AJ. "Oh yeah. There's that too."

He buried his head in his hands. "I was going to tell you, I swear."

"But?" I said. "Let's hear this excuse."

AJ met my gaze briefly then ducked his head. "The morning I was arrested, you came to see me early. Remember, Sam?"

I nodded.

"Then the both of you came back later that afternoon."

I gestured for him to speed up and get to the point.

"In between, I had another visitor. Another lawyer. Or at least, that's what he said he was."

I looked at AJ and Lockett. "I checked your visitation records. There's no one on the list but us. I looked because I wanted to know if anyone from the team or front office came to see you."

AJ shrugged. "Well, someone came." He gave us a description of the guy, but it didn't sound like anyone I knew. He continued, "He had pictures of my mom. Of Troy taking groceries into her house. Of her at the hospital, getting chemo." AJ picked his head up, tears in his eyes. "This guy, he said to keep my mouth shut about Keith sneaking out. He knew Keith had snuck out, away from the reporter. He even knew what time I brought Keith back. He said if I didn't keep my mouth shut, Troy and my mom would pay. He knew my mom's doctor's name. He knew everything about Mom and Troy."

I sank to the floor, resting on my haunches.

Lockett sat on the desk behind us. "Why didn't you tell us this?"

"It's my mom and kid brother. They're all the family I have!" AJ exclaimed.

I sat back on the floor and met AJ's gaze. "I'm still mad at you."

He nodded. "I know. I'm sorry. I truly am."

I looked up at the ceiling. "So why release a video that

shows exactly what they threatened you to keep quiet about?"

Lockett said, "Because they wanted to release it. Them having the video and Jenson's confession puts them in the driver's seat. We're behind the curve, doing damage control instead of actual investigation." He pointed at AJ. "He'll be tried in social media."

AJ looked at us. "Wait, what confession?"

I met his confused gaze with a hard one of my own. "As Precious would say, hold on to your titties, kitties, because you're about to have the ground pulled out from under you."

We played the video for him.

AJ was stunned. "None of that's true. I don't even have half a million on hand. After I pay my agent and taxes, I bring home under eight hundred thousand. I pay for my house, my mom's house, and Troy. Anything extra goes into investments."

I sighed, stood, and closed the computer, worried that the thumb drive could have put spyware back on my computer. "But you could come up with half a million if you needed to."

He shrugged because he had no argument. Then he held out his hands. "I was in jail when Brad died."

I nodded. "You have that going for you." I gestured at the computer. "I wasn't even sure they were real, but you confirmed the first one was. I'm going to assume the second one is as well. Toby's in the other room with the thumb drive and his computer, trying to verify both, just in case." I stood. "I'm going to have him double-check the visitation log at the jail."

I exited the room and went to my dad's office, where

Toby was working. I shared with him AJ's story about the visitor. Then I went back to the other office.

Lockett and AJ weren't talking. Lockett was writing on his notepad, a list with several question marks.

I sat on the couch next to AJ. "Why don't you tell us where you took McVay?"

AJ wiped his eyes and looked at us. "Keith was off-the-charts paranoid. Like I thought he was having a bad trip or something. And I asked him if he was okay, if he needed help. I'd never seen him like that. But he kept saying he was fine. We're eating, and he just gets up and walks to the pantry, saying he needs hot sauce and doesn't come back. I waited, but finally I followed him. I'm like, 'Hey, man, you need help reaching the hot sauce or something?' I go in, and there he is, standing in this little room with a wall of monitors and his finger to his lips, telling me to be quiet. It's like a panic room or something. I step in, and he closes the door."

"It's an escape room," Lockett said. "Because it has an exit. McVay's house was heavily bugged with both audio and video."

"And he knew it." I couldn't help but state the obvious. "What did he say?"

"He rambled about having been a part of some bad things but wanting out. Needing a change. He told me to get as far away from the Pioneers as possible. But he wouldn't explain anything. He asked me if I would drive him somewhere." AJ shrugged. "I agreed. He told me where to wait for him. Then he said we needed to go back to the kitchen and finish eating then talk about the game. Then I would leave and wait for him on the other side of the neighborhood."

Lockett flipped the page on his notepad to a clean sheet. "So this was early in the evening."

AJ nodded. "Yeah, like seven. We watched film, talked about the game. Then I said I needed to go. And I left." He pointed at the computer. "You saw what happened next."

I asked, "The guy that ran up to you was a reporter?"

AJ nodded. "Yeah, for the local paper."

I needed clarification. "Like you know he's a legit reporter?"

Again, he nodded. "Yeah, he's always at our press conferences."

I moved him down on my list of people to investigate. "So you take McVay where?"

"To the post office. In his backpack, he had a large padded envelope he wanted to mail. We drove around for about fifteen minutes then to a post office in downtown Portland."

"Fifteen minutes?" This from Lockett. "Any reason for that?"

AJ shrugged. "Keith wanted to make sure we weren't being followed. After we dropped off the envelope at the mailbox, I drove him home."

Lockett asked, "What was the package?"

AJ shook his head. "I dunno. Keith said it was insurance."

"Any chance you saw who the package was addressed to?" I said.

AJ gave a slight smile. "I didn't have to. Keith told me. Said he was sending it to a family friend, a lawyer named Chet Fuller."

I asked, "When you got the visit from this mystery guy while you were in jail, he told you to stay quiet about the video, right?"

AJ nodded.

I shook my head in confusion. "I can't come up with a

reason why he might ask this. Did he ask what you and McVay did?"

He nodded. "I told him we dropped off a letter at the post office. He asked me who it was addressed to, and I told him I didn't know." He held up both hands in protest. "I know I should have told you about him and the video. But I was scared. I didn't know what to do."

I was frustrated. If we'd had that information from day one, we might have already solved the case.

"But you weren't scared enough to tell him about the envelope," I said.

"Sam," Lockett said in warning.

AJ stared at me. "But I would have. At that moment, he was telling me they have access to my family. But they hadn't hurt them. I knew if I told anyone about the visit, they would hurt Troy or my mom or both. But they had no way of knowing if I knew who Keith mailed the package to or not. So I took a chance. But if they'd pushed me, I would have told them. Knowing the name was the one card I held."

"Did you ever plan on telling me, us?" I gestured at Lockett.

"I told you today," he argued.

"Because you had to."

He nodded. "Yeah. I'd like you to tell me what you would have done differently. My family can't hide out in Greece."

I wasn't sure what I would have done in his shoes. "Toby!" I yelled, hoping he could hear me next door.

A few moments later, Toby stood in the doorway, laptop in hand. "You bellowed?"

"Do a search for Chet Fuller. Lawyer. Minnesota." Minnesota is where McVay grew up.

He sat at the desk to type.

"Sam." AJ met my gaze, a deep sadness pulling on his features. "You have to see this from my perspective. The entire visit with Keith was weird, and once he put the envelope in the mail, I wanted to be done with it all. I wanted to get away from Keith as fast as I could. Honestly, and I'm ashamed to say this, I thought he was on something. Or bipolar or something. I never imagined all this would happen."

I began to put the pieces together. "Someone was there that night. Why are they filming? Maybe because McVay's behavior is so out of the ordinary they pick up on it. Maybe because you two go into the pantry for hot sauce and come out ten minutes later? Whoever had McVay's house bugged is tipped off somehow. That's likely who's filming. They do surveillance and see McVay come out of the escape room exit."

"That's how they entered McVay's house," Lockett said. "Keith comes out. Our criminal goes in and waits for him."

"And that's how they exit too," I said. "Which is why they aren't caught on any video." I looked at AJ. "What time did you drop McVay off?"

"Ten forty-five. I waited for him to get inside. He flicked a light to let me know he was good, and I drove home."

Lockett grunted. "There's no video of you dropping him off alive. And once this new video gets out, what do we have to counteract it? Nothing?"

I said, "I'll go to the neighbors, and see if any of them have Ring cameras or security that caught AJ dropping off McVay and driving away."

Lockett looked tired. "There's nothing to say he didn't just pull into another spot and cut across yards to get to the escape room entrance."

I looked at AJ. "I'll talk to all the neighbors. Maybe we'll get lucky, and someone will have a camera facing that way. You'd better hope someone does."

Lockett said, "Start with the neighbor, the rapper. He had motive and means. See if he's willing to share. If he resists, maybe that's telling us something."

My phone chimed, and I glanced at the screen.

AJ dropped his head onto his hands. "I should have told you both everything right away."

"Yes, you should have," I said. "But I get why you didn't, and it's a moot point now anyway." I held up my phone to show him a local news notification. "The media now has the videos and has released them to the public."

29

MONDAY

TOBY CLEARED HIS THROAT. "HERE'S THE LAWYER, CHET Fuller."

He swiveled his computer toward us. A website was pulled up with the lawyer's image on the screen. I watched AJ for any sign of recognition. Chet Fuller appeared to be in his late sixties with a comb-over, a friendly grin, and a flannel shirt.

AJ shook his head. "Don't know him."

Using the number on the website, I called Chet Fuller. A receptionist answered and put me right through.

"Hallo, Chet Fuller speaking," he said with a typical Midwest accent.

"Mr. Fuller, my name is Samantha True. I'm a private investigator working for AJ Gunn. You may know his name. He was charged with Keith McVay's murder."

"Ay, yah, I know who he is."

"I'm happy to send you a copy of my license for verification if you'd like. I have a few questions that I think you might be able to answer."

He was silent, which I took as encouragement to continue.

"On the night Mr. McVay was murdered, Mr. Gunn drove him to the post office where Mr. McVay mailed a padded envelope to you. Have you received such an envelope?"

"Why does it matter?" Fuller asked.

I glanced at Lockett while taking in a steady breath, trying to calm my racing heart and wondering how I could convince the man to share what might be confidential information with me.

"It matters, Mr. Fuller, because Mr. McVay knew he was in trouble. He told Mr. Gunn that night that what he was mailing you was insurance. If that's true, then what was in that envelope could actually be proof as to who murdered Mr. McVay."

Mr. Fuller huffed. "Well then, there's the pickle. Because I didn't see what was in the envelopes. I just mailed them out like Keith requested."

"Envelopes?"

"Ay, yah, inside the envelope to me were instructions to mail two other envelopes should something tragic happen to Keith. Seeing as how I got the envelope after your client had been arrested, I considered that as something tragic happening to Keith, so I mailed the envelopes out."

"Might you tell me where you mailed them?" I pleaded.

"And just why would I want to do that?"

I glanced at AJ. "Because I plan on bringing this killer to justice even if it turns out to be the guy who hired me. But something you should know, Mr. Fuller: Keith McVay was scared, even paranoid. He had an escape room in his house. Now he's gone. And you are my last hope of finding out the truth."

Fuller cleared his throat. "I've known Keith since he was a little tyke. Was one of his Pop Warner coaches. His dad and I were good friends. It breaks my heart that Keith's been taken away from us so tragically."

"So let's give him that last word."

Another long pause. "He asked me to mail one to that player with the hair—"

"Roman Castillo?"

"Oh yah. That's the one."

"And you said Keith asked you to mail two? Were these two envelopes the same size?"

"Oh yah, two. One was a padded envelope, a smaller version of what I received, and the other was a standard letter."

"Which one did Castillo get?"

"The padded envelope. I sent the other one to his house, per his instructions."

I repeated the information for those in the room with me. "You sent the other envelope to Keith's house in Lake Oswego? That's odd that he would do that."

"Oh yah, it is. Actually, I gave my wife the envelopes to mail. Let me check with her and see where she sent it."

"Okay, I can call you back in a few minutes if that's easier."

"Why would you need to? My wife is my receptionist. Hey, Barb!" he yelled.

I held the phone away from my ear and turned on the speakerphone.

"Barb, you mailed Keith's package, yeah?"

Barb yelled back, her voice more distant, "Of course I did, you loon. You told me to."

Fuller chuckled. "You sent it to his house in Portland, right?"

After a long pause, Barb spoke again, sounding closer. "No, I don't have that address. I used the cabin because that's where we sent his Christmas card."

"Oh, geez, Barb. I think the letter was supposed to go to his Portland house."

"Well, how am I supposed to know that? I don't even think we have that address. And why would he mail himself something to the house he was living in? Bless that poor boy's soul."

"Oh yah," Fuller said into the phone. "It looks like we goofed, Ms. True. Barb sent the envelope to the wrong house."

Lockett, AJ, Toby, and I looked at each other.

I said, "Maybe not. Might you be willing to share the address of the other house with me?"

"I guess it wouldn't hurt. He had a cabin out near Mount Saint Helens. Barb!" he yelled. "Get me the address for Keith's house."

"The cabin or the big one, because I already told you—"

"The cabin."

Moments later, Fuller gave me the address, and Lockett wrote it on his notepad. Then Toby started a search on his computer.

"Thank you, Mr. Fuller. The minute I know anything about Keith and who murdered him, I'll call you." I didn't bother to warn him to not talk to other people, believing his limited knowledge would work to his benefit.

I hung up and dropped onto the couch next to AJ, then I repeated what I'd learned to AJ and Lockett.

Toby's fingers flew over the keyboard. Moments later, he

said, "The house is registered to an LLC. I'm trying to get to the bottom of the LLC, but it's a deep rabbit hole. Probably why we never found this place."

Lockett summed everything up. "So McVay asked this family-friend lawyer to send out the envelopes in the event of his death, and one was to go to Roman and the other to his home in Portland, only it goes to a cabin McVay buried so deep that all our searches never found an inkling that it existed, much less an LLC was connected to him." He shook his head, looking frustrated.

I gnawed my lip then asked, "Why Roman? Why not Megalodon? They were neighbors and friends. Roman hated McVay. Is this letter a last dig at Roman?"

"What's Roman's connection to Keith?" AJ asked.

Lockett summarized the story for AJ.

"Oh no." I buried my head in my hands. "This is bad." I had connected the dots, and the final picture was scary.

"Sam?" Lockett asked.

I looked up at him with my palm on my forehead. "What's the connection to Roman? It's the Kami Bartell story. Kami Bartell's college years were ruined by a video of her doing a striptease for McVay. Fast forward to the present, and the sports world breaks with a story that McVay might leave the Pioneers. He's looking for a big contract, more than the Pioneers want to spend. He knows their cap and specifically asks for more. McVay and Roman get into a Twitter spat where Roman says McVay needs to go to prison, not get a new contract, and he says McVay is where he deserves to be."

"Yeah," said Toby, his tone asking me to go on.

I continued, "If you think someone might kill you and you think you have proof, who are you gonna send that proof to? The cops? The media? Both of those can be swayed. But if you send it to someone who hates you and the person you're accusing of being your killer, wouldn't you send it to that person?"

The guys nodded, each of them making their own connection.

I sighed heavily. "We're up against the worst possible person. He has means beyond what we have. He has far more to lose, which will make him more desperate."

Lockett swallowed then said, "You're saying the killer is..." He shook his head. "This is dangerous, Sam."

"Yeah, it's Austin Strong. And with all his high-tech capabilities, there's a good chance he knows we know."

30

MONDAY

ONCE AGAIN, WE WERE IN PRECIOUS'S SUV, HEADED NORTH UP Interstate 5 toward Toutle and Mount Saint Helens and the address Fuller had given us. We'd called Precious and told her we'd fill her in on the drive up.

Toby was in the back, typing away on his laptop. Lady M was hanging out back at my apartment with Lockett, who was doing damage control on the video. AJ was trying to reach Roman Castillo to ask him about the envelope. We had to assume he hadn't seen it yet because nothing was in the media.

Toby said, "Honestly, this property owner's identification is buried deep. Whoever handled this did an amazing job. I still haven't linked it to McVay."

My phone rang—AJ.

"You're on speaker," I said.

AJ cleared his throat. "Castillo says he hasn't seen it. He says any mail that comes to him at the training facility is bundled up and sent to his manager to sort through. Castillo's going to find out if there's anything on-site. If not, he said he would fly to his manager, who lives in Texas, by the way, and go through the mail personally. He said he would call us as soon as he found the envelope. I told him I'd call once you all found out what was at this cabin and in the envelope there."

We disconnected.

Precious said, "Okay, fill me in on everything. On the phone, you said we know who did it, and we're going to get proof."

I said, "It's Austin Strong." From there, I launched into the story and how I'd put the pieces together.

She glanced at me, stricken, her face going pale. "Oh no." She continued to look back and forth from me to the road.

"What?" I asked.

"Are you sure?"

I nodded. "Pretty much. It lines up."

Toby said, "Yeah, and now I can't make anyone else fit. It's Strong."

Precious stared straight ahead. "Oh no," she whispered.

"Precious," I said, "what's going on? You're acting weird."

Large tears coursed down her face, and I leaned toward her, afraid she might pass out or something and lose control of the car. She was not acting like herself.

"What's going on?" I asked.

"I'm sorry," she said. "So sorry." She shook her head and started those calming yoga breaths she always forced me to do.

"What are you talking about?" Toby asked.

I held my breath and waited for her to answer.

In a rush of words, she said, "Austin knows we're here."

"What?" Toby and I exclaimed in unison.

He nearly came from the back seat into my lap, his body between me and Precious.

She swiped away the tears. "Well, not *here* here, but that we're driving out to Saint Helens to look for a cabin that belonged to McVay."

My mind raced with a million questions. "When did you tell him what we were doing?"

Toby cried, "*Why* did you tell him what we were doing?"

She began to shake. "He asked me out for today, and I told him I couldn't because we were driving out to Saint Helens to look for McVay's cabin."

I knew she added the repeat because she knew I liked sequential information.

"What time?" I asked.

"While I was waiting for you two to get into the car. Outside your apartment."

I glanced at my watch and did the calculations in my head. We were about forty minutes away from the cabin. Given that, I figured Strong had done one of two things: either he or a henchman was planted somewhere, waiting for us to lead them to the cabin, or he'd found the info and could very well beat us there. I realized we might be walking into a bad situation.

I texted Lockett that Strong knew. Then I texted Leo, telling him to talk to Lockett ASAP.

"Pull over. I'm going to drive," I said.

Once we were back on the road, I put the pedal to the metal and raced toward the cabin.

Toby interrupted our silence. "You know, I feel like an idiot."

Precious, who had found her composure, blew her nose then asked, "How so? And for what it's worth, I feel like the biggest idiot. I was wooed by the prospect of having Austin Strong as a client so much that I set aside my normal checks and balances and opened myself up for manipulation."

Toby patted her on the shoulder. "Half my time is spent hanging out in dark web communities. No one there is being real, man. It's all smoke and mirrors. This whole case has been smoke and mirrors. But that's not what gets me. It's the tech. Tech's my jam, and still... Tech has been all over this. Those videos you got of your family, the videos of AJ, McVay's escape room. Tech."

"We can continue to beat ourselves up, but the point is we're here now," I said. "We got here. And Paulie Bea made a good point the other day. He said all the people on my suspect list have money. And money can buy all sorts of things. Like tech. So just because tech was all over this didn't automatically implicate Strong."

Toby sighed. "Easy to say. Hard to live with."

I said, "High tech, not amateur stuff—that's all for hire on the dark web, right?"

He nodded. "And hard to trace. I can only do so much."

I smiled. "And you're not willing to go to the dark side, right? So why are you expecting to have figured this out?" I punched Precious in the shoulder. "And you... Anyone in your position would have done exactly what you did. Austin Strong is a sociopath, a narcissist that uses people and discards them. We have to stop looking back. We can't change that. But we still have a lot ahead of us."

Precious smiled. "You're right. And that was well said."

Toby was clicking on his computer in the back. "I've been all around online, and there's little talk about McVay. No chatter about anyone claiming that they made those videos of AJ. Nothing more than what we know."

After an agonizing crawl at thirty miles per hour through Toutle, we resumed speeding through the winding roads of the Gifford Pinchot National Forest. Eventually, we turned onto a well-worn blacktop road off the main highway.

Toby pressed his face to the window as we drove through the woods where a handful of homes were nestled. "At least it's not the only cabin out here. I've seen two others since we turned down this road."

"Must be more than we think, because we just passed a community mailbox," Precious said.

I looked in the rearview mirror, and sure enough, a large metal box was there with eight individual locked boxes. "I wonder if there are already eight or if that's extra for future builds or something. And I wonder if our letter is in there."

Toby asked, "Should we go back and pick the lock?"

I shook my head. "I'd rather not commit a felony if I don't have to. I'm not sure which box, if any, is McVay's, and I'd have to pick all of them. Let's do a quick look through the cabin for a key. And make sure there's no box there."

Precious pointed at the tip of a driveway, the rest occluded by trees. "I think this is it."

I was making to turn onto the gravel road when Precious put out a hand, grabbing the steering wheel.

"Stop!" she cried.

I paused, not turning onto the drive, and Toby and I looked at her questioningly.

I asked, "Is something wrong?"

Precious faced us. "Remember when we went to the Olympics because you had a bad feeling?"

I nodded.

She swept her hand in front of the windshield. "Well, here we are, and now I have a bad feeling."

"Look, we aren't here for long. We're going to look for the mailbox, grab the envelope, and get out. But just in case, remember—"

"Don't eat red berries," Toby said.

I pointed at him. "Yeah, what he said. Honestly, though, I think your bad feeling might be because we've been so upset on the drive up. I've been watching. No car has followed us. I don't see any signs that anyone is around. I think we're okay."

Precious nodded. "Okay, but just remember that I said I had a bad feeling and you dismissed me."

Toby chuckled in the back.

"Whatever," I said. "We gonna sit here all day or go find this mystery package?"

Precious laughed and pointed up the driveway. I gunned her SUV, jerking the wheel to turn us onto the drive. We broke through the trees, and nestled in a flat field, with a backdrop of the foothills of Mount Saint Helens, was a small square cabin that looked like it'd been built centuries before. A wrap porch with rocking chairs skirted the small home.

Toby put his window down. "Not looking like the home of a millionaire."

Precious said, "I kinda like that he didn't build a mini fake mountain mansion out here."

I pointed at a helicopter to our south. "No matter where a person goes, they can't escape the modern world, sadly."

Precious shook her head. "When we go deep into the woods looking for Bigfoot, it's always a shock to hear a helicopter. Kinda ruins the experience."

I nodded in agreement and parked the SUV in front of the cabin. Hopping out of the car, I slung my backpack over my shoulder after taking out my lock-picking kit.

Toby said, "I'll wait here."

Precious had caught up with me, and we both turned toward him.

Surprised that he would come all this way without getting out of the car, I said, "Okay. But maybe do a walk-around, and see if there are any cameras and if they have a company name." We'd determined that McVay's Lake Oswego home was using Strong's security. In hindsight, that was another clue. In the moment, it had made sense.

Toby nodded. "Then I'm right back in this SUV."

"Fine," I said.

Precious looked toward the woods. "If you think you hear Bigfoot, let me know."

Toby also looked to the woods and paled. "Dang it, Precious. You got in my head earlier with your bad feeling about being here, and now I'm freaked out." He rubbed the area where Lady M typically hung in her pouch. He caught himself and smacked his own forehead. "And now I'm stroking myself. No emotional-support animal. No vaping because of that stupid lung disease they haven't solved yet, and no Doritos. Can you blame a guy for being edgy?"

We shook our heads. "Nope," we said in unison.

I said, "I'll leave the door open. Call if you need anything."

He nodded. "I'll need your stun gun if you want me to walk around this joint." He held out his palm.

I took my stun gun from my backpack and handed it over.

Precious and I went to the door, where a simple lock awaited.

"I think I can take this." I opened my picking kit.

Precious reached above the door to the lip of the jamb and felt around. "No key here. Try under the mat?"

I flipped over the well-worn welcome mat to find nothing but dirt and a few stink bugs. Next to the door was a flowerpot, and underneath that was nothing more.

I knelt before the lock. "I don't think we're that lucky, to have the key waiting for us. I stuck a lock-picking tool into the keyhole, but before I could begin, the lock clicked, and the door handle turned. Precious grabbed my shoulder as I shuffled backward hurriedly.

The door whipped open, and I fell back on my butt as Precious let out a high-pitched scream.

Toby, standing on the other side of the door, let out a matching scream.

I jumped up. "Stop!"

Instantly, they both stopped screaming. Precious was clutching her chest, Toby pressing the heels of his hands to his temples.

"Jeez, you scared me," he said.

Precious retorted, "We scared you? How did you get inside the cabin?"

Toby pointed behind himself. "I used the key I found under the mat at the back door."

Precious snort laughed and punched me in the shoulder. We'd had the right idea but the wrong door.

Taking my lock pick out of the keyhole, I told Precious, sotto voce, "And here I thought he was too scared and was going to rush back to the car."

"He's a constant source of happy surprises."

Toby said, "I'd be offended if she hadn't just complimented me. And yes, there are four cameras around the house. But they aren't run through the internet. Old-school wired to monitors with a clang-clang-clang alarm. I gotta give him props. No one can hack that."

"He was very paranoid, so I'm not surprised," I said.

Precious and I stepped into the house, and I closed the door behind us.

The cabin had a large front window that let in light, but the copse of trees limited it to bands of sunlight. I clicked the lights on.

"Look for a mailbox key," I told my friends. "I'm guessing he did have one of the boxes back at that community mailbox we passed. We find the key and get the *h-e*-double-hockey-sticks out of here."

The cabin was furnished with comfortable overstuffed leather furniture with blue-and-white-plaid throw blankets over the backs. Though the floors were wood, thick braided rugs softened the rooms. Photos of McVay in various stages of growing up, with who I assumed were his parents and grandparents, lined the fireplace and walls—catching a large fish, camping, in his Pop Warner uniform with Chet Fuller on the side, and in his uniform at Stanford while holding a championship trophy.

That was where McVay had lived. I was getting a sense of who he was as a person, of the person AJ told me he was.

"This place makes me sad," Precious said.

"Me too," I replied.

I moved into the kitchen. Because the cabin was older, the floor plan wasn't an open concept. The kitchen was square and had been updated with an island seating two in the middle, and off the end was a mudroom and the door Toby had come through. Fishing poles were resting in a corner. Back in the kitchen, a plate and a mug rested in a drying rack. On impulse, I opened the cabinets. Inside each was an assortment of mismatched dishes—until I reached the last cabinet. There sat two rows of monitors. I flicked them on, and images of the area surrounding the house came into view.

"This is the McVay I've come to know," I mumbled. *Paranoid.* However, I noticed his two residences were diametrically different. One was modern with state-of-the-art tech and an escape room. The cabin, though, was the absence of state-of-the-art. In fact, the only tech in the cabin was the TV and the monitors, which were essentially TVs. Paranoia didn't live here.

Tucked into the corner next to a monitor, hanging from its side, were two keys and a tag with the number seven on it.

"Found it," I said.

We quickly closed up the house and drove to the mailbox. Inside the mailbox was one plain white envelope. I tugged it out, held it up, and took a picture with my phone, wanting to make sure I documented what I could. Both the address and return address were the cabin's, just like Mrs. Fuller had said.

Inside the SUV, I opened the package and took out a letter. From between the folds, four Polaroids fell out: an aerial shot of a tropical island, a close-up of three kitchen cabinet doors, and two of house numbers. One of those showed black iron numbers reading 139, and the other, in silver, read 720.

31

MONDAY

I UNFOLDED THE LETTER AND HANDED IT TO PRECIOUS.
She cleared her throat and read:

Austin,

Enough is enough. You don't own me. Contrary to what you said.

And I no longer owe you. What we did in college is done. There is no going back. But there is going forward, and I am in control of what I do in my future. Not you.

If you're reading this, I'm dead, and I know it was at your hand. You greedy, maniacal son of a bitch.

You laughed when I said I wanted out. You laughed when I said I had proof of all the evil misdeeds you'd done. You said I was dumb and could never outsmart you.

Who's laughing now? I may be dead, but you're scared, and even from the grave, I'm going to bring you down. I was in possession of proof that shows how you set up Kami Bartell and all those other women at those colleges with your spyware just so you could launch your own anti-virus software and make millions of dollars from it. I have video proof of you threatening me to throw the game so you could win large on a bet. And I have proof that the guy driving the armored car that hit me that night after leaving the training facility was hired by you. I hired a hacker to find the paper trail. You're not the only one with computer skills or money, and it only took one of those to get what I wanted.

So let's play one final game, Austin. A Hail Mary, if you will. Here are the clues to where I hid all the proof. Good luck finding it. Hope you're smart enough.

You aren't the only one with this information. The clock is ticking. Go.

I tapped the envelope against the center console, thinking out loud. "This was supposed to go to the Lake Oswego house so that Strong would get it. McVay knew Strong was watching everything. But it didn't. Fuller's wife sent it here."

"Austin doesn't know anything about these clues," Precious said. "He knows McVay had evidence. He just doesn't know what or where."

"Well, he kinda has an idea where to start looking," Toby said quietly.

Precious looked at us again. "I'm so sorry."

I put up a hand. "None of that matters now. We have the clues. Strong doesn't." I pointed at the pictures. "I think this was a way to draw Strong's attention off of anybody else who might have this information. That would give Roman time to put something into action."

Precious asked, "Do you think it's a wild-goose chase? Nothing on the other end?" She gestured at the pictures.

I shrugged. "Only one way to find out. Because if, by chance, there's another set of proof, and we get our hands on it, then this will help us bring Strong down too."

"We better get to figuring out these pictures, then," Toby said. "Because the sooner we get Strong off the streets, the better I'll feel."

"Me too," I mumbled.

"Me three," Precious said.

We laid the photos out in a row on the dashboard.

"Toby, get a picture of the photos and the letter. Can you store the images safely?"

He rolled his eyes and mumbled, "Can I store the image somewhere safely, she asks. Like I'm new at this or something." Using his phone, he took pics, moved his thumbs over the screen for a few seconds, then smiled at me. "A better question would have been 'Do you have enough bars to send data out?'"

I gave him a thumbs-up. "Thanks." I pointed at the island picture. "Any ideas where that is?"

No one had any.

"How do we narrow down where these houses are?" Precious asked.

I shook my head. "They're too random, these pictures. I don't think we're supposed to look at them in context. Like, this is an island. Maybe that's the street name for one of these house numbers."

Precious held up a house-number photo and the kitchen photo. "So this could be 720 Kitchen Road?"

Toby whipped out his laptop and, using his hotspot, began searching. Soon, he said, "There's Kitchen Drive,

Lane, and Road, in multiples. We have about six of them that meet this criterion in this county alone. No telling how many are up and down the state."

"How about Oregon?" I asked.

"Or Minnesota," Precious added.

I shook my head again. "That's too many options. A wild-goose chase. He mailed this to Strong. He knew he could run a program to narrow down all the houses that meet the criteria of house number and Kitchen or Island being in the street name. McVay knew it would take time, and that's what I think he wanted. Time for Roman."

Precious gave me a puzzled look. "Why not mail what-ever proof he had to someone in media, someone like your dad?"

"Overly paranoid? I dunno." I thought about what Paulie Bea had said, that people with money have more options when committing a crime. "I think McVay knew Strong has endless cash flow and can do whatever he wants. So mailing this to someone like my dad only puts that person in the crosshairs. Mailing it to someone like Roman with more funds and a desire for revenge opens up opportunity."

I spread the photos out in a different order and studied them. Then I shuffled them again and tried to read them instead of seeing them. Reading photos was far easier than reading books—that was for sure.

I gasped and read the pictures again. "I think I have it. Go back to the cabin."

Looking at my friends, I held up two photos. "Kitchen and island. I think this might be the combination. Kitchen island. And these look like the cabinets in the cabin, don't they? Maybe there's a clue hidden at the cabin's kitchen island. Which, when McVay had this mailed, Strong knew nothing about the cabin. He would've had to find the property first."

Toby snickered. "And good luck with that. It's buried. Not being able to figure this out would have driven Strong insane."

Precious clapped with excitement then threw the SUV into drive and spun us around, kicking up pebbles and dirt. She took the turn into the driveway at a speedy clip, spraying even more dirt in her wake. I was out of the SUV before she had it in park. I ran around to the back and used the key Toby had found earlier, which we'd replaced. Precious and Toby followed.

In the kitchen, I studied the island. It looked like any other. One side was the sitting area. The other side had two cabinets for pans. I opened the cabinet doors and tried to see beyond the pans. Nothing looked out of sorts. I saw no false side or bottom or any lever to open a secret passage.

I wondered if I'd misread the photos. Not yet willing to give up on my interpretation, I felt around all the edges again and pushed on the panels. Toby and Precious stood back and watched.

"Maybe the pans need to come out?" Precious suggested.

I removed all the pans and felt around the shelves— nothing. I sat back on my haunches, the pans at my side, and stared into the cabinet. "I don't get it. Am I being too obtuse? Is the answer right in front of me but I'm looking too hard?"

"Maybe we're wrong," Precious said.

"Maybe." I reached to my side to put the pans back into the cabinet but lost my balance and had to catch myself by thrusting out a hand, only to knock over some of the cookware, the lids tumbling off with a loud clatter of clashing steel.

I scooped them up and thrust them into the cabinet. The last one, a large pot for cooking spaghetti or soup, lay on its side. The lid was still attached, but no clamps were keeping it in place. The lid, steel with a round black handle the size of an egg, looked like all the other lids in McVay's cabinet. Nothing about that pot and its lid stood out except the fact that it hadn't come off. Leftover food residue and a poor cleaning could have caused that.

I plopped onto my backside and grabbed the pot, tugging at the lid to take it off. It didn't move. I shook the whole thing, but nothing rattled inside. I ran my hand over the lid and its edge, looking for a latch of some sort. Nothing.

"Twist the handle." Toby squatted beside me.

I did, and it came away revealing a keyhole.

Toby sighed. "And who knows where that key is?"

I leaned back to pull the mailbox key from my front pocket. Two were hanging from the ring, but I hadn't given much thought to the fact that they weren't a set—until now.

I inserted the key, and the lid popped up. I pushed it aside, and the three of us peered inside to see a keypad between two round knobs, like drawer pulls.

I grabbed each in one hand and tugged. Nothing.

"You didn't think it would be that easy, did you?" Precious asked.

I shrugged. "It's always worth a try." I looked up at my friends. "Seven twenty was the number in one of the photos, right?"

Precious, who was holding the photos, checked and nodded. I typed it into the keypad, and... nothing. I typed in the other number. Nothing again. I typed in all the house numbers starting with the seven twenty, making the combination six digits. Nothing. I reversed the order, starting with one hundred thirty-nine then seven hundred twenty. I was awarded a green light and a clicking sound, like something had released. I grabbed the knobs and tugged, and the entire faceplate, keypad and all, lifted right out of the pot. I set it aside and realized the faceplate acted like a safe door. The faceplate was smaller in diameter than the pot and, therefore, when engaged, would deploy small bolts into the sides of the pot to lock it in place.

Inside the pot, under the faceplate, were a CD, a thumb drive, and a note.

I showed the contents to Toby and Precious. Each of them gave me a questioning and worried look.

The note read:

Congratulations, Austin. Now you have all of what I have. You win.

Or do you?

I said, "I'll call Leo. Precious, you call Lockett."

Precious moved away to make the call, but I stayed still, looking into the pot.

"Sam?" Toby asked.

Precious turned back toward us.

As I looked up at my friends, a shiver of fear ran down my spine. We were in possession of proof, evidence Austin Strong would kill for—literally. I sucked in a deep breath and blew it out slowly, trying to steady my nerves.

Then I said, "Game on, friends. Strong is coming for this."

32

MONDAY

PRECIOUS RUBBED HER HANDS UP AND DOWN HER ARMS. "You're freaking me out."

Toby stood. "Me too."

I reached into the pot and pulled out the thumb drive. "Your computer doesn't have a CD drive, right?"

He shook his head. "Most don't these days."

I waved the thumb drive at him. "You don't have to watch —not knowing what's on this could be beneficial—but I need to watch it ASAP. I need to know if what's on this is the real deal or just another way to stall Strong."

"What if it's the real stuff?" Toby asked.

"Worst-case scenario is he makes sure we don't live to tell anyone what we know."

Precious asked, "And best case?"

I shrugged, unsure. I'd never been in that situation. "We'll probably always be looking over our shoulders. Just because he'd be in prison wouldn't mean he couldn't harm us."

That was where Strong's endless dollars came into play,

giving him an advantage over us, the likes of which I would never know.

Toby stroked his chest again until he realized what he was doing. He slapped himself on the chest, sighed, and dug into his shirt to pull out his vape pen then put it to his lips. "Stupid empty vial," he mumbled. Then with shaky hands, he put the drive on the counter then rummaged through his messenger bag. Seconds later, he pulled out a vial and waved it in our direction. "I'm going to vape this, and neither of you can stop me."

I pulled myself up from the floor with one hand grabbing the counter and one hand holding the pot. "Toby, you know they still haven't figured out what's causing that vaping lung disease."

He shook his head. "I don't care. I'm going to have this..." He looked at the label and laughed bitterly. "Oh, that's perf. This flavor is called Bad Apple. Ominous, right? Now I'm freaking freaked out."

I studied the CD, debating what to do with it. *Leave it or take it?* Still unsure, I tossed it back in the pot.

"Okay!" Precious clasped her hands together with a resounding clap. "We have to get control. Toby, there's no reason to freak out." She bent forward while performing deep, calming yoga breaths. "No one freak out. I think I'm freaking out."

I was unnerved too. And that bad gut feeling I'd had a few weeks before was back. Knowing I could be holding evidence of someone's crimes was scary and humbling and, frankly, was giving me a power surge. Right then, all the cards were in my hand, but my foe would stop at nothing to change those dynamics. I opened the cabinet with the monitors and watched each of the screens of the outdoors, looking for signs that Strong was upon us. Everything outside looked quiet.

I had a better understanding of McVay's paranoia.

Toby got his pen loaded and blew out an apple-scented smoke plume.

"Ah," he said. "Starts out tart and ends up sweet." He closed his eyes and inhaled again.

I went to Toby and reached for his messenger bag. "I'm going to take out your laptop," I told him.

He slapped my hand away. "I got it." He pulled out the laptop and flipped it open. I handed him the thumb drive.

I glanced back at Precious, who was still bent over.

I glanced back at the screens. No change—yet the overwhelming sensation of claustrophobia ran over me from head to toe. The air felt thick, and the walls seemed like they were moving inward.

I glanced back at the screens. "I think we need to get out of here. Get in the SUV and get on the road. The sooner we get this to Lockett and Leo, the better off we are." Beads of sweat broke out on my forehead. "In here, we're sitting ducks."

Precious nodded in agreement.

Toby slammed his laptop closed and said, "I don't need further convincing."

We moved with lightning speed. I didn't bother to replace the key under the mat, instead sticking it in my front pocket. I hung the mailbox key back up by the monitors then shut them off. After that, I replaced the lid on the pot. My hope was that both the drive and the CD had the same information. And if, by chance, Strong found the clues and came there, something would be waiting for him. Maybe having the CD would make him think he'd won.

We rushed to the car. Inside, I told Toby to send Lockett and Leo a message that we would soon be uploading potential evidence against Strong to my cloud. Lockett would be able to access it from my laptop.

I peeled out of the drive and onto the road, kicking up a shower of rocks and dirt. "Don't skip the seat,belts, gang. It's pedal to the metal."

Clicking his seat belt in place, Toby said, "There are seven files. Three are videos. Four are documents. One of the videos is labeled Watch Me First."

I scanned the road ahead and behind on a steady rotation as if my head was on a swivel, waiting for something to come at us from any angle. "Play it," I said while catching sight of that helicopter in the distance far behind us. A forestry helicopter wasn't unusual in those parts, and if needed, we could try to flag it down to help us. But I didn't want to think about what would have to happen to make me resort to that unlikely assistance. But I was a girl who liked having options, and that helicopter represented an option.

From behind me, where Toby was sitting, came McVay's voice.

"My name is Keith McVay, and if you're watching this video and I've died under circumstances other than old age or cancer, then that means Austin Strong killed me. Maybe not by his own hand, but he definitely had something to do with it. Let me explain. Included with this video are several documents and two MP4 files that will substantiate my claim."

My phone rang. "It's Leo."

Toby paused the video while I answered, putting my phone on speaker.

"You're on speaker, Leo. Did you get my text?"

"Yes, Sam. Where are you?"

I glanced around, seeing nothing but trees and narrow roads. The GPS on the display in Precious's SUV gave more information. "We're about half a mile from Spirit Lake Highway. That would put us two hours from home."

Leo asked, "But where are you right now? If I had to come find you..."

I explained how we were leaving the cabin. Saint Helens was on our left, to the east, and the town of Toutle was to our right, the west.

Leo said, "No one can find Strong. Either he's truly not in his office, or he's playing a game of hide-and-seek with us. I'm driving your way. You'll reach Toutle before me. When you get there, call me, and give me an update of your location."

Toutle was the town between us and the interstate home.

"Okay, Leo," I said.

A flicker of something dark to my right caught my eye.

Precious screamed, "Sam, watch out!"

A second later, we were T-boned by a large dark truck, its front end colliding with our middle pillar.

The impact forced my phone to fly across the car toward Precious. My head whipped in the same direction, only to be shoved back into the driver's-side window as the curtain airbags deployed. Glass shattered around me. The force of the steering-wheel bag felt like someone had slapped me directly in the face, stunning me. The seat belt cut across my body, squeezing breath from me as it held me in place, fighting against the momentum that wanted to send me out the window. The crunch of metal bending, glass cascading to the ground, and an engine revving with a loud whine while my teeth knocked together filled the space, bringing disorientation. No sooner had the airbags appeared then they deflated, and I swiped at them to get them out of the way.

Precious's SUV skidded sideways on the road, the tires squealing in protest. We met resistance when the SUV came off the road and was pushed into a line of trees, the edge of the forest.

The truck that had hit us revved its engine higher, pushing more force into our SUV.

I shook my head and tried to get my bearings. Metal creaked as it buckled, giving in to the force of the truck.

Precious groaned.

Toby suddenly appeared between the front seats.

"Hey," he said, shaking my shoulder then moving to push away the deflated airbag. "We have to get out of here." He shifted toward Precious. "Precious. Talk to me."

My senses came back to me in a rush of fear powered by adrenaline, a sensation so strong that it left me breathless for a second before flooding me with a million commands. I released my seat belt and faced my friends.

Where the truck was pushing against our vehicle, the SUV was buckling inward toward us, inch by inch. The truck was acting like a trash compactor.

"Toby, your computer?"

"Crazy, right? But it's okay. So is the thumb drive." Blood was trickling from his temple down the side of his face.

He touched the spot tenderly. "I'm okay." He pointed at me. "You got your own."

Like him, my left temple and forehead had taken the brunt of the impact against the window, and I'd been cut. Blood ran in a warm path down the side of my face, those two areas throbbing.

"Precious," I asked, "are you okay?"

Her SUV creaked again and gave up a few more inches.

She looked at me, dazed. Her nose had taken the brunt of her airbag and was bleeding. She was pale and her eyes wide, pupils dilated. "I think I might be sick."

I released her seat belt and brushed hair from her forehead, where it was sticking to several small cuts she'd received across her face. "Hang in there. Deep breath. Visualize getting out of here alive. Toby's right—we need to get out of here, now. This guy is trying to crush us." I scanned the car for an exit.

Toby said, "We have to go out the window. The doors are pinned."

And going out the back cargo door would expose us to the madman in the truck.

I shifted, pulling my legs up so that I was squatting on the seat. "There's enough room, for now. But not much." The trees we were being pushed into would eventually block us. I took off my coat and laid it through my broken window, hoping it would block any remaining shards of glass. The deflated curtain airbags were useless as I lifted myself onto the window ledge. My muscles screamed in protest, my chest and neck burning where the seat belt had held tight.

I dropped to the ground and doubled over in pain, taking a moment to catch my breath, the sudden movement having made my head throb with blinding severity. The high revving of the truck's engine stopped suddenly, pulling my attention there. The truck reversed a few feet then stopped while the driver shifted.

"Hurry!" I held out my hands.

Precious took them, with Toby coaxing her from behind. With his help, we got her out the window seconds before the truck T-boned the SUV a second time. The impact threw Toby against the door and onto the floor, his eyes closed.

Toby!" I helped Precious to lean against a tree, where she lost her stomach as I went back for Toby.

The truck backed up a second time.

"Toby!" I rushed to the window to find him squatting on the driver's seat but reaching across the console to the floorboard, toward the truck and where the next impact would be. "Get out now!"

"I can't find Precious's purse." He handed me his messenger bag and my backpack, which I'd forgotten all about, then practically vaulted out the window, falling to the ground, and landing on his butt.

A moment later, the truck rammed the SUV, the force of which echoed the creaking and bending of steel throughout the forest.

I helped Toby up while simultaneously pulling him toward Precious. The truck's revving had ceased, and at any moment, the driver would be out of the vehicle and after us.

I grabbed Precious by the arm as Toby and I ran beside her and tugged her along while we sprinted toward the protection of the trees.

Unlike our hide-and-seek game at the Olympics a few weeks before, we had no trail to follow. We had to maneuver over thick brush, fallen branches, and large ferns that covered the land. All of that was creating an easy trail for whoever was in the truck.

I pushed them deep into the forest before pulling them behind a tree and signaling with my hand for us to stop.

I whispered, "We need to split up."

Peeking back in the direction we'd come from, I could

see no one. We were likely being stalked like prey, the hunter waiting for the right moment to strike.

I held out a hand to Toby. "Please tell me you have the thumb drive."

He nodded and dug through his messenger bag before finding the drive and putting it on my palm. "It never dislodged from my laptop."

Thank the heavens for small miracles. I handed the thumb drive to Precious. "Tuck this somewhere."

She put it in her bra, near her armpit.

"Get somewhere safe, and try to get that stuff on the cloud." I pointed at where she'd hid the thumb drive. "We need to separate. You two fan out but go in the same direction. You're going to need to reconnect to get the drive online. But Toby, if you get caught, I don't want you to have it on you. I don't want them to find anything on any of us. There are three of us and, I'm hoping, one of them. Let's fan out. Each of us should head toward the main road but stay out of sight. We can't trust any cars unless we know who's behind the wheel. Leo is on his way."

Toby shook his head. "I think we need to find a cabin to hide in."

Precious crouched low and hugged her knees. "I don't want to be out here alone."

A twig snapped behind us, sounding closer than expected. The hunter was upon us.

33

MONDAY

TOBY WHIMPERED. PRECIOUS'S EYES WENT LARGE AND ROUND. I patted my back pocket, searching for my stun gun. I looked at Toby and mouthed the words "stun gun."

He pulled it from his front pocket and handed it over. I pointed at each of them and then in the direction I thought Spirit Lake Highway was.

"Go," I mouthed. "Run."

Toby looked at me with uncertainty. Precious shook her head. We were banged up, scared, and panicking. I was rattled from being hit by the truck. But we didn't have the luxury of processing our shock normally. We were out of time.

The *whop-whop* of that helicopter drew near, and hope sparked. I would need to get into a clearing to get their attention. I peered between the trees, trying to catch sight of the helicopter to gauge its direction. A second later, it flew directly overhead in the direction of the crash. I couldn't make out who the chopper belonged to. *Forestry? Wildlife?*

Then it made a banking turn, and the text on the side of the helicopter was clear: Strong Protection and Software.

My heart dropped as hope was snuffed out. No rescue was coming. The only positive aspect of that helicopter was the cacophony of noise from the blades. Maybe they would draw the attention of locals or police as well as giving cover for any noise we might make. I grabbed my friends, signaling we should move deeper into the woods, using the sound to cloak our movement.

They followed me as we crept along, picking our way slowly to limit any chance of drawing attention, though I was desperate to break into a full-on run. We stopped every five minutes to listen. The helicopter continued to circle the area of the accident. I waited until we were close to Spirit Lake Road but still under the cover of the trees before I pitched my idea again.

"We need to separate. If we get caught together, then Strong has the evidence and all of us. One of us has to get away."

Toby leaned against a tree and sighed. "I don't like it, but you make sense."

I pounced. "Here's what I think. One of you stays on this side of the road. One of you goes across. Use the road to guide you out of here. But stay under the trees so you can't be seen. Watch for Leo."

"Where will you go?" Precious asked.

I looked into the forest in the direction we'd just come. "I think I need to draw them in a different direction. Maybe confuse them. I don't know how many are on foot. I'm guessing two. I'm also guessing the helicopter has more, maybe even Strong himself. We're outmanned and outgunned. We need help. If I go back toward the cabins, then maybe I can find some help." I looked at Toby. "Do you have your cell phone?"

He pulled it from his front pocket. The screen was cracked, likely from being tossed around the back seat during the accident.

"No service." He showed me the lack of cellular bars.

I said, "Maybe a cabin will have a phone line."

"Strong will be searching all the cabins," Precious said.

I nodded. "Hopefully, I find one he's already searched. I don't like the idea of separating, but I think we need to do it."

We stood in silence for a few beats. Then Precious wrapped her arms around me and hugged me tightly. "Please be careful."

"You too."

We separated and wiped away the tears gathering in our eyes.

Toby offered me a fist bump. "Don't eat the red berries."

I smiled. "First chance you get, go through everything McVay gave us. And if you can, get online and destroy Strong. That's the only way we get out of this alive. Right now, his secret is still that, a secret. We need to expose him. We can't count on Roman finding his envelope anytime soon. Until then, I'm guessing Strong will do whatever it takes to keep his secret hidden. Including making us disappear."

Toby nodded and swallowed. His Adam's apple bobbed convulsively. "I got a few ideas on how to bring him down."

Precious held out her fist to him. "Rock, paper, scissors for who has to cross the road."

I offered Toby my stun gun, but he shook his head.

"Okay," I said. "Good luck."

"Good luck to you," Precious said.

"May the Force be with you," Toby said.

I gave them one final look then slipped back between the trees, cutting a diagonal toward what I hoped was McVay's cabin and the ones surrounding it.

Honestly, I wasn't sure about my plan. Maybe we shouldn't have separated. Maybe the helicopter had thermal imaging and could watch our red-outlined forms run through the woods.

What I did know was that Leo was on his way toward us, that we needed Toby to get online and expose Strong, and that time was against us in both of those cases.

So I was working with what I knew and guessing the rest, assuming the worst, of course. My goal was to give Leo and Toby time even if that meant I had to be a decoy, a sitting duck—the honeypot, if you will.

I came upon the road to McVay's sooner than expected and hung back in the tree line and ran perpendicular to it, putting the accident behind me.

From memory, I knew a cabin was coming up. We'd passed two before reaching McVay's drive. I could only hope to find people living in one of them or a phone line, at least. I didn't dare risk going back to Precious's SUV to look for my, or Precious's, cell phone.

Ahead, the trees were thinning, indicating the clearing around the first cabin. I slowed to a walk, pausing before leaving cover. I rested against a tree, pushing my hand into my cramping side. My head was throbbing. My nerves were shot, my hands were fisted, and no matter how hard I tried to take deep, steady breaths, my body quivered from fear combined with the adrenaline of surviving a collision. If I lived through everything, I was going to eat all my favorite foods and sleep for two days.

The "cabin" before me was a trailer on a concrete slab, likely used for hunting and little more. No electrical or phone lines were evident, but maybe they were underground. I crouched low and looked for movement. Had the sky not been overcast and gray, I could've looked for shadows—just one more way the day was working against me.

I picked up a rock and chucked it across the yard, pinging it off a corner of the trailer then waited for someone to come check it out.

Nothing.

I did it again.

Nothing.

I sucked in a deep breath and slowly stood straight, my muscles screaming in protest as they stretched. I counted to three then sprinted across the yard when I got to four because fear was making me stall. I kept my head low, tucked between my raised shoulders and made it to the back door without getting shot, tackled, or harmed bodily in any other way.

I jiggled the handle and found the door locked. Dropping to one knee, I tugged off my backpack. From inside, I dug out my lock-picking kit. The lock was the standard, like the one on my bedroom door, which I'd practiced on. I had it open before I could count to ten.

After stepping inside the dark trailer, I eased the door closed. The smell of closed-up musty house greeted me. I took out a penlight and cast it around. Inside was a small one-counter kitchen with a two-burner stove, a small round wooden table, and two chairs, and the living room furnished with a sofa and love seat likely bought in the seventies.

I stuck my nose against my shoulder for a breath of different, albeit not much better, air.

Next, I searched the place for some way to communicate —a ham radio, walkie-talkies, or something. Anything. But I came up empty.

I cleaned the blood off my temple and splashed water on my face then dried it with the underside of my shirt.

Then I walked the perimeter of the trailer, looking out all the windows for signs of activity. When I thought the coast was clear, I exited the way I'd entered, leaving the door unlocked behind me. That trailer could be a place to hide if I needed it, and I didn't want to risk the time it would take to pick the lock if I was running from someone.

I dashed back into the woods and ran a zigzag in case anyone was following me.

Minutes later, I came to the second clearing and paused at the edge of the trees, again looking for activity. I tossed three rocks that produced no inquisitors. That cabin offered promise. The place was a home, more like McVay's. Larger than the trailer, it looked more like a getaway home than a hunting cabin. On a small concrete slab outside the back door was a covered grill. An awning offered the small space protection from the elements. Someone regularly took care of the place.

Three solid wood chairs were stacked against the house, and flower boxes decorated the windows but sat empty. Hope plummeted with my realization that the cabin appeared to have been winterized.

However, I wasn't giving up. I could only hope the owners had a landline.

I sprinted to the back door as I'd done at the trailer and knelt down to inspect the lock. The door had two. One was a dead bolt. *This will take some time.* I tried to look in the window of the back door, to search for a phone, but the curtains were all drawn. From my viewpoint, the curtains appeared to be closed on all the windows.

The snap of a twig in the direction I'd just come from startled me, and I fell back on my bottom, my head swiveling in that direction. I couldn't make anything out, but I wasn't going to wait around to see who or what had made the sound. I grabbed my bag and ran into the woods opposite the sound.

I had just exited the clearing and was reaching cover among the trees when I ran smack into Austin Strong.

34

MONDAY

STRONG GRABBED ME BY THE THROAT AND SHOVED ME AGAINST a tree, my backpack saving me from any bark digging into my back.

Instinctively, I grabbed at his hands, fighting to pull them away, which only encouraged Strong to tighten his grip.

I was able to take in small pockets of air, enough to keep me conscious and give me the ability to talk, albeit strained. But any more pressure on his part meant no air on mine.

"You're quite the troublemaker, Samantha True. Lucky for such a stupid person."

I held his wrist while he held my throat. "I'm not stupid," I whispered.

He laughed maniacally. "Are you so sure about that?"

Something from my pack jabbed me hard in the lower back, and my brain shifted to wondering what it was. *My stun gun? No, that's in my front pocket.*

In my front pocket.

In a second, I had a plan. I stepped into Strong's choke

hold, moving my body closer and hoping he wouldn't notice my other hand reaching into my pocket.

I said, "I'm going to bring you down."

He snarled. "I'd like to see you try it."

I slid my hand into my pocket, pulled the stun gun out, and flipped it in my hand, my thumb searching for the switch. I didn't care where the gun made contact as long as it took him out.

His snarl became more prominent. "See what I mean about stupid?" His gaze flicked over my shoulder.

While I was bringing up the stun gun, hoping to make contact with Strong's body, the awareness that we weren't alone was my last thought as blinding pain crashed through the back of my head. Then darkness claimed me.

I came to in McVay's cabin. Flat on my back, I looked around slowly because my head was throbbing, and quick movements made me nauseous. One hand was flex-cuffed to the leg of the stove, a steel appliance more than four times my body weight.

I closed my eyes and steadied my breathing, holding back panic by using slow, steady yoga breathing.

Heavy footsteps sounded across the floor, the vibrations in the floor rumbling through my inert body as they approached me.

Someone with a deep voice said, "She's still out, boss."

Strong asked, "How hard did you hit her?" He chuckled as his voice came closer.

I felt him stand over me. I recalled being a kid, scared in my bed, imagining someone or something evil standing over

me, ready to do me harm. Just thinking about that helpless-
ness would suck the breath from me.

But I was actually having that experience in real life, and
the fear was far worse than I'd imagined.

Strong kicked my foot. "Wake up, stupid."

Do I feign coming to? Or do I give up the ruse?

I figured pretense was pointless. I opened my eyes and
blinked a few times because my vision was still blurry. "Call
me stupid again, and you'll regret it."

He lifted his lip in disgust. "Gonna haunt me from the
grave? Because your time for vengeance is over, sweetheart."

Strong, dressed in jeans and a sweater, looked every bit
the average man with money. Behind him stood one of his
goons, whose muscles bulged as he crossed his arms. He was
dark and lethal looking, the stereotype of a movie bad guy,
only uglier with a pockmarked face, crooked nose, and
receding hairline.

I curled up on my side, hoping it hid my fear. "I'm not
dead yet."

Strong held up the photos of the island, the kitchen, and
the numbers. Then I realized my backpack was gone.

He waved the pictures. "Let's see how smart you are. Did
Samantha the private investigator put these clues together,
or could she not get them to add up? Lucky for you, Keith
didn't write the clues out. You'd have been stumped for
sure."

"I know how to read," I said.

He smiled an ugly grin, reminiscent of those who used to
tease me in elementary school. "But you couldn't always
read, could you."

"What's that have to do with this moment right now?
Nothing. So why bring it up? Because you're an asshole. But

we already knew that about you." I'd dealt with guys with personalities like Strong's all my life. I knew where his buttons were. "I'm sorry," I said.

"Sorry for messing everything up? Sorry because you're stupid? Why are you sorry?" He stuck his hands on his hips and leaned over me, glaring down.

"I'm sorry no one likes you. Not when you were a kid, and not now when you're a billionaire. I'm sorry that no matter what you've done, you have no real friends."

Strong's lips pressed into a thin line before he kicked me in the side.

I grunted while balling up into the fetal position, one arm extended toward the stove. Tears burned my eyes as bolts of pain shot across my ribs and stomach. I closed my eyes, forcing the tears back. They would only satisfy a lunatic like Strong.

"I have something better than friends. I have power. You think just because you have a group of freeloaders who hang out on your couch, eating takeout Italian food, you have friends?" He shook his head. "They'll turn on you like that." He snapped his fingers.

His reference to Italian food took me back to the night AJ was released. Strong had witnessed it. I wondered how. I'd discovered the bugs that morning and had cleaned out my house and car and removed the app from my phone. "How did you get that app on my phone?"

His smile was smug. He enjoyed getting one over on anyone. "You gave me your phone, remember? At the coffee shop."

Of course. Score one point for Strong.

"How did you get the videos of my family?"

He shrugged nonchalantly. "I own the cable company.

My installer upgraded your town and slipped in a few extra wires and cameras. You'd be amazed at what I see out there." He swung his arm wide to indicate the world outside the cabin.

From his back pocket, Strong took out several palm-sized square objects, the photos McVay had put in his letter. Strong slapped me in the face with them. "Look at these. Did you figure out what they meant?"

I shook my head. He already thought I wasn't clever enough to do my job, and I didn't want to convince him otherwise.

"I didn't think so," he said. "Let me tell you." He slapped one against my forehead. "This is a kitchen sign, and this one a picture of an island. Put those two together, dumb-dumb, and you have 'kitchen island.'"

I kept my eyes closed and said nothing.

Strong grabbed me by the hair. "Look at me."

I opened my eyes. Strong's face was close. Spittle had gathered in the corners of his mouth, and his pupils were dilated. I'd seen the look before. Nobody could reason with him.

He grabbed the front of my shirt and pulled me up, my handcuffed arm pulled back at an awkward angle.

"Sit up and watch my brilliance." He let go, and I scooted backward on my butt, adjusting to make myself as comfortable as possible, all things considered.

He tossed the photos onto the island and continued, "I have everything I want. I have enough money to buy a country, a nation of politicians, or whatever my heart wants. And I can destroy you and your friends, and no one will care."

He pointed at the island. "Clue number one." He then

pointed at his goon. "Tear this island apart. We're looking for a secret compartment."

I gave a silent thanks that Precious had the thumb drive, that I hadn't held on to it.

Goon Guy took a hatchet to the walls of the island, tearing away the outside, exposing nothing but the pots and pans inside. Once that was done, he stood back and waited for more instructions.

Strong surveyed the mess, hands on his hips, eyes squinted in fury.

I couldn't refrain. "What now, smart guy?"

He pointed a finger at me. "Shut up, or I'll kill you now."

"And have me miss out on your moment of glory? I doubt it." I met his glare with one of my own.

My courage was bolstered by the fact that Strong hadn't mentioned Toby or Precious. Not that he was hunting them. Not that he had caught them. Nothing.

He stalked toward me, hand raised to strike, but the whirling of helicopter blades made him pause. He glanced at his watch and then at Goon Guy.

"Tell him I need ten more minutes. Finish getting the cabin ready."

Goon Guy paused. "What about the clues?"

I almost smiled, not having expected Goon Guy to care about unsolved mysteries.

Strong pointed at Goon Guy. "Did you hear me? Do I pay you to stand around?"

Goon Guy shook his head. "No, boss." He averted his gaze then headed for the back door.

Strong picked up the hatchet, and bile rose up my throat. I could fight back in many situations, but getting hacked up was not one of them. I felt for the secret pocket pinned to my

jeans and thanked the heavens I'd tucked the small pocketknife there. It wouldn't be helpful against the hatchet, but
if Strong got close enough, I might be able to jab it somewhere awful.

The thought made me cringe.

Strong kicked a pan, sending it across the room. He
kicked another one, that time harder, and it bounced off the
wall and headed back toward us.

Strong faced me and smiled. The fake pot was between
us. He stepped back then took a running kick at the pot,
aiming it directly at me. I put an arm up to block it from
hitting me in the head.

Bam! The heavy pot slammed into my arm, and pain shot
up to my shoulder and down to my hand, leaving the latter
all tingly and numb. The pot bounced back, the lid still
intact. I glanced at it then Strong. He was staring at the pot.
He picked it up by the round lid handle, and I knew he knew.
I rested my injured arm against my waist, placing my hand
near my secret pocket. Attempting to slowly ease the pocketknife out would be difficult with the loss of feeling in my
hand.

Strong tossed back his head and laughed, a wicked, scary
sound that sent chills through my body. No wonder McVay
had gone to such extremes.

"You killed McVay because he was going to out you," I
said. "He was going to tell the world that you were the one
who had invented the spyware and put all those videos
online, and then you capitalized on it by creating protection
software."

Strong grabbed the photos of the house numbers from
the island and plugged them into the safe. He pulled off the

cover and looked inside. Then he pulled out the CD and pointed it at me.

"You see how stupid Keith was? He put his confession on a CD. Did you know these can rot? Keith was an imbecile when it came to tech."

"But he was a good quarterback."

Strong nodded. "All this started because he wanted to leave. What if we didn't win the Super Bowl this year? He knew winning one was on my bucket list and we were in the zone. We were headed for the opportunity."

"So why didn't you just pay him?"

Strong's eyes went wide. "Why did I have to? I owned him."

"And you held it over him to make him do whatever you said. But I'm guessing he grew tired of it. That's why he was willing to give everything up to get away from you. So what happened? He asked for big money. You said no because then you'd have to lose some other players due to the salary cap and he... what?"

"He tried to play with the big boys. Make no mistake— Keith was a good ballplayer. Talented. But he was a soldier. He took orders—orders from the coaches and from me. I warned him not to let his ego get the best of him, but it did. He wanted more money. And when I said no, he decided blackmailing me was the answer." Strong laughed derisively. "Stupid people surround me."

I said, "Only I don't think he did want money. I think he wanted away from you."

Strong shook his head. "But don't you see? I was never going to let Keith out of my sight. He knew too much. And once he was no longer worth anything to me, I would dispose of him like I do all my other problems."

"Except Kami Bartell. She's still around."

Strong stood. "Have you met Kami? She's afraid of her shadow. I just have to remind her to be afraid every so often. She'll crack soon enough and do herself in. Problem solved."

I met his gaze with my unwavering one. "So you snuck into McVay's house from the escape room door, a room you only just discovered that night when you saw him come out of it. And you knew then that McVay had kept this secret from you, so what else might be out there? You went in and were waiting for him when AJ dropped him off."

"I bet you didn't figure that out alone, did ya? But yeah, I was there when he came home. He wasn't surprised to see me. Said he knew I'd be coming. But he tried to play me for a fool. Changed his tune. Said he was gonna stay with the team and go all the way. Said he didn't have the proof, that I'd called his bluff."

"But you didn't believe him?" A paranoid guy like Strong wouldn't ever be able to trust another person.

"Nope. And he turned his back to me just once, and I put both of us out of our misery."

"You hit him with the dumbbell."

Strong made like he was dropping a mic. "Problem solved."

"And Brad Jenson? AJ? What roles had they played in this?"

Strong shook his head. "When you have a weakness, prepare for it to be exploited. That was Brad Jenson. He had gambling debts. I paid them off, and all he had to do was switch the medicine shot the doctor gave Keith with the one spiked with the PEDs. Your pal AJ was a convenient scape-goat—nothing more, nothing less."

I shook my head, confused. "It doesn't sound so smart to

tip your hand to someone I imagine you saw as insignificant as Jenson."

Strong rolled his eyes in annoyance. "I didn't deal with him. Lennie did." He gestured toward the outdoors, where Goon Guy had gone. "Then you started snooping around, and I couldn't take any chances, so Lennie took care of him."

"After you made an incriminating video regarding AJ. A fake confession."

Strong's brows wagged. "Of course. We live in a world of deep fakes. I went old school and didn't have to use artificial intelligence to modify the video. The confession is the fake." He tapped his temple. "Brilliant, really."

I smiled. "Only your guy Lennie forgot about his shadow, and it's visible, moving across the room. He also forgot to have Jenson start and stop the video. It's clear someone else is in the room." I gave him a serious face. "You really should get better editing equipment or fire the guy who did the editing. Even a dumb-dumb like me picked up on the errors on the first watch."

Strong's nostrils flared.

The back door flung open, and Lennie the goon stepped in. He said, "The other two jumped into the back of a truck and are headed toward town."

Strong's cheek twitched ever so slightly, then he looked back at me. "Goodbye, Samantha. I win. You lose." He turned to Lennie. "Burn her down."

Lennie waited for Strong to leave the room then approached me, but not before he picked up the hatchet. I tried to scoot away, curling into a ball to protect myself. He stepped over me, flicked on the gas stove without lighting it, then took a swing at the stove with the hatchet. The knob flew across the room, leaving no way to turn the gas off.

Lennie looked down at me and smirked. He feinted with the hatchet, and I flinched, which made him laugh.

He tossed the hatchet into the other room and moved to stand by the back door.

Then I noticed a stack of newspapers and magazines next to the counter. Lennie pulled a lighter from his pocket and flicked it. He dropped it onto the newspapers.

Then he stepped outside and closed the door.

35

MONDAY/TUESDAY

I'D BEEN WORKING ON TAKING THE LITTLE POCKETKNIFE FROM my secret pouch safety-pinned to my jeans when my situation escalated to critical in seconds.

One minute, Strong was standing over me calling me stupid, and now the counter by the back door was on fire, the room smelled of gas, and the countdown clock to an explosion was ticking loudly in my head.

That could also have been my racing heartbeat.

I fumbled to get the knife out as my hand throbbed, not working well. If my arm wasn't broken, it certainly was bruised, which was the root cause of my dexterity issue. Once the knife was free, I used my teeth to release the blade and sawed at the plastic cuff.

Burning the house down was smart. I would die in the explosion, and the plastic cuff would melt, leaving no proof that I'd been trapped.

I sawed with reckless abandon, not caring that the knife occasionally slipped and jabbed my wrist or cut across my skin instead of the cuff. I was a woman desperate to survive and didn't care about a few scratches and cuts. Stitches, I could live with... because I would be alive.

I shaved away at the plastic binding while begging the universe or a higher power for more time.

Tears ran down my face, mixed with sweat from the heat of the fire.

My parents would be so upset if I died. I wouldn't get to see Cora grow up or tease Rachel about her helicopter-mom tendencies. No more sharing beers and laughs with Leo on my balcony. No more Precious or Hue. If I survived, I might consider getting my own emotional-support animal.

Toby. I hoped he was destroying Strong on the internet. I hoped he knew how much of a friend he was to me.

I blew out a shaky breath. "Please, please, please," I begged. I needed more time, less fire, this plastic to give. I kept sawing. My wrist was wet with blood. The fire was climbing the outside wall and moving in my direction.

I bore down, and seconds later, the cuff snapped free.

I jumped to my feet, afraid of wasting a second, but my stomach roiled, and bile rose up my throat. The blow to the head had made me woozy and slightly disoriented. I put out a hand to steady myself against the fridge.

Run! my mind screamed. *Run!*

I forced myself to push through the pain in my head and the nausea in my stomach, and with my arms out in front of me, in case I crashed into something, I ran to the front door.

I flung it open and dashed outside. The cold air slapped me, instantly chilling me, and I found it refreshing and invigorating. The newfound energy spurred me forward, and I ran down the driveway toward the road. My head was throbbing with every footstep that slammed against the earth.

The cabin would explode at any moment, and I wanted to be as far away as possible. I was nearing the edge of the drive when it happened. The force of the explosion threw me forward, and my body rose from the earth and was briefly carried on a blast wave of heat, only to come down as quickly as I'd gone up. My body slammed across the ground, skipping like a rock across a lake.

My body screamed in pain, and starbursts exploded in my head, the pressure of which forced me to cry out in agony while squeezing my eyes closed. Rocks, grass, and debris from the house rained down around me. The heat from the fire felt like the worst sort of sunburn, making my skin tingle and my clothes—what wasn't shredded from my slide—cling to me like plastic wrap.

I slid to a stop a few yards from the end of the drive. Another wave from the blast roared around me, that time sucking debris back toward the fire.

The initial blast was behind me. Next, I had to worry about the woods catching fire and burning around me. But that realization and ensuing worry were distant thoughts. My entire being—my skin, my bones, and my awareness—was beat to hell, and the darkness was begging me to visit. I was too sore to roll onto my back, too tired to crawl to the street and where a car *might* pass, too broken to care if Strong circled back and saw me. I had come far but was desperate for a break.

So I stretched toward the void and let it claim me.

"Sam, Sam." A voice was beckoning me from the abyss.

I struggled to find it. Opening my eyes, a mere slit showed Leo staring down at me.

"Leo?" I mumbled, but even to my ear, it didn't sound like his name but a garbled mess of sounds.

"I got ya. Stay with me. An ambulance is on the way." He sounded worried.

I tried to reach out to him, to comfort him, but the darkness called me back, and it was easier to sink into it than to stay with the light.

"We're going to roll you onto your back on the count of three. Ready?"

That voice I didn't recognize. I lifted one eyelid to see whom it belonged to. I didn't recognize the face. The man the voice belonged to lifted up my eyelids and shined a light into each of my eyes. He then slid a brace around my neck. Oddly, I found it comfortable.

"Okay," he said again. "One. Two. Three."

I was jostled and rotated, and when the cold air hit the front of my body, its touch on my wounds was excruciating.

Death by a thousand cuts. Exposing the wounds made them sting and scream in protest. It made me do the same.

"It's okay, Sam," Leo said. "The blast must have pushed you down. You got a little road rash."

I turned toward his voice and tried to smile, tried to let him know I was okay. I hated that he was seeing me like that —not because I was likely beat to hell but because he'd seen me after a battle before, and he didn't like it. And when he didn't like it, he reminded me of it all the time.

I was lifted up and moved through space, the sensation disorienting. I closed my eyes to get my bearings, and the darkness waved me over. We were becoming close companions.

. . .

I awoke again as they rushed me into a hospital, the doctor saying something about X-rays. I wasn't interested in being awake for that part.

The next time I woke, my dad was leaning over me, his hand pressed to my forehead. I was in a bed, but the room wasn't mine.

"You have a fever," he said. "I'm going to get you some ginger ale."

Ginger ale was Dad's go-to. Stomach ailments, fevers, headaches, and even boy problems were treated with ginger ale.

I didn't feel like ginger ale, so I closed my eyes and looked for my friend Mr. Darkness.

"Samantha." The voice was familiar, but I couldn't place it.

"Samantha. Don't you worry. I'll take care of Strong for you."

I opened my eyes and blinked several times. I took in the face of the man looking down at me. He was leaning over my bed.

"Carson?"

Am I dead? How can Carson be here if I'm not dead? And if I was dead, that was not how I expected it to be—very much a disappointment.

"You get better," he said.

I closed my eyes and pulled the blanket of darkness over myself. When the light beckoned me again, I refused to go.

If I was dead, I needed the afterlife to be much better than what I'd last experienced. Therefore, I was giving the afterlife time to get its act together and spruce things up. If I was dead, I expected to not feel any pain, to experience no confusion, and to have clarity. I certainly did not expect to feel like crap run over by a semi truck.

And to shove my dead husband at me on day one was just a cruel joke—cruel indeed.

36

SATURDAY

THE NEXT TIME DARKNESS SHOVED ME TOWARD THE LIGHT, I was ready... but hesitant.

I slowly opened one eye and was not greeted by the blinding pain light had been bringing with its presence. I slowly opened the other.

I blinked and took in my surroundings. I was in a bed in what looked to be a hospital, if the track curtains dividing the space and a TV mounted across the room were any indi-cation. And the smell—antiseptic mixed with cleaner. *Gross.* I groaned my displeasure.

Something rustled behind me, and I rolled, albeit slowly, toward my right. Leo was asleep in a high-back recliner, his arms crossed over his chest.

"Leo," I said, but it came out a croak. I smacked my lips, which were dry, and when I rubbed my tongue over them, it was like licking sand. I tried to clear my throat instead then repeated, "Leo." I sounded hoarse and not like myself at all.

He popped awake, sitting straight up in the chair, blinked twice, then focused on me. "You're awake?"

I nodded.

He narrowed his eyes. "For how long, though?"

I tried to roll mine. "Drink," I croaked.

He jumped to his feet. "I'll get a nurse."

Just as quickly as he was out the door, he was back with a woman my mom's age wearing green scrubs and a necklace made of Christmas lights.

"It's great that you're finally with us, she said. "You've been out twelve hours."

I blinked in surprise.

"You're telling me," she said. "We all thought you'd be awake sooner. I'm Ellie. I'm your nurse. Let me get something for those lips." She bustled off then came back with a damp washcloth to blot my mouth. "I'm going to do this for a moment, then I'll put ChapStick on. After that, I'll get you some ice to suck on. Baby steps, here."

I said, "What's wrong—"

She waved me off. "Save your voice. I'll give you the list. You have one humdinger of a concussion. No surprise there. Your left arm is broken, the ulnar bone. That's the one that lines up with your pinkie. You have some second-degree burns on your body from the blast and some road rash that'll be uncomfortable for a while. You have two cracked ribs. You needed nine stitches on your wrist from various cuts. And you're going to need a good manicure when you're released."

All said and done, it wasn't that bad. The concussion worried me the most, but I was in the right place to be monitored. I gave her a thumbs-up.

She rolled a ChapStick tube over my lips, and I felt the slightest bit of relief as moisture sank in.

"Let me get those ice chips," Ellie said and scurried off.

I looked at Leo. "My dad?" I thought I'd seen him earlier.

He glanced at his watch. "His plane should be landing anytime. He had to catch several flights to get here. Your mom stayed behind with Cora and Rachel. Though I don't think she was happy about it. She made me promise to call her every hour. She'll be happy to know you're okay."

Weird. Like Carson, Dad was a dream? Funny how they both felt real.

"Strong? Precious and Toby?"

Leo smiled and sat on the edge of my bed. He took my hand. "Toby and Precious are fine. Worried about you. Like me. Like Lockett. You know who isn't worried about you? Hue. He said you were tough; you can handle anything. But I told him next time *he* could find you lying on your stomach, bleeding from the nose—"

My eyes went wide.

He waved it off. "Apparently, that's normal with an explosion." He met my gaze. "An explosion."

"I was there," I whispered.

He closed his eyes and sighed. I gave his hand a comforting squeeze.

He opened his dark eyes and stared at me. "I'm sorry."

"Strong?"

He nodded. "Yeah, Strong. That son of a bitch. Toby got him good. By the time the ambulance got to you, the world was learning all about Austin Strong's part in the creation of the spyware and posting it online and then the creating the anti-virus to combat it. That pastry chef you interviewed?"

I nodded to indicate I knew whom he meant—Kami Bartell.

"She came out against Strong. Talked about how he sent her threatening emails every few months, videos of her in

her house and at work. Roman Castillo did a press confer-
ence and told how McVay had sent him proof of Strong's
crimes. He also showed McVay's video, which has gone
viral—"

I tugged at his hand, drawing his attention. "Video?"

He looked at me in question. "Yeah, the video was part of
the information you all retrieved from McVay's cabin."

Ah. We'd been hit by the truck before I got to finish the
video. I gestured for him to continue.

"McVay's video outs Strong on everything. Apparently,
Strong had a crush on Kami, but she didn't reciprocate. So
he stalked her. Tried to ruin her. He saw her go into the
restroom and come out without her drink. Because he knew
her every action, he knew she'd go back for it—nonalcoholic
drinks were hard to come by at these parties. He put ecstasy
in the drink, and when Castillo took her home, Strong
convinced McVay to film her. Apparently, McVay didn't have
any problem with what Strong was doing back then, but
over time, it started to wear on him."

"Contract negotiations," I said.

Leo nodded. "Yeah, the only reason McVay was pushing
for high salary was because he knew Strong didn't want to
pay. Wouldn't pay it. He was trying to use it as an out. From
what I can figure, if Strong had let McVay go, then McVay
would have gone and kept his mouth shut. He just wanted
away from Strong."

"But Strong would never have that," I said, recalling our
accident and how Strong liked to use car accidents as a way
to cover his crimes.

Ellie came back in with a small pink pitcher and a clear
plastic cup with a spoon inside.

She said, "Here ya go, hon. We're gonna start slow with

taking in fluids. You keep this down, and then I can bring you some more liquids. Maybe even some chicken broth." She wagged her brows.

I grinned and gave her another thumbs-up. She moved around, taking my vitals, checking the machine I was connected to, and she wrote it all down while making small talk with me and Leo. Moments later, she left us to finish our conversation.

"Strong?" I asked again.

"He's been arrested. He was caught trying to fly out of a private airport in Seattle. His flight plan was for Switzerland." Leo shook his head.

I pressed a palm to my temple.

"You okay? Headache?" he asked.

I shook my head. "Strong scares me." I wanted to say that I wouldn't sleep until Strong was dead, that I would always be looking over my shoulder for him whether he was in jail or not. But I didn't have the energy. I would deal with that problem after I dealt with getting better.

Leo pushed a lock of hair from my forehead. "He's a concern, no doubt. Lockett has some thoughts. We can talk about them when you're discharged."

"AJ?"

Leo smiled. "Lockett thinks the court will clear him of all charges in the next day or two. But if the reaction on social media means anything, the community is already rallying around him."

I rolled my eyes. Half that community had turned on him the minute he'd been arrested. "The team?"

Leo shrugged. "I think there's a lot that has to happen with ownership. Strong was a control freak, and he hasn't left anyone in charge. But the general manager is running the show until all that gets dealt with. AJ was announced the starting quarterback."

I widened my eyes though I don't know why I was surprised. AJ was under contract after all. Talk about awkward situations... I would hate to go back into the locker room after everything that'd happened. However, AJ had nothing to be ashamed of.

"AJ's cool with it, though he said it's not the way he wanted to get a starting job. Precious reminded him to enjoy what was in front of him."

Leo's phone chimed, and he pulled it from his pocket and checked the screen. "Your dad's landed. He should be here in a few hours."

I waved a hand. "Tell him to go home and sleep. It's late."

Leo laughed. "It's six in the morning. Your clock is jacked."

I laughed, which came out hoarse and husky. I followed the laugh with a yawn.

Leo stood and stretched, reaching over his head. "I have to work. I'll be back this afternoon when I get off duty."

I nodded.

He looked down at me, a smile playing on his lips. "You're tough, you know that?"

I nodded again. "I've always had to be."

"One day, when you're feeling better, I want to know what all happened in that cabin, okay?"

I gave him a thumbs-up.

Fat chance. No way would I tell him everything. He was never going to know I'd been flex-cuffed to an exploding stove. He would lose his mind.

He bent forward and delivered a light kiss on my forehead. "Will you really tell me everything?" he asked, standing back up.

I shook my head.

"Will you tell Hue, and then he can tell me?"

I chuckled. "I'll think about it."

He nodded once in understanding, squeezed my hand, then left. Ellie came back in and told me to get some more rest.

But my mind wouldn't let me sleep. With Austin Strong still alive, the rest of us were still in danger. Strong lived for revenge.

37

THURSDAY

LOCKETT, TOBY, PRECIOUS, LEO, AND I SAT ON MY BALCONY and watched the hustle and bustle of the town. Christmas was right around the corner, and locals were getting in some shopping while supporting small-town businesses.

AJ was out of town for a game. Simon was back home with Troy, AJ's brother, since he was back home. Dad was downstairs, putting a breaking story to press.

Using my unbroken arm, my dominant one, I took a beer from the cooler, popped off the cap, then snuggled back in my chair, pulling the heavy blanket around myself.

"Tell me again what happened," I said to Lockett.

He rubbed a hand down his face. "It's incredible, right?"

The group mumbled their agreement.

Lockett continued, "As the Multnomah County jail report reads, Strong was with the general population. They said they had no reason to believe he was in danger. A fight broke out among the inmates. A few of the correctional officers tried to break it up. A custodian got caught up in the mix, and somehow—no one knows how—Strong was stabbed and killed."

"Where did the knife come from?" I asked.

Lockett shrugged. "I interviewed three people. No one saw the knife. No knife was found at the scene. All we know about the knife is how long the blade was."

Precious asked, "And the custodian? Bad luck on his part?"

Lockett nodded. "He'd recently taken the job. Only his third day at work."

"Were you able to interview him?"

Lockett shook his head. "Can't find him. He gave his statement, cooperated with the investigation that day, but when he was okay to go home, he never came back. He's in the wind. Just like that visitor AJ received the day after he was arrested. Can't find him either."

"You think the custodian was there to kill Strong?" I asked.

Paulie had said people with money have all sorts of options available to them.

Lockett nodded. "I do. Just don't know who hired him."

Precious said, "A guy like Strong probably has enemies lined up. If he was blackmailing McVay and the baker, there had to be more."

I said, "We may never know who all he blackmailed or stalked or whose life was ruined by Strong. For all I know, Roman Castillo could've done it. His grudge ran deep."

From under the blanket, Lady M cooed. Toby had brought her over the day I came home from the hospital, two days before, and I'd been loving on her ever since. Having her to hold and cuddle was doing me a world of good. And knowing Strong was dead was a giant weight off my shoul-

ders. I was still sweeping my house and car and Dad's newspaper for bugs because some habits were hard to break. I
still woke up in a panic sometimes, covered in sweat, afraid
he was trying to break in. But that would all fade with time.

I confessed to my friends, "I know I shouldn't say this,
but I don't care who hired that custodian. If he's the one who
took out Strong, I don't have a problem with him. In fact, I
owe him because now I have peace of mind."

Toby said, "The enemies of my enemies are my friends."

I nodded. I could spend my life trying to guess who
might be behind Strong's murder. But I had better things to
do. And those didn't include telling my friends that I dreamt
Carson had come to the hospital or that a part of me thought
Carson might've been behind the murder. That was simply
crazy talk. Carson was dead, and I'd received a head injury
during my altercation with Strong.

Toby continued, "Lots of stuff coming out on the dark
web about Strong. I'm gathering what I can and sending it to
the prosecutor. Strong may be dead, but his company still
has access to people's homes, whether they have his security
system, anti-virus, or his internet service, like he had in
McVay's. It's not unreasonable to think Strong had other bad
actors in those organizations working for him. We need to
know who they are and clean up those companies."

A jingle from down the street caught my attention. Lark
Ogilvy had come outside the coffeehouse, holding a tray
with tiny cups on it. She was offering them to passersby,
many of whom were declining.

Leo said, "I went to the coffee shop yesterday, and she
said my aura was yellow. She said a straight black coffee
wouldn't be a good move and kept trying to push some tea
on me. Eventually, I got frustrated and left."

I looked at Leo, puzzled. "You mean she wouldn't sell you what you wanted?"

He shook his head. "She refused to sell me coffee. She said she respected my aura more than I did and she wouldn't do that to me. She's nice and all, but that's not good business."

I agreed. "And no one is taking what's on the tray."

Precious said, "I went by earlier. It's a cranberry-infused coffee with an Irish cream whipped topping."

"Did you try it?" Lockett asked.

Precious shook her head. "Sometimes, you want life to be clean and simple."

I held up my beer. "I'll toast to that."

The others held up their drinks too, and we all clanked our bottles against the others. Then we all went back to studying Lark Ogilvy as she attempted to peddle her unique coffee mixes.

As people crossed her path, Lark appeared to be forcing the mini cups on them. The giftees showed their gratitude by dumping the cups in the trash right in front of her.

Poor Lark. But as bad as I felt for our newest resident, I wasn't about to go down and get any coffee.

Paulie Bea came out of the yoga studio and headed our way. Rocket wasn't with him. He was dressed the same: sweats, hoody, puffy jacket, and white high-top tennis shoes.

Lark jumped in front of him and shoved the tray in his face.

I half expected Paulie to flip the tray back at her, but he voluntarily took a cup. *This isn't going to go well. Unless something's wrong with Paulie.* That might have been the case as he was standing there talking to Lark and about to take a sip.

They exchanged a few more words, and Paulie walked

away, taking a sip as he headed toward us. He then stopped and spat the drink on the ground. He tossed the cup into the garbage and said something to Lark. Based on her shocked expression, it probably wasn't very nice. He strode off.

"I wonder what he said," Toby said.

Lockett said, "Maybe it wasn't the coffee. Maybe she called him on his aura."

"Doubtful," I said.

Precious said, "Or his clothes."

We chuckled. But Lark drew our attention again by screaming at Paulie's back, "It does not taste like swill! It tastes like the holidays!"

Paulie didn't respond. Instead, he crossed the street to my apartment and came pounding up the stairs.

Lark dumped the remaining cups in the trash and stormed into her coffee shop.

Paulie stood at the top of the stairs and met my gaze. "Had to see you for myself. Good to see you're alive. You don't look so bad," he said.

I nodded. "Thanks. It's good to be alive."

"You're a tough nut to break." He reached into a pocket and pulled out a laminated rectangle the size of a credit card. He flicked it to me. "I made you this."

The card landed on my knee, and I picked it up, turning it over to the front. He'd given me a fake driver's license.

I read the information. "Tamantha Blue?" I showed the card to Leo.

He chuckled.

"Is this in case I need to go on the run?"

Paulie gave a one-shoulder shrug. "Yeah. I made the name similar as I figured it might be hard to answer to something unfamiliar."

Sound logic, I suppose. "Did you color my hair in with a brown marker?"

Paulie nodded.

Toby said, "Dude, they have programs that can do these sorts of things. Coloring hair, change eye color... Using a marker is so 1950s."

Paulie glared at Toby. "Using those programs ain't my thing. And I figured Sam might be in a hurry to get outta town, but now with Strong dead, the urgency is gone." He glanced at me. "Keep it for backup."

I smiled. Paulie had been worried about me.

"Thanks," I said. "I will. And thanks for all your help. I couldn't have done it without you."

Paulie gave me a thumbs-up. "Okay, I'm off to the range. See you around."

We waved goodbye.

He paused at the top of the stairs. "Also, Sam, your client Renee Foote with the possible philandering fiancé? Turns out your gut was right. He's a good guy. Also, don't drink any of that coffee from the flittering bird down there. Nasty stuff. Plain nasty."

Lockett coughed into his hand as Leo ducked his head. Even though we agreed, we couldn't help feeling bad for Lark.

"Noted," I said.

Moments after Paulie was gone, Lark came out of the coffee shop. She locked the door, closing up.

"Calling it a day?" Lockett asked.

She looked up at us and came down the sidewalk to be closer. She pointed at Leo and his beer. "I see you heeded my warning and avoided black coffee. That's good."

He smiled and nodded.

She put her hands on her hips. "You had black coffee, didn't you?" He nodded again.

She glared at all of us, making a point to go down the line and make eye contact with everyone. "You all are giving off bad juju. It's so bad I was being affected down here."

No one corrected her by pointing out that maybe the coffee had been the bad juju.

Hitching a thumb in Leo's direction, I asked, "Is his aura still yellow and sunny?"

She lifted her chin a notch. "Yes, but it's getting darker by the minute. And it's because of you. You have black dots in your aura."

"Black dots?"

She nodded. "Yeah, that means trouble follows you everywhere."

The others laughed.

I said, "Don't I know it," and held up my broken arm, the cast painted blue and green for the Seahawks—my dad was so proud. "But trouble can come find me. I'm waiting. And trouble should know I fight back."

Lark shook her head. "You're crazy. You're all crazy." She threw her arms in the air. "This town is crazy, and this coffee shop is jinxed."

I said, "It's got a black aura."

Precious said, "With that attitude, the coffee shop will never do well. You need to visualize changing that aura. And what will happen once you do."

Lark shot us daggers. "I hate this town. I'm out." She swiveled on her heel and marched toward the shop. At the door, she reached up and pulled the shop sign off the wall.

"I hate this town!" she screamed and tossed the sign next to the garbage before marching away.

Toby said, "I think her aura is getting darker by the minute."

Precious said, "That's a self-fulfilling prophecy. With an attitude like that, she's destined to fail. She needs Sam's attitude. She looks trouble in the face and challenges it to up its game."

"Darn right," Lockett said.

Toby and Precious clanked their beers. I stroked Lady M's head and smiled.

Leo groaned. "Maybe she could ask trouble to back down its game."

I said, "I think I'm going to need a bigger secret pocket to pin to the inside of my pants."

Leo ducked his head and rubbed at a temple. "I can't imagine what else you might need besides handcuff keys and a knife."

I took his hand and squeezed it. "Me neither, but I think I'm about to find out. I got one of those feelings in my gut again."

BOOKS BY KRISTI ROSE

Samantha True Mysteries- Laugh out loud twisty mysteries

One Hit Wonder

All Bets Are Off

Best Laid Plans

Caught Off Guard

A Liars Island Suspense (written under pen name Robbie Peale)

Perfect Place

The Wyoming Matchmaker Series- Whether marriage of convenience or star crossed lovers, everyone earns their happily ever after in this series.

The Cowboy Takes A Bride

The Cowboy's Make Believe Bride

The Cowboy's Runaway Bride

The No Strings Attached Series- A flirty, fun chick lit romance series

The Girl He Knows

The Girl He Needs

The Girl He Wants

The Girl He Loves

The Meryton Brides Series- A wholesome romance series with a Pride and Prejudice theme

To Have and To Hold (Book 1)

With This Ring (Book 2)

I Do (Book 3)

Promise Me This (Book 4)

Marry Me, Matchmaker (Book 5)

Honeymoon Postponed (Book 6)

Matchmaker's Guidebook - FREE

The Second Chance Short Stories can be read alone and go as follows:

Second Chances

Once Again

Reason to Stay

He's the One

Kiss Me Again

or purchased in a bundle for a better discount.

The Coming Home Series: A Collection of 5 Second Chance Short Stories (Can be purchased individually).

Love Comes Home

MEET KRISTI ROSE

Hey! I'm Kristi. I write romances that will tug your heart-strings and laugh out loud mysteries. In all my stories you'll fall in love with the cast of characters, they'll become old, fun friends. **My one hope** is that I create stories that *satisfy any of your book cravings* and take you away from the rut of everyday life (sometimes it's a good rut).

When I'm not writing repurposing Happy Planners or drinking a London Fog (hot tea with frothy milk).

I'm the mom of 2 and a milspouse (retired). We live in the Pacific Northwest and are under-prepared if one of the volcanoes erupts.

Here are 3 things about me:

- I lived on the outskirts of an active volcano (Mt.Etna)
- A spider bit me and it laid eggs in my arm (my kids don't know that story yet)
- I grew up in Central Florida and have skied in lakes with gators.

I'd love to get to know you better. Join my Read & Relax community and then fire off an email and tell me 3 things about you!

Not ready to join? Email me below or follow me at one of the links below. Thanks for popping by!

You can connect with Kristi at any of the following:
www.kristirose.net
kristi@kristirose.net

JOIN KRISTI'S READ AND RELAX SOCIETY

I hope you enjoy this book. I'd love to connect and share more with you. Be a part of my Read & Relax Society and let's get to know each other. There, I'll share all sorts of book information. You're guaranteed to find an escape. You'll also be the first to know about my sales and new releases. You'll have access to giveaways, freebies, and bonus content. Think you might be interested? Give me a try. You can always leave at any time.

If you enjoyed this book I would appreciate if you'd share that with others. I love when my friends pass along a good read. Here's some ways you can help.

Lend it , Recommend it , Review it
XO, Kristi

CPSIA information can be obtained
at www.ICGtesting.com
Printed in the USA
BVHW032147010421
603991BV00005B/142